DRAGON MATED

DRAGON MATED
Supernatural Prison #3

Jaymin Eve

Dragon Mated: Supernatural Prison #3

Copyright © Jaymin Eve 2016

All rights reserved

First published in 2016

Eve, Jaymin
Dragon Mated: Supernatural Prison #3

1st edition
No part of this book may be reproduced, stored in a retrieval system or transmitted in any form or by any means, without the prior permission in writing of the publisher, nor be otherwise circulated in any form of binding or cover other than that in which it is published and without a similar condition, including this condition, being imposed on the subsequent purchaser. All characters in this publication other than those clearly in the public domain are fictitious, and any resemblance to real persons, living or dead, is purely coincidental

To Leia Stone, thank you for being the best BAFF a girl could ask for. We are totally Jessa and Mischa, twin souls separated at birth. (Dibs on Jessa ... because, you know, Braxton) ;)

It's said that if you lie with snakes long enough, you either become a snake or you get bitten. Makes perfect sense. Except, if you're a wolf, you lie in wait, you bide your time, and right when its guard is down, you kill that fucking snake.
Jessa Lebron

Chapter 1

To say I was upset about being kidnapped by Larkspur, the self-proclaimed dragon king and all-around asshole, would be one of those grand understatements, like saying a cyclone was just a little storm, or Braxton Compass just a little deadly. No, I wasn't *upset*, not *upset* at all – my emotions were running hotter than the depths of hell, fire burning in my gut and utter hatred swamping every feeling in my body.

It felt like weeks since my entire world had been turned upside down, but I knew it was no more than a single day. Twenty-four hours—nothing really in the eight hundred plus years I could live—and yet it was the longest day of my life so far.

My mind continued reliving the moment Larkspur had snatched me up from Krakov, the Romanian supernatural prison, and flew like a freaking human lizard through his step through. I had no idea where the frig we were—some sort of castle floating through the sky. I was pretty sure we were nowhere on Earth. The tall, honey-blond dragon king had dumped my butt into this room and then left without a word.

Mutha-flaming asshole.

I stepped gingerly through the mess of wood, feathers, and linen that covered the floor and made my way to the one, tiny window. I took my time examining the landscape and grounds again, memorizing the visible stone paths that led from this building, trying to orient myself so I might have a shot at escaping. The castle seemed to consist of a weird mixture of rough, grayish stone, and a cream-colored, porous granite, all of which swirled together into large turrets and a mile-wide series of smaller buildings, a mess of mazes which would make escaping extremely difficult.

Not to mention the entire concoction was floating about ten miles in the air.

If I didn't hate the dragon king so much, I'd admire his genius.

My wolf and dragon were restless inside. We did not like the strange magic surrounding us. It was not natural—it felt like the fey, only a million times stronger. Yeah, I was taking a guess here, but it made sense that Larkspur would hide in Faerie. Few supes lived here, and the land was pure magic. The perfect world in which to hatch his dastardly plan.

A low thud at the door had me swiveling and falling into a semi-crouched position. The door was heavy and metal, reinforced and bolted. I knew this because I'd spent the first part of my time here trying to smash it down. Even calling on my dragon hadn't helped, and she was strong. Obviously, old Larky had planned for that. *Larky.* I was totally calling him that from now on. I just knew it was something he'd hate. He was all regal and proper and king-like, and Larky sounded like a baby bird or some shit.

I stalked closer to the door. Whoever walked through was going down. I could already feel my body changing as my wolf shifted closer to the surface. We did not like to be caged; we would kill our abductor and we would make it hurt.

I was about three feet from the massive door when I felt the stirring of magic, and then a small gap appeared in the stone, just above my head. I caught a flash of a face, skin which looked to be a scaly green. Then a tray was pushed through to my side.

I lunged forward, prepared to pull scaly through also. I was not above using a hostage to try and get out of here, but the magically-reinforced opening only allowed one-directional movement. My hand slammed against the gap like it was solid rock. Which kinda hurt. Cursing, I yanked the tray out and flung it like a Frisbee across the room. It smashed against the far wall and joined the rest of the rubble on the floor.

"You should eat," a low voice murmured through the door. "I won't bring you more food for six hours."

Truth. Even the demi-fey couldn't hide truth from me.

My stomach protested. I hadn't eaten for a while, but I'd be damned if I took any of king asshole's food. I would rather starve.

Okay, that might be some crazy talk going on there. Maybe I'd just make a decent attempt at a self-induced starvation protest.

Shut it, I mentally chastised my stomach.

I focused on scaly again. "Come in here and make me eat it," I said. I could only hope the supe on the other side was one who couldn't resist a challenge.

There was a brief pause, then I swear I heard a chuckle before the magic dissipated and the opening was gone. New waves of anger and frustration rose up in my mess of emotions. I wanted to scream loudly. It was on the tip of my tongue. But I would not give them the satisfaction. I had no doubt the dragon king was watching me. I was getting a creepy vibe, and he was as creeptastic as all hell.

I stepped away from the door again, making my way over to the last space on the floor clear of debris in the large, round room. I settled down and crossed my legs, my back against the gray stone wall.

Time to connect to my dragon.

Closing my eyes and settling my thoughts were step one. I breathed deeply, deliberately, trying to calm the tumult of emotions. It took some time, but finally, when I felt that I was as Zen as I could be under current circumstances, I reached for my beast.

For most of my twenty-two years, I thought the dragon was a demon living inside of me. My dragon mark had been spelled and she was hidden away, which had damaged the bond between us. I could feel her there. I practically saw her as she prowled around inside, but I couldn't shift on command. The wall between us was always present; the only time it busted open was when I was in mortal danger.

Braxton had said that my dragon and I needed time for our bond to properly form, that after this all the issues would disappear. So since I had nothing but time right now, I was going to try and bond with the biggest weapon I had at my disposal.

I let my consciousness drift toward her, bypassing my wolf, who was content to let our dragon sister have the floor. I hovered on the near side of the wall, trying to seep through, trying to figure out how to reach her. She roared at me, sensing my need. We needed to escape. We needed to find our family. We needed our Compasses. We needed Braxton.

Calm had slipped out of reach again; my thoughts were red hot, anger mingling with a tinge of sorrow. The Compass quads were my best friends; we had been a pack since we were two. That was all, just pack and best friends. Until a few days ago.

What happened then was the best thing in my life. Braxton Compass. Six and half feet of chiseled hotness, with double dimples, hair as black as the darkest night and eyes so blue the sky was jealous. We'd both fought the attraction for years, me because I was a hardheaded dumbass who was afraid to break our friendship pact and possibly ruin the pack dynamics, and Braxton because I was a hard-headed dumbass and he was waiting for me to figure out that there was so much more between us than friendship.

He had been waiting for me for years. Which was new knowledge for me, and it totally had my emotions on overload.

My body still tingled thinking about the few brief times we'd been together, and as luck – and fate – would have it, Braxton was my true mate … well, sort of. Something had malfunctioned with the bond; it was only partially there, but I didn't give a flying crap on toast. He was my true mate, chosen by the gods, and for me there was no other choice, no matter if Larky thought otherwise.

Just behind Braxton in my heart were the rest of the Compasses. They were my best friends too, just minus the romance. Their faces crossed my mind, images tangled together, each one more beautiful and badass than the next. Tyson, the wizard with his brown-auburn hair and honeysuckle eyes; Jacob, the slightly more fine-boned fey, with his white-blond hair and leaf-green eyes; Maximus, a massive vampire who rocked some sexy dirty-blond hair and dark brown eyes; then lastly Braxton, dragon shifter and badass. They were quads. They were beautiful. They were arrogant assholes with dimples and attitude problems and I missed them so freaking much it actually hurt to breathe.

My wolf and dragon both started to howl then, and deciding I didn't give a single shit if the douchey king was watching, I threw back my head and let my anguish pour out of me in one long stream of hoarse screams and growling curses.

My grief was cut off by a low, measured voice. "In my time, ladies did not speak so … vulgar. I think I kind of like it."

I was on my feet so fast the room spun. The amused voice was close. Somehow douche king had managed to get into my room and was standing before me without having set off a single one of my senses. Goddamn sneaky shifter.

Air exhaled rapidly from my nose as I stared the asshole down. He was handsome, there was no denying that. Though that cold, regal thing he had going on did nothing for me.

Gray eyes flashed as he looked around the room. The amusement did not fade from his quirked lips. "I see your accommodations weren't to your liking."

I didn't take my eyes from him but I knew what he was referring to. Upon my arrival the room had contained three pieces of furniture: a large four-poster bed: heavy, dark timbered, with netting on all sides; a dresser; and a small side vanity. All three were now in a million pieces strewn across the slate floor, most of which was hidden by the ton of feathers I'd ripped from the mattress. It was almost pretty in here now, a snowy massacre of wood.

He paused, as if waiting for me to join his conversation. I didn't say anything; I was not playing nice with Larky. His eyes shuttered, and in an odd movement he almost stumbled forward, as if he couldn't help himself.

That's right, asshole. Come a little closer.

His hands were clenched at his sides, those eyes turning from light gray to a dark tumult of emotions. I remained stationary; my expression did not shift, and as he tilted that golden face to the side – in a movement very much like a predator – I knew he was trying to understand what was going on in my head.

My guess was that in his previous life this handsome, charismatic, and powerful piece-of-shit usually had women falling all over him. Looked like it was time to introduce him to few home truths about Jessa Lebron. She fell at no one's feet.

"You should eat, Jessa," he said as he moved forward again, smoother this time, stepping around the mass of debris which separated us. "I know you love food."

How? Seriously, how did he know anything about me? He'd been stuck in the land of asshole souls for the past thousand years. I wondered if his daughters, the bitch twins, had managed to stay in contact with their father.

I couldn't keep quiet any longer. "Where are we?"

Larky's grin widened, as if he'd won some sort of dominance challenge in getting me to talk. I was just information gathering so I knew where the frig to run when I managed to get free.

And I would be getting free.

"This is my castle in the sky; it has to stay in Faerie. You know how the humans get when things are outside of their control or understanding. Plus, it's much easier to float here with all of the magic in this land."

Dammit! I had guessed right. Faerie. I had no idea how to get out of this realm, but ... Louis had tracked me here before. I hoped he could do it again, just as soon as I got out of this place – there'd definitely be some sort of spell here cloaking my energy. The entire castle was probably hidden.

"How can you be here? I thought this land was dying. That's why there was a mass exodus of fey and demi-fey, right?"

Those gray eyes were calculating as they locked on my face. "Are the leaders still spinning that story?" He continued to stare, and I kind of got the feeling he thought I was an idiot.

"Yes, they're still spinning that story!" I snarled.

He laughed, like out-loud, grab-at-his-belly laughter. It hurt my ears and gave me those tingles down my spine in the bad way. The really bad way.

"Come," he finally said when his eerie laughter ended. "Let's dine together. In the meantime, someone will be in to fix up your room."

He held out a hand for me – like just held it out, expecting I would take it. Worst part, a very small part of me did want to take his hand. The dragon mark on my back, which was large enough to encompass my entire side, was warm, like it knew its master was close by. The dragon king basically owned all of the dragon marked; we were his little army of brain-dead minions. He could control us, communicate with us, and lots of other joyful facts.

So far I'd heard or felt nothing of him in my head, I wasn't sure if he hadn't bothered to tap into the mark yet or if it was only something he could do in the Earthly realm. Either way, I was hoping like hell he would not use this connection between us. I would fight him to my dying breath, but if that control was wrested from me … shit. I was really hoping that would not happen.

I stepped closer, my booted feet kicking up a few planks as I plowed through them. I was still dressed in my dirty, torn clothes from the prison. I'd only been in Faerie for about a day, but it already felt like a year. Time moved so differently here; I wondered how much time had passed on Earth. I had no doubt my family was losing their shit. Braxton had probably already razed half of Romania to the ground. The other quads wouldn't be far behind him.

I forced my expression not to change, eyes motionless on Larky as he waited for me. I managed to swallow down the flood of hatred that wanted to pour from my mouth. Acting nice might be my one chance of catching him off guard.

"I'll show you where you can get cleaned up," he said.

"A shower?" I asked with a dickish level of false enthusiasm. Like he could soften me up so easily.

He nodded. "Yes, of course. Shower, clean clothes, and then food. You don't need to live like an animal. You're my beloved, and we're going to rule over the five races."

Oh, like wow, he was really pulling out the big guns today.

I forced myself to smile, just a little, as if the thought of being his beloved and ruling over the five supernatural races was a pleasant thought for me. Reality was, I'd rather cut my own head off than be in the same room as this slimy piece of crap.

Actually, scratch that. I'd prefer to cut *his* head off.

When I was close enough to touch him, I pretended I was about to reach for his hand, but just as his fingers were about to wrap around mine, I leaned back, kicked up a long board from the floor, and using every ounce of my strength swung it directly into his face. His eyes had been locked on me, so he was a beat too slow to get out of the way. I clocked him directly in the temple and actually knocked him down. I was over the top of him faster than he could blink, straddling him and slamming my elbow directly into his throat. He wheezed out, his cheeks and eyes darkening. He was not a happy camper, and I gave zero fucks.

I knew I couldn't kill him. I'd stabbed him directly in the heart and the bastard had just pulled it out and went along his merry way. But I was still going to enjoy causing him pain. His nose crunched as my fist pushed it to the side. Blood poured from it, which told me he was real enough to bleed. Of course it basically healed in an instant, which was very annoying. He reached for me, and I sprang backwards, my boot landing in his gut. Despite that lame grab attempt, he wasn't fighting back. He was just sitting there and letting me hit him.

What the hell?

"Fight back!" I growled at him. "Don't treat me as weak."

He gracefully arose, sort of levitating to his feet. "This would not be a fair fight. Even though I haven't tapped into the thousands of marked souls at my command, I'm still much stronger than you. And once I do draw upon the marked power ... there will be no stopping me."

I had some scary thoughts racking me then. *Is he actually saying that...?*

"If the dragon marked are alive, you can't die? I would have to kill every single dragon marked before I can kill you?" My tone was low, mingled with disbelief and what-the-fuckery.

He reached up and rubbed away the few drops of blood still lingering around his nose.

"Yes, which would be impossible, as you're the strongest of all the marked, and would have to die also."

This was bad, really freaking bad.

"I'll just have to make sure we imprison you again."

Larky shook his head, like he was feeling sorry for me. My hands clenched as I itched to punch him again. "When I tap into the marked power, there's no one in any of the worlds who could contain me."

I stilled. How could he be so sure there was no one? He'd been locked away for a thousand years. My mind flashed back to the sanctuary and the training hall where my boys had joined their powers for the first time. They had a calling – to fight and destroy the dragon king. I was guessing that even with this calling the boys would still have to figure out a way to break the ties between him and the marked. They'd never kill me, I knew that without a shadow of doubt. They would let the rest of the world and all supernatural races fall before harming me, and I'd do the same for them.

"Come, Jessa."

Larky was blood free and on his feet. He turned and walked out the now-open door. I followed him, wanting out of this room. Plus, I could use this as an opportunity to get a layout of the castle. Intel was important.

I kept a decent distance between us as we stepped out into the long, stone hallway. He turned to the right and continued on at a nice even pace.

So arrogant, turning his back on me like that.

I was going to guess he'd never met a female like me; I was going to fight him all the way. I took a running jump and two-foot-kicked him straight in the back. My hit was hard and solid, and he ended up face-down on the stone. I heard the *oomph* as all the breath whooshed out of him, but I didn't stick around to see his recovery. I started running and never looked back.

I sprinted as fast as my legs would go, looking for a stairway or exit from this shithole. I heard a series of curses behind but knew better than to turn back. The odds of me escaping were slim to none, but I had to try. Maybe if I could just get outside…

"Jessa! You can't escape from me."

His voice was closer than I would have liked. The hallway seemed to be never ending, but there was a lighter section in the distance. I needed more speed. My wolf came to my call in an instant. It took me mere seconds to slip free of my human skin and clothes, and I let loose with a long howl as the canine in me took over.

My senses sharpened and we were so much faster on four legs, the green-gray landscape zooming by in a monotonous array. The end of the hallway was fast approaching and this gave my wolf an extra burst of speed. There were no clear exits, just a few doors scattered about. My nostrils picked up furniture and linen scents from within. Bedrooms most likely.

Just as I was about to reach the junction where the light shone brightest, a figure stepped out into my path. I skidded to a stop, my eyes darting over the newcomer. I dropped lower; growls ripping from me, rumbles in my chest, the fur standing up on my back. I didn't hesitate to attack. The wolf didn't understand that this creature was dangerous, maybe even more so than the dragon king chasing us. The wolf just wanted to be free, and I wanted that too, so I didn't stop her.

The jinn did not step back. It glided across the hall and knocked into my side, smashing me against the wall. I yelped. *Asshole*. How the hell was there a jinn here anyway? At least this one didn't have the markings of an elemental, but still, was he teamed up with the dragon king?

I attacked him again, from the side this time, my movements slower so I could dodge if he swiped at me. He was sidetracked for a moment by the arrival of Larky; the shifter was hard to ignore as he strolled up to us. Using that distraction, I managed to latch onto the jinn's arm, mainly grabbing at the layers of black cloak he wore. I jerked back and ripped it free, exposing his long, sort of oddly shaped limb. I couldn't tell in the wolf vision, but I guessed he would be marked in shades of red and black, like the last one I'd seen.

"Do not hurt her, Kirik, or I will end you." Larky was all protective and shit, and I really wished he'd do everyone a favor and kill the jinn and then himself. Was that too much to ask?

"She's your weakness, Larkspur. You will do well to remember your promises. This one cannot go free. If the bond is not fulfilled, you have no course with the gods. You have no firstborn and you made the deal."

This conversation was confusing to the wolf. I knew I should still listen so I could examine it later. There was something disturbing there. Firstborn … seriously? If Larky's dick came anywhere near me, I was cutting it off.

While the pair were focused on their argument, I took off in the opposite direction, but Larky was faster than a freaking bullet. He zipped across the corridor and enclosed my wolf in his strong arms before I could make it more than a few feet along the hall.

"Come, my little wolf. We have a dinner to attend."

I struggled, clawing and biting the shit out of him, but no matter how much flesh I tore free, nothing loosened his grip. His whole no pain, total-chill-about-everything attitude was starting to annoy me. I needed to figure out what his buttons were and I needed to push them. Hard.

He took me back in the direction we had originally walked, past the door of my smashed-up room and all the way to the end, where a spiral staircase led down.

Three floors down, we emerged out into a massive space. It was all marbled floors, fancy artwork, and shelves filled with books, like a big recreation room slash library but completely decked out for the rich and famous. The bastard had taste. I ignored the opulence and continued my mission to scratch his arm off.

I was getting really sick of being treated like a piece of décor he could just cart around. His blood flecked my fur and his clothes, but all of the wounds were healing fast. It was impossible to inflict enough damage to escape; he healed before I could even sever the muscle, and my wolf and I were getting both frustrated and tired. Supernaturals had a lot of stamina, but I had not eaten or slept in many hours. It was starting to take its toll.

"You have to learn to stop fighting me. We are meant to be together. I'm patient. I've never taken a female against her will, and I'm prepared to wait for you to come to the realization that we are meant to be. You can't escape your fate. The gods have spoken."

Lie. I think. He was good at using lie and truth in the same sentence, which confused the detector.

I bit him again, harder this time. If it was fated, I wouldn't have formed a partial bond with Braxton. There was something else at work here, some sort of dark magic, and there was no need for two guesses to figure out who had messed with the strings of fate. Larky had done this to me, I knew it, and I planned on rectifying the situation as soon as my ass got free.

It took us quite a few moments to pass through the beautiful room. The king continued to regale me with the most boring tales ever about how he won that piece of art in a spelling contest or something equally lame, or how that large mahogany duchess was acquired in his years as a knight. Dude was so old he made Louis look like a toddler.

Finally, we crossed into the next room, a large dining room. Off to the side I could see and scent the kitchen. *Goddammit*, I was starving.

I rationalized it in my head for a moment … really, there was no point denying myself food. I would only be weakened, and I needed to fight.

Plus, I was really effing hungry.

"I'm going to leave you here in the sunroom," Larky said as he pushed open a set of double doors.

My wolf eyes were quick to catalogue the cozy little nook, with its large windows and scattered couches. "The glass is magically reinforced. You can't break out of it. Someone will be with you shortly. There's a small bathroom just through there."

He dropped me down, gently, before moving like a shot to the open door. I lowered myself and snarled at him, showing every fang in my mouth. I would never accept this situation. I would continue to fight him until one of us was dead.

His genial tone cracked a little as he gave me one last glance. "Don't attack my ... maid. I will be unhappy if she's injured."

What the crap? He cares about his maid?

He swept from the room, the doorway closing behind him. Just like in the bedroom upstairs, there was no handle or lock on this side. I pulled on the wolf energy, calling it back into myself, shifting into human.

Rising from a crouch, I ran toward the glassed windows, wrenching up the couch which was closest to me and flinging it with all my strength. The noise was deafening, but little happened besides it bouncing off the glass and rebounding back toward me.

Motherfucker! He hadn't been kidding about that magically reinforced glass. I was starting to freak out. What if I never escaped from here? *Shit, no way.* That just wasn't even an option.

Through the window I could see miles of green grass, flowers, hedges, and landscaped gardens. It was beautiful, but with that sheen of fakeness; everything was just too perfect. Magic. My wolf senses usually detected magic with ease, but Faerie world was so doused with it I was on overload, numb to the energy.

The door clicked behind me and I spun, crouching down again, hands aloft. Larky was crazy if he thought I wouldn't use his maid to get out of here. This was the first weakness I'd seen in him and I was taking full advantage.

As the door widened even further, I stalked myself closer. A waif of a girl wearing a simple cotton shift dress slipped in around the corner and the door closed behind her.

She held up both hands in front of her. "I can't reopen the door. They have it locked down with magic. He's always one step ahead of us. I'm sorry."

Truth.

Her low, sweet voice halted me momentarily, my claws retracting slightly as I examined her. She was totally not what I had expected, and while I didn't want to fall for some I'm-weak-and-innocent trick,

I could sense nothing truly untoward about her. Still, she might be Larky's wolf in disguise.

Neither of us moved for a few moments, and I tried to figure out why she was so important to the dragon king. Her long, light brown hair hung in shiny strands along her face, which was small and elfin, pretty but unforgettable. She had brown eyes and a petite nose. Her skin was the most defining thing about her. It was a rich, creamy cocoa color, like she was a blend of more than one nationality, although I was pretty sure she was fey, or half at least, and in that case she could be from anywhere.

"Who are you?" I took another step closer, lowering my arms. "What do you know of old Larky?"

Those dull brown eyes met mine, and as she registered the hostility vibrating from me she flinched. Great, she worked for one of the scariest bastards in existence and she was afraid of me.

"Who the hell are you?" I demanded again, more venom this time, and I took another step closer. I realized that she was actually a little taller than my five feet four, but she was so waif-like that she seemed smaller.

"I'm … I'm as he said, the maid, and, uh … his wife."

I blinked once. And then twice. *What the what?* Did she just say *wife*?

Chapter 2

There was nothing I hated more than disloyal men. Sure, the Compasses were as free and easy as any male, with a revolving door of ladies through their beds, but if they ever committed to anyone, that would be it, there would be no others. That was what true honor for a man was, and Larky was neither true nor honorable. In the short time I'd known him I'd found out about his wife, his chosen mate – Lemon and Orange's mother – and me, whatever the hell I was supposed to be. Did this dick really think he could have a whole menagerie of women stashed around and that was all okay?

Fey wife was still staring at me, and I really had to ask her: "Why? Seriously … what the hell were you thinking? You could do a lot better than a weird, dead-for-a-thousand-years megalomaniac."

She lowered her gaze before it shot back up again; her eyes flashed as if she had only just realized I was naked. She went all wide-eyed with a sort of deer-in-the-headlights shock on her face. There was something very odd here. She was sweet, innocent, not the sort of plaything I expected Larky would keep around.

"Tell me how you came to be Larkspur's wife." "Wife" was such a human word to use.

She cleared her throat. "My parents sold me to him when I was fourteen and one year. There was this dragon terrorizing our village, in France. Master saved us, and in return I was promised to him when I turned sixteen."

Holy golden donkey balls. *France?* There had not been a prison community there in the time of the dragon king, which meant she was not fey … she was human. "What year were you born?" I asked.

She pushed back strands of her shiny hair. "Uh, I don't exactly recall." She took a few moments, seeming to be calculating in her head. "I've been in the castle for more than a thousand years."

"How are you still alive?"

She shrugged. "I don't know. I've lived here since I was acquired. I never age or change and it's okay. I do my duties, and the … the king leaves me alone."

I'll bet. She must have loved it when he was gone for most of her thousand years. No wonder she looked fey, she'd been living in Faerie, surrounded by magic. It had slowly been infusing itself into her, shifting her humanness. Now she was no more human than I was.

"What happened in this castle while Larkspur was in the land between?" I asked, hoping like hell she might have any insider information. The dragon king had chosen well when he sent her to me. I would not attack one of his victims, not even to save myself.

Dammit.

"The castle does not need him to continue its journey around the fey lands. We – the other captives and staff – just lived day to day."

She had to have been bored out of her freaking brains. I'd only been here for five minutes and I already wanted to carve out my own eyeballs and throw them against the wall just for something to do.

"What's your name?" I tried to put on my nice and gentle voice. She seemed easily spooked and I needed her help.

"They call me 'maid,' or 'wife.' I don't recall what my name was before that."

Maid or wife ... what the holy fuck? That's it, I'm killing every single one of the assholes in this castle.

"Okay, well, you need a name, because I'm not calling you either of those things. Let's go with…" I examined the timid female, trying to think of something which would suit her. "You look like a flower, all delicate and pretty so … Rose. That's what your name can be. Rose." Hopefully she had some hidden thorns too.

She did that blushing thing again, and I found myself shaking my head at the innocence of her. I'd thought my twin was naïve, and she had more than proven she was by trusting the bitch twins, but Rose was almost child-like. She had only been sixteen when she was taken, which was very young in the supernatural world. Not so much in the human world, especially back in her time of birth. They'd had very short lives then.

I put my general blunt nature into play. I didn't have time for bullshit.

"Would you like to escape from here, Rose?" She stepped closer to me and I realized there was a basket at her feet. She must have dropped it when she first walked in.

"I can't leave. If I betray the king, he will hunt me down and inflict the worst torture you can imagine. I'm the first of the dragon marked. We're all tied to the king of course, but I'm more so than any other. He can end my life with nothing more than a thought."

"So there were dragon marked before he was killed and sent to the realm between the worlds?"

She nodded. "There was me. He disappeared in Faerie for some time, and when he returned, he cast this spell. I was his experiment to see if he could create a bond between himself and other creatures. The spell allows him to infuse small pieces of himself into each marked, and then their life essence bonds to him. While there is even one marked alive, he cannot be killed."

I'd guessed as much, but it was still painful to hear that.

I straightened, blinking rapidly, trying to process her information. "Why are you telling me this?" I asked. "Surely, he doesn't want us to know anything which might help to defeat him."

She shook her head, before reaching down to yank up the basket. "I'm forbidden from giving you any information which might help you escape. He has not forbidden me from talking about the marked."

Her large eyes were flashing at me, and I knew she was trying to tell me something more. That the key to defeating king of the dickheads had to do with the marked.

"Come, I must dress you. He's expecting you for dinner."

"No," I snarled. "I will not dine with him. I'll tear apart any clothes he puts me in."

Rose did not argue with me, she just waved her hand and suddenly I was frozen in place. Great, so the rose did have some thorns – but she wasn't supposed to use them on me.

"I don't want to force you," she said. "If you give in to him a little, you have more chance at him granting you the freedoms you'll need to escape. In my time we had a saying: the snake in the grass will catch more with silence than with fear."

Strange she brought up that analogy, when my personal feelings toward Larky was that he was a snake. But okay, she had a point with the try-and-be-nice thing. It was just so much fun to smash his belongings and rip the shit out of him, but ... it definitely wasn't getting me anywhere. I was disadvantaged here. Everyone in this damn place seemed to have more magic than me. Even the human.

Rose released her hold on me, and this time I didn't fight as she shuffled me across to the bathroom. I cleaned up quickly, trying my best not to think about how out of control I felt. I would just have to be smarter at this game. Fighting, no matter how right it felt, was not going to work. I had to manipulate him to get the information I needed – lull him into a false sense of security. That way, when I figured out how to kill him, he would never see it coming.

Once I was dry, Rose handed across underwear and a dress. Ignoring the silky and expensive feel to each piece, I just pulled them on and dropped the lilac-colored shift dress over my head. It was old-fashioned, falling to my knees and draping across the rest of my body. The straps were thin, with lace edging.

I reached up and ripped the lace free, the material giving away easily. I hated lace. At least there were no ruffles. Rose said nothing as she sat me in front of a large, ornate mirror and pulled a wide-toothed comb through my black hair. It was getting longer now, falling in a dark cascade to my mid-back. As it draped around my face, the blue highlights made the dark blue of my eyes pop.

"We really need to ugly you up a bit," Rose said as she looked over my head. "The king likes pretty things. He's going to be even more obsessed with you now."

I snorted. "My mouth's not pretty, and he's sure as hell not going to like what comes out of it."

Rose's expression was scrunched, her thin eyebrows drawn together. "He's a dragon shifter. They like fire. They like fight. Maybe you'd be better acting like me. Invisible."

We both stared at our reflections. The contrast between us was strong. I wasn't sure I could tame the fire inside of me. I too was a dragon, and a wolf, and both of them were wild.

"I'm going to beat him," I said to her. "I'll figure out how to break the marked bonds, then I'll kill him. We'll be free one day."

Her scrunched expression did not ease, and I knew she had given up hoping a long time ago. My words meant nothing to her.

When I was groomed to her satisfaction, she ushered me toward the door.

"Why do you think Larky took you from your family?" I asked as we paused before the barred doors. "There must have been a reason he helped your village. He doesn't strike me as the kind of supernatural to just offer his services out of the goodness of his heart."

What had he wanted from them?

"For a long time I wondered the same thing as you," she said, a spark of fire lighting up those dull eyes. "Then one night I woke and found him in my room. He was draining my blood and life force. I believe that for some time he'd been sneaking in, spelling me to sleep and stealing from me. The sleep elixir must have been weaker that night. I was able to hear some of what he said. He spoke of how my blood worked the best in his spells, that it was the closest thing he had to the blood of the shining ones. My father always told me we were descended from fey, and I think that was what he needed in my blood."

So not totally human after all. Probably why she had adapted so easily to this land. The shining ones were the gods of Faerie, and if what she said was true, her blood would hold elements of their power. Blood was used a lot in spells. It was filled with life and essence; its strength was unparalleled. I wished Jacob was here, he'd know more about this than me. Faerie secrets were well guarded.

Hell, I really needed all of my boys. Most probably they were locked up right now for rampaging, pillaging, and killing stupid fuckers who wouldn't tell them where I was. I stumbled then as the full-body ache of being away from my pack crushed in on me. Rose mistook my fumble as weakness from hunger.

She touched my arm. "Come, you must replenish your strength."

I didn't understand this girl. Sure, I had no real experience with humans, although she wasn't really human, but she didn't seem to hate or love Larky. It was almost as if she was indifferent, which was a coping mechanism I had noticed in some of the long-lived members of our races. They had endured through so much that eventually they just shut down their emotions. Of course, there were always exceptions to that rule. Louis, my powerful sorcerer friend, had proven that by finally coming back to the land of the living after the death of his chosen mate.

Rose grabbed her basket and moved across to the door. Her cotton dress swamped her slender frame and looked easy to pull on and off. Why couldn't I have worn that style instead of this lace number? I swear to the gods, if Larky's eyes lowered to my boobs for even a second, I would forego all of my fake calm and rip his head off.

Rose knocked a few times on the door. There was a pattern to it; I guessed she was alerting the guard on the other side. My sensitive hearing picked up the click as the magical locks released, then the door swung open soundlessly. Rose didn't seem concerned to have her back to me. She was either stupidly trusting, or she had already sensed that I was not going to attack her.

To save my boys I would destroy anyone, but if I was the only one to think of, I could be more altruistic. Besides, I would have plenty of opportunities to escape. No doubt king dickhead would make a wrong move sooner or later.

My bare feet padded silently behind her, the floor cool but not uncomfortable. Like most of Faerie, the weather here probably did not change – not to mention everything here was infused with magic, so the floating castle and its surroundings would just respond to Larky's will.

Rose led me back to the kitchen area, and then off into a large round room. The stone floor merged into a thick, warm carpet and my feet sunk into the luxuriousness. Despite my fatigue and hunger, I remained focused on my surroundings, cataloguing windows and doorways. Noting that the large wooden table was ornately set.

"This is where I leave you. Please take a seat and someone will be with you shortly."

Rose nodded at me once – there was that spark of something in her eyes again – then she was gone. I watched her leave before refocusing on the table. It was made from what looked like a single slab of wood. It wasn't perfectly square; the shape mimicked the natural stretch of the tree it had been cut from. It reminded me of the stunning wooden piece in the boy's house in Stratford, the one that had been lovingly carved by Braxton. My dragon was talented with his hands, in more ways than one.

The ache crushed in on me again and I had to reach out a hand to steady myself. I knew I would struggle being away from the Compasses, but this felt so tangible, as if the partial mate bond between Braxton and I was actually causing me pain. Or was I feeling Braxton's pain? *Shit.* I really hoped it wasn't that. Nothing would make me lose my mind faster.

"Hello, Jessa. You look lovely."

I froze, my hands clawing into the back of the chair. I took a few deep breaths, and by the time I turned to face him I'd reeled my emotions in and schooled my face to show nothing but indifference.

Be nice. False sense of security. I had to repeat it more than once, my fist already clenched in preparation of punching that smug face.

"Thanks," I said, my voice bland, monotone. I wasn't going to go as far as acting enthusiastic – he knew I wanted to kill him. Better for him to think I had simply resigned myself to this fate.

He waited for me to take a seat at the table. There were at least twenty settings. I chose one furthest from the door. I wanted to be able to see who was coming at us. Larky sat across from me, and involuntarily my body leaned back. The width of the table top was at least two meters, but we were still way too close.

My eyes lowered to the setting in front of me. There had to be a hundred pieces of white and gold-trimmed dining ware, not to mention an array of silver objects which looked like old-fashioned cutlery. Nothing which would work as a weapon though – not that I needed one. Couldn't stab him to death unfortunately. I needed to break those magical bonds first, and I had no idea how to do that.

"I really love you in purple. Your eyes almost look lavender."

Really? He had to be shitting me.

Be nice, I repeated to myself again, but before I could stop myself my hand smashed out and crashed into the stack of white and gold plates – stupid perfect pieces of his life. They clattered to the floor. Some broke, but the soft carpet protected the rest. Of course, once I started I couldn't stop. I launched myself out of my chair and kicked out, upending the entire table. It was heavy – felt like it weighed a ton – but I was a shifter so I barely broke a sweat. The wooden top crashed to the floor, chairs and plates flying around the room. Larky had shifted himself back a little, but still sat in his chair, staring at me with that stupid friggin' grin on his face.

I screamed long and loud before launching myself at him. We collided and his arms went around me, but I was having none of that. My elbow whipped out and cracked him in the jaw, splitting it wide open. I avoided the spatter of blood, hating when any of his essence touched me.

The grin finally fell from his lips, and deep emotion lit up those stormy gray eyes. He lifted up a hand as if to slap me.

Bring it, bitch.

His hand jabbed out. I managed to deflect it, before returning the favor with a punch in the gut. Either he wasn't that hot at hand to hand fighting – I supposed in his day it was probably more about swordplay – or he was again just humoring my little rebellion. Stupid Ass. I was so ready to bail.

I drew on my wolf speed, and took off for the door. I had pieced together the basic layout, and this floor was definitely my best bet of getting out of the castle. It was ground level. I just had to find a window to smash or a door to break down.

I reached for my dragon. *Come on.* I needed her now. She was strong enough to crash through the damn brick if required.

King asshole's voice followed me as I ran: "Jessa, you cannot escape from me."

Still tooting that tired old trumpet. I focused on escaping and blocking out his energy.

My dragon and I continued to smash against the wall which separated us. Why the hell was this so hard? Shifting into dragon should be natural for me.

I crossed through the large room with all the beautiful books and paintings. The windows were high and barred; there was no escape from here. I took another hallway, one which I had not been down before.

"Follow me," said a soft familiar voice. I caught a glimpse of shiny brown hair and knew it was Rose.

Following her scent, I zoomed along even faster. Straight, left turn, right turn, and then left again. It was a maze of halls and I had to hope like hell Rose wasn't directing me on some wild-goose chase. I slowed as she came into sight, her petite frame before a large arched entrance, that low, unnatural yellow light of Faerie pouring through.

"I see you did well with the laying low and false sense of security thing," she said. A grin lit up her unique features, making her look extra young and pretty.

I shrugged. "What can I say. Guess it's not in my nature to lay low."

She nodded, not looking at all surprised. "You have a chance to escape now. I crisscrossed the path many times to confuse our scent, but you don't have much time."

"Are you going to be okay?" I knew she was forbidden from helping me, and I hated to think Larky would follow through on that torture thing.

She swallowed. "I'll most likely be punished for helping you, but I don't care. I feel you are the one chance for … for all of us trapped in a world of living but who do not truly live." She handed me a small brown sack which I had not even noticed her carrying. "Go now, find your family and break the bonds of the marked. It can be done. The answers lie on the island of the shining ones."

"The castle is in the sky. How am I supposed to escape?"

She gave me a bit of a shove then. "When you reach the end, take a leap of faith."

What the hell did that mean? She wanted me to just jump off? She gave me another push, and with a shake of my head I clutched the soft material of the bag – it was surprisingly heavy – and took off. I was loath to leave Rose behind, but she was tied too closely to the king. He'd be able to find her in a moment. I was hoping he didn't have the same direct tracking beacon to the rest of the marked.

Rose's exit from his castle led out into what looked like a courtyard garden surrounded by a stone wall about six-feet high. *Damn, I wish I wasn't in this dress.* The draw-string pack in my hands had straps, so I quickly threaded my arms through them and secured it across my back. I was going to need both hands to make it out of here. If I could have touched my dragon, it wouldn't have been a problem, but no, we still had a wall between us.

I sensed my beast's frustration too. Smoke was pouring from her nostrils as she struggled to reach me. I forced my focus outwards again; the gardens were filled with low bushy plants, twirled brambles of thorny vines and lots of flowers, most of which I had never seen before. Crazy things grew in Faerie, that was for sure. As I was closing in on the wall I heard shouts from back at the castle and knew that Rose's crisscrossed path had been discovered. I never looked back. I was not returning to the castle. I was not spending one more second with the king.

Avoiding most of the deadly looking flowers, even with their very tantalizing scents, I traced a path across the large courtyard garden. As I closed in on the wall, which was taller than me by quite a bit, I leapt up and landed cleanly on the large sandstone surface which lined the top of the barrier. On the other side of this wall was nothing but clouds, a massive expanse of white.

Well, eff me.

The breezes were buffeting me, and since I couldn't see more than a speck of land below, I knew there was no way to survive a drop this high. Sure, I'd done it once before in Faerie, but that had been when the dragon marked were indestructible. Now that the king had returned we could very easily be killed. My only choice was to "take a leap of faith," or return to the castle.

Trusting in Rose, I stepped off the side.

I stifled my scream, but thankfully only dropped for about three seconds before a mist swirled around my waist, and then, just like that, I was on the ground.

I shook back my hair, flipping my head up so I could see if the castle was above me. It was. Miles above. But it was as if I'd only fallen a few meters.

Was it some sort of optical illusion? Damn, no time to worry about it now.

I took off again. As soon as I had some distance between myself and those pursuing me, I would change into my wolf. I was faster, smaller, and harder to detect in wolf form. Magical tracing didn't work on my wolf either. Of course, I wasn't forgetting that Larky was a dragon. He'd definitely track me from the sky, so I had to find some sort of cover – this wide open expanse of grassy plane was never going to work.

I could see undulating hills in the distance and decided to head in that direction. They would limit the dragon's ability to both track and fly low enough to snatch me up.

The ground was still soft under my bare feet, which helped a lot with speed. I had a bad feeling I wasn't going to be fast enough. Sure enough, when I was only about halfway to the mountain, there was a distinct change in the air around me. Shifter energy lashed out and I almost stumbled at the sheer power. Larky was one powerful bastard – which was really annoying.

I sensed the dragon long before I saw him. Looking up, he was only a black dot in the sky behind me, glints of red and black flashing, yet I still clearly heard the distinct whoosh of wings.

In my dreams the king always had dark, heavy black scales, but in real life his black undertones were lit through with flames of red and orange, the colors shimmering in the light.

I skidded to a halt. There was only one chance for me now. I pulled off my bag and got naked in about five seconds, shoving my clothes into the pack. I called for my wolf, and within a few heartbeats I was changed, the bag in my teeth as I took off. I was at least three times faster in my wolf form – not to mention the dulling of my human fears was a nice relief. The wolf knew we were being hunted, but her emotions weren't quite as broad, nor strong, as my human ones. She would not panic until she was caught.

I heard the roar behind and there was a tingling heat in the air. The dragon drew closer, but my extra speed was enough for me to make it into the first valley between the mountainous ranges.

Chapter 3

Despite the mountains offering the smallest sense of security and freedom, I did not slow or lose my focus. If Braxton had taught me anything, it was that dragons were relentless. Larky would hunt me forever. He thought I belonged to him, and he would do everything in his power to retrieve his possession. The bag was a little annoying; its weight pulled at my lower jaw and the string dragged on the ground, but I couldn't escape without my clothes and what was hopefully food. I could smell varying scents from within and was reasonably confident that Rose had given me provisions.

The air still shimmered with tendrils of energy and lightning power. The dragon king was pissed, like mega pissed, and he was not hiding it. I could tell that here, in this land of pure magic, the dragon was extra potent. So why the hell couldn't I reach mine?

I could barely even sense her now in my wolf form; there was an even greater barrier between us. The two animals did not hate each other or anything, but it was almost as if one could not be present when the other was. It sort of made sense. It wasn't natural to have two shifter animals. There was no other shifter in history – even those from hybrid parents – who was a dual like me.

A roar echoed over my head; it sounded so much closer than before. I lowered my wolf muzzle as much as I could whilst carrying the bag, and picked up the pace. My paws were aching from the rocky ground but I was holding up. I'd be doing even better if I had some food and sleep to fall back on.

I was thankful that the valley I'd chosen to take through this mountain seemed to run the entire range. The path was worn, with strange colorful plants dotting the edges, very similar to the ones I'd seen in our jungle adventure here, just less overgrown. Shadows flashed across my head; I glimpsed Larky's brilliantly-colored sunset dragon through small gaps from above. He knew I was here but was too large to make it close enough to grab me. I really wanted to find a place to lay low until I figured out a way to contact Louis, but I could hear someone on the ground following as well. I was being pursued from all angles.

I needed another plan. They were tracking me too easily like this; I would eventually falter and be caught. Especially since I was not running at full capacity, and I'd already learned multiple times today that there was no real way to fight the king. I had to escape him and find my people again. We needed a plan to sever the ties between the king and marked. Like yesterday.

A shimmery visage caught my attention then, and it was odd enough that I faltered slightly in my full on sprint. *What was that?* I knew it wasn't safe to investigate strange things in Faerie. This was a land of weird and dangerous shit, but the shimmer had caught my wolf's attention. She wanted to move closer. So we did. My wolf and I were the same but there were also times where her curiosities had more control than my caution.

The ground pursuers were still some distance away, so I had enough time to change directions and dart between two thorny bushes which led toward the strange vision. I halted, my head tilting to the side as we tried to determine what this was. Some sort of portal is what I would guess. The sparkling depths could lead to anywhere, and for a second I wondered if there was anywhere worse I could end up than back in the clutches of the dragon king.

Behind me, rocks were shifting, feet pounding toward me, and I knew my time had run out. I could no longer hear the roar of the dragon from above, so Larky was probably also on the ground now.

Shit. I made the split second decision and dived into the shimmer. Wherever it led, I'd deal with it when I got there. My snout was first to enter, but by the time the rest of me followed, my feet were already off the ground and I was spinning in arcs and swirls across what felt like time and space. The inside of my head was spinning too, and even as a wolf I had to close my eyes against this nausea-inducing travel.

It wasn't hot or cold. No breeze. No scents. I had thought for sure that this was just a portal or step through, so what was with all the swirling? Someone was totally messing with me and I was going to rip their freaking heads off when I finally got off this ride.

The tendrils of air around me started to ease, the pressure which encased the wolf dying away, and I hoped that meant we were almost done in here. In a blink I was back on my feet and the world was again the right way around. And in that split second my nostrils registered the familiar scents around me.

No! No! No! For the love of my freaking sanity! No!

I was back in the castle. Back in that first goddamned room I'd destroyed. The swirling portal was gone now and there was no visible means of escape. How the hell had he set that up? How had he known my wolf would be enticed by that sparkling portal?

Looked like I was the winner of dumbass-of-the-day award. Angry with myself, I gathered energy and in a rush of red-hot rage shifted back to human. I picked up the bag which had fallen from my wolf's snout and yanked the strings open to look inside. Pushing past the purple dress, I was relieved to see jeans and a tank, not to mention new underwear. Rose was a regular genie of the castle. Too bad our plan hadn't worked.

Once I was dressed, I wasted no time hoovering down every morsel of food which had also been tucked into the satchel. Just a sub roll and a bottle of water, all of which tasted like double-dipped chocolate cake to my empty stomach. I needed the energy. Larky was going to be so far up my ass now, there'd be no easy escape again.

Muffled noises could be heard outside of my room, and before the magic door was even open, I managed to yank up a sharp stick, broken off from the bed. The door slid across; tingles of magic coated my tongue. I was one of those shifters very attuned to magic. I could always sense it being used. I leaned into my fight pose, letting my energy seep through me as I rose to the balls of my feet. I was prepared to leap, to fight. But it wasn't the expected blond dickwad who entered.

It was Rose.

I relaxed slightly, before dropping my stick and launching myself across the room to the fey-human. "What are you doing here?" I said, grabbing her arm and pretty much lifting her slight form up and back out the door. "Larky's going to kill your ass if he finds you helping me again."

A smile bled across her elfin features. "I love that you call him Larky ... he would hate that nickname." *Yes!* I knew it. "And he hasn't returned to the castle yet. There was a disturbance within the walls and he's very occupied."

I focused closely on her, eyes narrowing into slits. "How did you know I was back here?"

Things weren't adding up with Rose. She was human and yet not at the same time. She was a maid but could still sense when I returned to the castle. I mean, how strong was the shining ones' blood in her?

She didn't answer immediately, choosing instead to start ushering me forward. We were out in the hall, our steps picking up to a sprint before she answered me.

"I have lived within the walls of this enchanted castle for a thousand years. The king did not quite realize how much of the control and power would bleed into me. He tied himself to me, and therefore I became the mistress of the castle. I don't have complete control or anything, but nothing goes on in here that I don't know about."

Oh man, Larky was a dumbass, the sort of high-level-dumbass who would probably engineer his own downfall. That's what happened when you got so arrogant and powerful you forgot about the people around you. Tyrants often create the adversaries strong enough to fight them. Larky didn't realize what a weapon Rose was, but I did, and I would be taking full advantage of that.

As we hoofed it along the now-familiar stone passage, I remembered what she'd said before.

"What disturbance is Larky dealing with?"

A stillness crossed her face, like she'd just shut down on me. "Nothing you have to worry about. There are intruders in the courtyard, and their timing couldn't have been more perfect. I'm going to make sure you're far away this time, out of his territory with all of its traps."

Intruders!

The tugging sensation which had been rocketing across my spine since I entered that damn whirly portal increased; my pulse picked up speed. I'd felt this type of pull before. It felt like the partial mating bond. Were my boys here?

I yanked back on Rose's grip. She was surprisingly strong, but in the end I was stronger. "Who is it? Is it my pack, the quads?"

Rose still wore that poker face, which told me so much more than her words. She was totally hiding shit from me, and there could only be one thing this important. I pushed in close to her, making sure to let the wolf bleed into my eyes. Rumbling growls rocked my chest. I was struggling to stop my body from partially shifting.

"Take me to them right now. I like you, Rose. You seem like a good person who got dealt a shit hand, but if you attempt to keep me from my pack, I will destroy you."

I was not kidding either.

Slithers of color flashed across her eyes, like small fireworks. She swallowed audibly. "You have to understand, they're keeping the guards occupied, and they can more than hold their own. This is your one chance to escape. I can send you on a direct path to the isle of the shining ones … the fey gods. Like I said before, this is the only place I can think of to find answers. They'll know how to defeat Larkspur. Your pack will find you there. They sensed you the moment you were outside the castle walls."

I huffed. I was growl-yelling at her now: "If they can find me, Larky can find me, so there's no point running from him now. Let's go downstairs and kick his ass."

She didn't shift away from me, although those sparks were really zooming across her eyes. "If you make it to the Isle of the Gods, then you will be safe from Larkspur. The king's not welcome there. He has issues with the shining ones and he'll not risk waking the shadows when he doesn't have what they want."

I was reminded of what Louis – all powerful sorcerer and big brother figure – had said to me the last time we were in Faerie. Something about *lucky they did not wake*. Was he talking about these shadow ones?

My heart and soul were aching to knock Rose down and take off. My pack was here and I needed to go to them.

"Please, Jessa. I promise you there's no other path. No one can defeat the king without first breaking his ties to the marked."

As I opened my mouth to argue again she did something odd. Her eyes slammed shut and an energy zipped across her skin. I was about to yell or shake her when my vision went fuzzy. *Shit!* What was this bitch doing to me?

Then the first image shuttered across my mind, like an old school projector. It was a little dull and out of focus, but there was no mistaking what it was. A battlefield.

The images continued to shoot at me, one after the other, and all of them depicting the same thing. A field of death. I was blind now to the outside world, but there was no masking my cry of anguish as the cold, unmoving faces of countless members of the supernatural races buffeted my mind. Why was Rose showing me this? What the hell was this supposed to prove?

By the time the male stepped onto the scene, I was starting to understand. Tall, and deadly, he made a slow progression through the field of death. *Larky.* The dragon shifter looked different, wild, dressed in battle armor, chain mail, sword and head piece. He spared no notice to the dead, kicking through them with ease. He had no issues splashing across the rivulets of blood coating the ground, not surprising since he was well spattered already. Ahead of him, a vampire, who was crushed under a pile of other supes, lifted a hand and tried to scrape himself free. The dragon king noticed the movement, and even though I knew this was many years in the past, I wanted to shout at the vampire to be still, to play dead, even if it went against his predator instincts.

Larky moved with speed, his sword slicing through the supes neck, severing the head, and leaving another victim behind. I could hear screaming, and for a moment thought it was my voice, but it was actually Rose. Old-time Rose, dressed in a shift style dress of muted tones, with multiple layers of material. She also had a silky looking scarf wrapped around her hair. She was being held on the edge of this field by a bunch of gray-haired males. The king's mystics stood in a group, watching as the king continued to search out every single survivor. One by one he murdered helpless supernaturals, Rose's screams the background soundtrack. I focused long enough to hear words in her bellows.

"Why? They surrendered."

The king finally reached his advisors, and took a casual step forward before backhanding Rose, hitting her with the hilt of his sword. She collapsed into the arms of the closest gray, and only then did Larky answer.

"I gave them one chance, and they chose to fight my rule. No matter if they surrendered later, I expect total loyalty."

I was shaking now, and wasn't sure I could see one more dead face and keep the contents of my stomach. We had learned of these battles in history class, the dragon king had been involved in some of the bloodiest of all, but seeing it in graphic detail like this was stomach churning. Not to mention that Rose had actually been there, so these were memories tinged with her emotions. It almost felt as if I was standing on the battlefield too.

I wasn't sure if Rose let me go, or if I finally managed to pull myself free. We were both breathing heavily, and I fought hard to slow the trembles of my muscles.

"Now do you understand?" Her voice was low. "We have waited a long time for the one who could defeat him, you cannot stray from this path."

I understood, I really did, but I was also stronger with my boys. "You know that the quads have a calling, they can defeat the king."

She gave a huge sigh and my hand twitched. I almost bitch-slapped her. Typical of me: freaked-out to psycho in 2.3 seconds.

"They have the power to hold him off, nothing more. He cannot be killed. Their calling will be useful after you find a way to break the marked ties."

I was sort of stalling on the hope that the decision would be taken from me. Unfortunately, even though more noises were filtering up from other parts of the castle, no one approached us in the corridor. Rose reached out then and grasped my elbow, and before I knew it we were moving again.

My gut wasn't saying much at the moment. Usually it was a great indicator of what I should do but after seeing that field of death, my mind, at least, knew Rose was right.

"So you're sure they'll be able to find and follow me, and king-dick will not?"

Rose flicked around to shoot me an exasperated face.

"Explain it to me like I'm an idiot," I said. "I know nothing about Faerie."

"The land of Faerie is divided into four quadrants. There's the Isle of the Gods, the Land of the Dying, the Land of Sea and Forest–" *Been there.* "And right now we're in the Land of Illusion and Bespelling. All four lands are joined at the center of Faerie. This path I'm sending you on takes you to the center. He'll be able to reach you on the path, which is why we need to hurry, but once you're on the Isle of the Gods, you'll be safe from him."

It was annoying to know so little about this world, and it seemed the one thing I thought I knew – that Faerie was dying – was not even true. Why then had all the fey fled to Earth?

"So Larky has this entire castle rigged as some sort of illusion?"

I'd guessed as much from my short trip to the ground, but had also wondered if maybe it had been a large step through which had caught me when I jumped from the castle.

Rose was facing forward again, her grip still firm on my elbow as she continued dragging me down the spiral stairs. "Yes, it's a security system. Not many would have faith to jump from the sky. You've already proven your bravery."

Or stupidity.

We finally finished our descent and stepped out into a dark, narrow space. It had an underground, dank smell, and immediately my wolf wanted out. She wanted fresh air and freedom to run. My dragon didn't mind so much; her breed could easily adapt to caves and cold.

"These run beneath the castle. They're an old system that were used for smuggling."

"Smuggling of what?"

Rose shrugged. "Lots of things. Money, treasure, people. You'll be able to escape from here. This journey is not going to be easy, and once you enter the labyrinth you cannot leave until you reach your destination."

Okay, when had the *path* suddenly turned into a *labyrinth. Shit.*

"A labyrinth? As in a really long, complicated maze?" This was not going to be the easy journey Rose was spouting before.

"It's a path really. We call it the labyrinth because it has the ability to change its way … throw up obstacles."

Great, it was totally going to be filled with lots of Faerie inspired dangers. I sucked in a deep breath, closing my eyes briefly to center myself. What the hell, might as well get going. Wasn't like I had anything else to be doing right now.

The tunnel widened more and we were able to walk side by side. Rose was paying close attention to the walls and I could hear her counting under her breath. Great, we were lost in the freaking tunnel *before* the labyrinth. Lucky she wasn't going to be my tour guide for much more of this little Faerie journey. Girl's sense of direction was whacked.

I heard her murmur eighty-seven, then she pulled me to a stop. It was difficult to track her every movement in the dim light, even with shifter vision, but it kind of looked like she was pressing both hands into the brick. Before I had a second to think on this, she yanked us right through.

I braced myself, expecting to hit brick, but we just stepped out to the other side. Magic … even though I'd grown up with it, sometimes still took me by surprise.

We were outside. It was warm here, a garden again, but with less flowers and more hedge-type bushes.

"I'm guessing this is the beginning of the labyrinth," I said.

It looked like a secret garden, all sunshine and chirping birds. I had expected it to be dark and spooky, but I'm sure that horror would pop up later.

"This is the path that will lead you directly to the center of Faerie. Once you enter, there is no turning back. You must not be distracted by anything you see. Go directly to the island. Keep your wits about you. The shining ones do not encourage visitors. I've never been there, but I imagine there will be many traps and misdirections along the way. Do not lose focus, it could cost you everything."

I was listening to her, but the way she spoke in the ridiculous half-riddles of fortune tellers was really shitting me off. I hated those confusing bastards. Just say what you mean, straight up, no more damn mumbo jumbo crap.

This time I left with only the clothes on my back. The moment I crossed the threshold into the secret garden, I was surrounded by a plethora of new scents. The air was dry and sweet, like summer when flowers were in full bloom. I detected nothing out of the ordinary, nothing which was screaming dangerous. Still, just after I took my first step into the labyrinth, the hairs stood up on the back of my neck. The hedges looked different on this side, like they were closer and much taller. I risked one glance back to the entrance, but Rose was already gone.

Great, I was on my own, and I wasn't supposed to turn back. I shook my head a few times, almost stumbling as the realization slammed into me – Braxton had been back there. My Braxton. And I had let Rose lead me into this fucking path. What the hell was wrong with me? Okay, sure, she'd shown me the images of that battle, the horror of

Larky, which had spurred me forward. But she'd also done something with her touch afterwards, calmed me down, laid some Zen over my emotions, and I'd blindly followed like a pet wolf. Hell to the no! She was totally going down.

I turned back at a run, uncaring that I wasn't supposed to leave. Rules were for bitches. As I tried to burst out from between the hedges, my nose smashed straight into a barrier and I yelped, flung back to land heavily on the ground. Okay then, so when Rose said you weren't allowed to leave, she had meant it very literally. You could not actually leave.

My wolf and dragon both snarled. They wanted their mate. They wanted their pack. All three of us did. Looked like the only way I was going to end this crap was to get through this maze – get to the isle of the shining ones and ask them for help, or hope they had a weapon to cut the ties between Larky and the marked.

I wondered, for a moment, why I had never heard king dick in my head. He was supposed to be able to communicate, possibly even control us marked as a mass of minions, but so far … nothing. Maybe his Jedi powers didn't work in Faerie. There was an awful lot of magic in the air here, and it could definitely interfere with the mind-connection.

With a loud exhalation of annoyance, I pulled myself to my feet, dusted my pants off, and started trudging along between the tall hedges of this labyrinth path thingy. I scanned my surroundings constantly, bemused by how boring and mundane it was so far. I wasn't sure what I expected, having only had a few minutes to wrap my head around a Faerie labyrinth, but surely they could have expanded out from green hedges…

Green hedges which appeared to be pushing up into the sky the further I walked.

As they grew, the darkness around me increased. Great … I just had to open my big fat brain and start thinking about how things were not scary enough here. I should have learned my lesson about that the last time I was in this shithole. The land of Faerie read thoughts and then had a good ol' laugh creating your worst nightmares.

Despite the growing darkness, my footsteps did not falter. I was not scared of much. Even when I was alone I always had my animals to keep me company. And if Rose was right about my boys tracking me, they could very well be there when I got to the center of Faerie. I freaking hoped they were.

As I walked I periodically reached for my dragon. The wall was still between us, but for some reason it seemed thinner. Maybe Braxton was right.

Time was the only thing that could break down these barriers, cement our bonds. I had spent so much of my life pushing her down, forcing her to stay caged – not to mention Louis' magic subduing her – that now I didn't know how to bring her to me. I would figure it out though. She would be hugely important in the fight against Larky.

I wondered how much time had passed on Earth since I disappeared. No doubt they were well into the new year now, late January maybe. It was almost the quads' birthdays. They were born on the first of March. I was the thirteenth of October. We were all twenty-three this year, though some days I felt closer to a hundred and twenty-three. All I could say was that we'd better not still be in the middle of this shit when the quads' birthdays rolled around.

They were only two years away now from taking over as leaders of the American Supernatural Council. Now that Kristoff was gone and not trying to frame them for murder, they might actually have a shot at learning something. *Kristoff.* That sorcerer was totally still on my shit list. As soon as I had a spare second I was hunting his ass down and killing him. That's if one of the quads didn't beat me to it.

My tumultuous thoughts were cut off by my wolf perking her head up inside. She had sensed that we were not alone any longer. I slowed my pace, stepping lightly, keeping my presence as hidden as possible. The hedges had grown at least a hundred feet high. It was very dark on the ground, but I could still see quite clearly. A slight mistiness was invading, but I didn't let that deter me as I continued along. About six feet separated one side of the hedges from the other, hopefully keeping out anything too massive. Mind you, I should have known that in Faerie, it didn't have to be massive to whoop me in the ass.

Two figures stepped out of the misty shadows, blocking the path. Identical in every way, it took me a moment to figure out what I was seeing. My first guess were chipmunks, about three-foot-tall, brown fur with tan stripes across the bridges of their nose and along their tummy area. They stood completely upright, like humans, and had more than a little intelligence shining in their large globe-like eyes.

Still … how much trouble could two little rodents really cause?

The three of us remained motionless, our stare-off silent, although my wolf was urging me forward. She was hungry and chunks of chipmunk sounded like a perfect end to the day. Personally, the Jessa part of me preferred my meat a little less alive. Raw was not my favorite way to eat.

It didn't take long for me to be over our stare-off. Time to give my wolf what she wanted. Moving forward, my movements were swift and sure, arms already elevated in preparation of grabbing each chipmunk around its fluffy neck.

One of them opened its mouth and I expected squeaks or something to come out.

"What are you doing in our labyrinth, bitch?"

I pretty much tripped over my feet then and did a flip before sprawling out on my ass.

What the actual fu…? Did it just call me a bitch? Wait … did it just talk? Chipmunks don't talk. Not on Earth anyway.

Chipmunk number two piped up then. "I am totally going to eat your ass."

Um. Laughter exploded from me. I doubled over holding my stomach, trying my best not to choke. This had to be a joke, seriously. Between fits I could see that the two chipmunks looked uncertain, exchanging worried glances, which only made me laugh harder.

I finally managed to pull myself together. "You two … thanks, I needed that." I wiped at my eyes. "But I'd really prefer it if you didn't eat my ass."

"That's right," a deep voice said from right behind me. "There is only one creature that gets anywhere near Jessa's ass."

I froze, my entire body going into lockdown as it tried to figure out if that voice was really there or if it was a figment of my imagination. I knew I had to turn around, I had to move my goddamned feet so I could see with my own eyes. He'd snuck up on me, which was happening a lot lately, and neither my wolf nor dragon had detected him. That had to mean he wasn't real. It was just my heart and mind trying to bring my pack to me. Bring a piece of home.

Of course, I still had to turn, to see him for a second, even if he was only an illusion.

White teeth and dimples assaulted me, and a muffled sob caught in my chest. *Jacob*. The male standing before me might not have been the number one Compass of my heart, but he was a close second with the rest of the quads. I hesitated. Was this just the labyrinth screwing with me? Was he some sort of shape-shifting, killing machine?

The moment my wolf started to howl and push me forward I knew it was really my boy. I scrambled toward Jacob. His white hair glowed softly in the dark labyrinth as he used super speed to meet me half way. I wasn't sure if I was crying or laughing, or even breathing as I wrapped myself around him, absorbing everything about him, his fey scent, the elemental power that was so much Jacob, especially the fire he loved to keep closest.

He started to hum as I attempted to pull myself together. His strong arms held me tightly, enclosing me in his warm and familiar body. A million memories burst through my mind as the song of birth or *de la entréed* started to pour in a haunting melody from his lips. He knew I loved that fey ballad the most. It had been a comfort for me my entire life.

I held on to him as tightly as I could, and for just a few moments let all of the stress and worries fade away. But of course, there was only so long I could hide my head in the sand, and as the last notes of his beautiful voice faded into the darkness, I was back in the nightmare which had become my life.

Pulling some of my focus from Jacob, I sensed that the chipmunks were both confused and cautious. I was about to turn and see what those little fuckers were up to when one of them must have edged a little close – possibly to eat my ass – because Jacob let loose a fireball. The whoosh of heat was distinct as it left his body. The first flame would be a warning, but if they tried it again we'd soon be dining on crispy critter.

I knew it was time to remove myself from Jacob's arms. We had to find our way through the labyrinth and I had a million questions to ask him. Top of that list: where were the other Compasses? Still, I struggled to step away from his comfort.

After an eternity, and nowhere near long enough, I pried myself away. Jacob set me gently on my feet but stayed in my personal space, crowding me, one hand tangled in the hair at the nape of my neck as if he couldn't let me go yet. We remained like that for many silent moments, my wolf and I simply breathing in the pack bonds. Being without my pack was like being cut off from part of myself. You can survive, at least for a short time, but it's not comfortable.

"How long have I been gone?" I blinked a few times to clear the rimming of tears. "Have you been in Faerie the entire time?"

Jacob shook his head, those grass-green eyes slightly shiny themselves as he focused completely on me. "We were on Earth trying to find you, trying to keep Braxton in line while he carved a path of destruction through the sanctuary and every single being who ever had contact with the dragon king. We didn't know you were on Faerie until just recently. Even Louis couldn't find you, so whatever sorcery the king had around you was very strong."

I took a few long, deep breaths through my nose. "How is that possible? Louis knows everything. Larky somehow managed to get one over on the most powerful sorcerer on Earth?"

Jacob smirked and I wanted to reach up and touch his cheek. I was so happy to see that smile. "Larky. That's gold, Jessa babe. I'm totally stealing that. And yep, old Louis has been well and truly duped, which pissed him off a tad. Not to mention that Brax pretty much ripped his arm off and tried to beat him to death with it."

I felt my face scrunch up. "Why?"

"For all the times Louis knew more than he said, and for the fact that he promised to act as your big brother and then he let you disappear without a trace. Brax is a loose cannon right now. It takes literally nothing to set him off. He killed one of the fruit twins the moment you were taken, and the second followed soon after."

I tried to feel sympathy for those bitches, but … I just didn't care. They signed their death warrant long ago. I realized there were so many more things I had to be asking him, but at the same time I knew it wasn't smart to be standing still in this place.

We had to keep moving before the really scary shit came out to play.

Chapter 4

Jacob and I shifted apart as we turned to observe the path. I swiveled my head, taking in the complete circle of our surroundings. The chipmunks were gone, having scampered away at the first sign of a fireball-wielding fey. Still, even though nothing was around us, I sensed eyes out there. We were being watched.

"We should start walking," I said. "We have to make it through the labyrinth and to the isle of the shining ones."

Jacob just gave me a nod before holding out his hand, and together we started to stroll along the darkened path, the green grass swishing around my feet.

"Tell me everything else," I said as we crossed the distance at a reasonable pace. "How did you finally find me in Faerie? Why are you the only one in here? Where's everyone else? How are Dad, Lienda and Mischa?"

I had thought about my family a lot during my time in Larky's castle. When I wasn't tearing his shit to pieces, that was.

"I won't lie to you, Jessa babe, it's been really bad with you gone. I never expected it would be fun or anything, but shit fell apart in an epic, mammoth, gut-wrenching way." He had to clear his throat a few times then, and I gave his hand an extra squeeze.

"We were fucking devastated," he said, "not knowing if you were okay, if you needed our help. We were doing anything we could to find you, chasing down every goddamn lead which ever existed on Larky and his lairs. It's been weeks, weeks of nothing, dead ends, and dead supes – especially after Brax was through with them. Then, yesterday, when we were back in Romania dealing with shit at the sanctuary, which mainly involved a lot of interrogation of marked and mystics, Louis and Brax felt you. After that, the sorcerer knew you were in Faerie and he opened a portal straight away."

"I escaped," I mused out loud, doing the math on when they had appeared. Right after I managed to break free of the castle illusion. "When I jumped from the castle, I must have broken some of the spelling which was hiding my essence."

Jacob nodded. "Whatever it was, those two felt you just long enough for us to find the castle. We were intercepted by the king and his men before we could get to you. Did you know he has an entire army of elves?"

I blinked a few times. "Elves? I didn't even know elves were still a thing."

Jacob laughed. "I didn't either. They were definitely some sort of elf or half breed. Their skin was very green. Probably for blending in the forest."

That explained the green-skinned food bringer in the castle.

"In any case there are a lot less elves in the world now. Brax tore most of them to shreds. The rest of us got about eight seconds of fun. Your mate hogged all the killing for himself."

I had to push down my agonizing need for Braxton. I was starting to get all jittery, like a crackhead overdue their next fix. I had to not think about him or I was going to go crazy.

"What about Larky? You fought him … you guys know he can't be killed, right?"

A flicker of something flashed across those green eyes; the skin tightened along his brow. "We'd just finished off the elves and were facing down Larky when some sort of ripple went through his illusion world and he took off. He was heading in this direction right before he disappeared."

He probably felt my energy leave. I had no doubt he was hunting me right now and could still reach us here. We had to move faster.

Jacob picked up the pace with me, continuing his story as we dashed along. "We gave chase but were intercepted by this weird human-fey creature. She told us where you had gone, and with her map we found this labyrinth no problem."

Good old Rose. Well, it was nice to know she wasn't a complete bitch-face. She might have sort of whammied me to get me in here, but she sent my boys after me, so it wasn't all bad.

"We all tried to follow you, but I was the only one not repelled by the barrier. They decided to send me in so I could scout for you. Louis knows another way to the center of Faerie. They'll meet us there."

Hold up. "One: how do they know what's at the end of this path? And two: why couldn't they get in here?"

Jacob got that look on his face then, the one which appeared whenever he couldn't talk about fey secrets. Well, screw that one sideways on a horse. Not today, buddy. The fey owed me, because I was in their land and in an ass-ton of shit. I wanted answers and I wanted them now.

I must have been growling without realizing, because Jacob started to laugh. He wrapped me in his arms. "Calm, Jessa babe, my loyalty is always to you. You know that. It's just that there are some things which I am forbidden to talk of. I've sworn oaths and will be held to them."

I sighed. "Okay, I understand that, but with most oaths there is a way around them. What can you tell me?"

"Well, your sister is back in Stratford with your mom. Jonathon thought it was the safest place to stash the pair for now. The sanctuary is compromised because of all the marked there. The king hasn't called them yet, but if he does, there is a veritable army right there ready to detonate on the supernatural world."

I was relieved to hear that Mischa was back home, and clearly okay, or Jacob would have mentioned something more. She had been badly injured in Krakov, and it was really screwed up for me to have been taken before I knew if she had survived. Jacob's news relieved tension I hadn't even know I'd been holding onto.

Mischa and I had issues. Big ones. She'd acted like a complete fucking moron, trusting the fruit twins. She should have known better. She grew up with humans, for shit's sakes, and humans were fraught with deception and disloyalty.

I'd be a liar if I didn't admit that her stupidity did worry me. I hoped that wasn't a permanent part of her personality. I was prepared to give her the benefit of the doubt this one time – this one time only. Mischa better have pulled her head out of her ass by the time I got back to Stratford, or we were going to have a much bigger issue than a lack of trust.

What we really needed was time to bond. We should have always had a bond – which would have ensured she had less human weirdness in her – but our life together had been stolen from us the day of our birth. Hopefully when this shit with Larky was all over, we'd finally have our chance.

The labyrinth stretched out in front of us, so far nothing crazy was jumping out, but I doubted this peace would last much longer.

Jacob continued, "The four of us have been working on our bond and our abilities to fight the king. And yes, we do know that for now we can't kill him. He's surrounded in these layers of protection, millions of ties which are like a cushion against any blows we deliver."

I had information to add to that now but I didn't want to interrupt him. I needed to hear about my pack.

"I don't know for sure, but I think the others couldn't enter the labyrinth because it's a direct link to the Isle of the Gods. You can use this path to access any one of the four quadrants. You need strong fey blood to be allowed in here."

I felt my face crinkle as confusion swamped me. "Well, how the hell am I in here? Don't tell me I'm a dual shifter and somehow fey also."

Jacob laughed then. "Yep, you'd be even more of a super special supernatural then, wouldn't you?"

I snorted. That was a mouthful. Super special supernatural. Had a nice ring to it though, except I did not want any more specialness, especially if it meant the dragon king could use me for whatever diabolical scheme he had planned. And we all knew he had something crazy-assed planned for me.

"Am I allowed in the labyrinth because of the mark?" I wondered out loud. "I'm pretty sure Larky made some sort of deal with the shining ones before he died, and the marked was one of the things he received in return."

Jacob tugged me closer to him and I wondered fleetingly if he had sensed something out there. My wolf and dragon didn't seem alarmed, but that didn't mean there wasn't something alarming around.

"I doubt they would have made a deal with him, but if that's the case he'll owe the gods a massive favor. The fey started to flee these lands because a great evil sleeps here. The shining ones battled them, but something happened and the great ones lost a lot of their power. The fey were afraid that if the evil ever awoke, there would be no one that could contain them."

That was the most Jacob had spoken on Faerie in all the years I'd known him – which was okay with me, everyone is allowed their secrets, and I knew he never kept anything important from us. Our pack was very open with each other.

"So you all abandoned ship just in case it ever got into rocky waters?" I asked, my brows raising.

Jacob nodded. "Pretty much."

Well, that explained a lot. I jumped subjects: "Are Cardia and Grace okay?"

"Yes," Jacob said, "they're back in Stratford too."

Maximus' mate, Cardia, I didn't know very well, and I wasn't sure I was going to like her that much. But I would give her the benefit of the doubt, for my vampire. He held such a huge part of my heart and that meant his true mate would be a large part of our lives.

I didn't know if I'd ever be fully okay with sharing him with his mate, but so far he was making it work. Of course a lot of that was due to the fact that he still continued to put his pack first, and I had no idea how long it would take before Cardia decided it was time for her to be his numero uno.

"Louis was right about Grace too," Jacob said, as we continued to stroll. The breeze was just starting to pick up; there was an iciness to the air now. "She saved Mischa's life. The moment the immortality lifted with the king's arrival, Mischa was in grave danger. I don't think there would have been time to get her back to a healer."

Another thing I needed to thank the sorcerer for. Louis was powerful and enigmatic and I loved him like a brother. He hadn't been around as long as my Compass quads, and did not come close to their place in my heart, but he was still hugely important to me.

Our conversation was cut off then by a loud rustling of the hedges. We fell into defense mode, Jacob shifting so he was to the front of me in case anything flew out suddenly. I hated it when they did that; I didn't need a supernatural shield.

I took a step back, creating a distance between us. We needed space to fight, both of us already in our favorite stances. I had my arms in a loose, slightly raised position. Something was definitely stalking us, and I was pretty sure they were ready to attack.

Magic seeped into the air around us, ruffling through my hair, standing my wolf and dragon at attention. Some of the elemental magic was from Jacob. He had called on fire. A flaming ball rested in one of his hands. But the rest was from something else. Something fey, but not like my Compass. This was cold and metallic.

I recognized the magic a second before the figure stepped into view.

"Shit!" I said, low but audible. Jacob reacted immediately, shoving me further behind him before he stepped into the middle of the path.

A jinn. Seriously? These fuckers kept popping up everywhere I turned. They must have missed the memo where they were supposed to be nothing more than a myth.

I took two steps to the side, standing with Jacob. I threw him a glare to let him know I didn't appreciate being shoved aside like a damsel in distress. He flashed me a grin and some dimples, which was the quads' standard fare to get them off the hook. He was lucky I had missed him a lot.

Both of us returned our attention to the figure blocking our path. It took me a few seconds to recognize it as Kirik, the jinn from Larky's castle. *Shit!* Was he here for the dragon king? Had he been following me the entire time? Seeing him for the first time outside of my wolf vision, he was red and black, like the one from the sanctuary. Though upon closer inspection Kirik's features were different, more elongated and defined, with larger eyes and teeth. His markings were not very prominent, just your regular run-of-the-mill jinn. If you could call any of them run-of-the-mill.

"What the hell do you want?" I snarled, unable to hold my tongue a moment longer. "Why are you dickwads always stalking my ass? I thought you stayed out of the business of others. I'd appreciate it if you'd fuck right off and well, stay out of my business."

Damn, I had this politeness thing down.

The jinn just continued to stare at me with those dark, depthless eyes. I glided a little closer, shaking off the warning hand from Jacob. I wasn't sure where my lack of concern for my safety or wellbeing sprung from. The reality was I was far more breakable now than ever before, but I was running on no sleep or decent food – no *cake* – and I had had enough of this shit.

I got right into his personal space. "Answer me," I said, my mouth inches from his face.

I realized then that we were practically the same height. Jacob towered over us. These demi-fey creatures held so much power, I often forgot they were quite frail in appearance. "Why do you all stalk me?"

A rush of winds was my answer, the previous iciness growing. Then, when I was about to lose my shit completely and throw down with a supernatural that could probably squish me with no more than a thought, it spoke.

"You're not natural, Jessa Lebron. You hold something which is not yours to hold. Larkspur stole the essence and you were forcibly dragon mated, and that cannot be allowed to continue. The jinn read the future, and for now you have none. We debate whether to end you, or to simply bide out time and let you work it out ... the right way."

Whoa! Okay, that was a little full on. No future? Surely they must see something for me. And what the hell was dragon mated? We had mates in the supernatural world, but how did that specifically refer to dragons?

"Give her a chance," said Jacob. "She always does the right thing. Even if it takes her a little while to reach that conclusion."

Jacob was standing against my right shoulder. He was apparently going for the diplomatic approach today. Although I wasn't sure if that was an insult or a backward compliment. Either way, he deserved an elbow in the ribs, which I delivered.

"If you make the right choice, then you'll have no more issue with our kind," the jinn said.

In a flash, the air around us filled with fire and ice, a strange combination of the two elements. Jacob and I jumped back and I still felt the burn of flames and the sting of frost. By the time I blinked a few times and looked again, the jinn was gone. That elemental fire and ice show must have been its grand finale. I took a few shuddering breaths before locking eyes with the fey.

"He was in the castle with Larky, I thought they were in cahoots, but it seems that the jinn are keeping tabs on him and me." I all but whispered. "Do you think he'll return?"

My dragon roared then and urgency overtook my mind. Jacob hauled me closer.

"The jinn's gone," he said, "but seems like everything else is coming out now."

Noises crashed in around us and I was getting the distinct impression that the jinn had been keeping the creatures of the labyrinth away so that it could deal with us directly. Now it had left again, taking with it whatever barrier it had erected. Shit was getting real now.

Jacob and I ran, hauling ass as fast as our supernatural legs could carry us, neither of us pausing or looking back. "You need to stop drawing the attention of the jinn," Jacob said as we powered along the dark lane. The noises grew around us, reminding me of the ape-bears that had chased me last time I was in Faerie. "They have the power of the fates behind them. They can rewrite the fabric of the worlds. They can create and they can destroy." His pause was dramatic. Typical fey.

"Don't give them a reason to rewrite you, Jessa babe, not even a small one."

I managed to sigh, roll my eyes, and keep running like my butt was on fire. "Jacob Compass, what the freak do you think I did to draw their attention? I didn't even know they were still in existence until the last couple of months. Whatever is up with me, it's because of the dragon king. That asshole did something to me, something before I was even born. All of the marked have been manipulated by him, but for me it's something more."

And according to Rose, the shining ones were the only beings with any answers. Now ... what were the odds they would be willing to tell us?

Jacob got all serious then. "You know Brax and the others will be waiting for us at the center of Faerie. If we make it out of here, there's a great chance you'll run straight into your mate's arms."

I swallowed roughly, my throat and body tightening at the mere thought of being with Braxton again. I knew Jacob was giving me this little motivational speech for a reason.

"How bad is it?" I asked him, unwilling to turn my head and see for myself. I was not tripping over a log or some crap right now. I needed full focus in case the maze threw out any obstacles.

He didn't answer immediately, which of course allowed my mind to imagine the worst shit possible. Before I had a chance to beat the information out of him, the world exploded around us. Creatures flew out of every bush and crevice, so many that there was no way to accurately assess their level of scary. We had no choice but to slow, the path blocked on all sides, with more continuing to fill in the gaps.

Jacob brushed closer to me. "How bad is it, you asked? Well, on a scale of one to apocalypse, I'm going to go with an eight," he said casually.

Eight … if this was an *eight*, what the hell was *apocalypse*? Dammit, okay, we could deal with this, we'd been here before and we would be again. I was not getting taken out today, not by a bunch of chipmunk freaky Faerie creatures.

As they pressed in closer to us I could see there were more than just the chipmunks here – though they had brought fifty thousand of their closest friends. There were slime-coated fire slugs about the size of a small poodle, their tails lit up like a very orange fireball. And also a weird rabbit thing, almost shaped like a kangaroo, but wider and shorter, its ears long, and with some lethal looking claws on its front paws – not to mention large, webbed feet and bucked teeth to finish off its ugly-ass-ness. Elements danced in the air around us as Jacob pulled his power. The fey were so much stronger here than on Earth. I'd never seen fire and air respond to him so quickly. The rumble beneath our feet indicated he was shifting the plates, using the ground as a weapon of sorts.

"Don't forget about Braxton," Jacob said with his jackass grin on. "He's waiting for you and you need to survive this, Jessa babe. If you don't, then none of us do."

The odds were against us, but he had given me the best incentive of all to slay these fey creatures. I just wished I could shift into my dragon; she would pretty much eat all of them up in one gulp. Jacob pulled a knife from his belt and handed it to me and in the next instant we were under attack.

I focused on the creatures around us, my grip firm on the long-handled blade. Most of our stalkers might be smaller than us but they had fey power and it would be the epitome of stupid to underestimate them. Three came at me from the left, and at the same time at least half a dozen flew at Jacob. Neither of us hesitated. I hit the ground, rolling clear of their attack and coming up beneath them. My blade hummed and then seemed to actually move of its own accord, eviscerating two of them in a rapid succession. I loved when I used fey-made blades, they pretty much had a mind of their own. My partially shifted left hand was useful too. The third was taken out by a claw to the brain.

Pain grabbed at my spine then, right near the base. I dropped backwards, directly to the rough ground. I heard multiple squeaks, and whatever rodents had attached to me were either squashed or jumped free just before I landed. Of course, now I was down, and that left me vulnerable.

I rolled across to the side, just in time to receive multiple slashes in my arm. My wolf and dragon started to growl as pain rocketed around my body. I was not in a good mood. These little assholes were going to die, seriously.

Dislodging a few, I jumped to my feet. The pain was dull, pounding across my lower back, and I wondered if they'd done some real damage there. A quick glance told me that Jacob was cleaning up his section, making me look pathetic with my half a dozen dead. He had dozens fried, drowned, suffocated. His elements were a distinct advantage, but there is nothing like getting your hands dirty. I was a down and dirty sort of girl.

I let the shifter energy course through me, and as I felt the wolf respond; the hum of dragon power dipped across the wall between us. A flood of panicked confusion welled within my mind, and immediately the blocks fell back into place.

Shit!

That had been the perfect opportunity to connect, to break down the barrier once and for all. I had a sense that if I figured out how to break this wall between us, and not because I was about to plunge to my death, then it would be gone for good.

If there was one opportunity, more would follow.

My train of thought was cut off again as more chipmunks, fire slugs, and mutant rabbits dived toward me. They were working in larger teams now, two of each Faerie creature forming a ring and coming directly at me. I could feel the heat of the slug's tails and as I slashed out with blade and claw, the fire was close enough to bubble skin and singe clothing. I was killing them as fast as they dived, but there were just so many of them.

I need you, I cried out to my dragon, and she smashed herself against the wall. Inside my mind I started to holler, expelling every ounce of my frustration, fear, and anger. It was a pure expulsion of energy, and as my beast came at me just as fiercely, the very first fissure appeared in the wall between us. I sucked in rapidly, still slicing and dicing my way across the thousands of creatures that were trying to stop Jacob and me from making it any further through the labyrinth.

Internally my dragon and I continued to smash away; there was finally a weakness to work with. A burning pain licked across my ribs and I realized the side of my shirt was completely ablaze. I hit the ground again, rolling to douse the flames, staring up through the mass of towering hedges and curved vines into the endless sky above. Jacob stepped into view and hauled me up, dousing the last of the flames. We fell in back to back and I was a little annoyed to notice that he looked a hell of a lot better than I did. Just some mussed strands in his blond hair –though, okay, that was actually pretty messy for my fey pack mate.

My dragon was still working at the barrier. "Keep me covered for a second," I murmured. "I think I might have a shot at shifting into dragon." No point tipping these little critters off. I wanted to make sure they were all here still so I could stomp them into the ground.

Jacob reached back and gripped my hand, squeezing tightly, and I knew as always he had my back. *Fuck. I wish my other boys were here.* We were strongest as a team and right now we needed their strength.

I felt the pull of elemental power again, stronger than before. A ring formed around us, a very large, blue circle of flame. Jacob's fire had sprung from the fey power in his chest. I'd seen one before, and knew it took a lot of energy to maintain.

The circle started close to our bodies and began expanding out to incinerate anything caught in its path. That I was pressed right against Jacob allowed his magic to recognize me as not-enemy, and I was unharmed. But the rest of the creatures weren't so lucky. They started to fall back, shrieking as their bodies burned. Nonetheless, they were relentless, and even as some burned others continued to try and reach us. Jacob was strong, and could keep this up for a long time, but eventually they would overpower us with sheer numbers. I had to reach my dragon. It was our only hope.

Chapter 5

I wasn't big on focus. The Jessa part of me liked spontaneity and change, got bored easily and tried to create drama. The wolf part of me was another story. Wolves locked in on their prey and stayed locked.

Flashing back to that moment before, when connecting with my wolf had weakened the dragon wall, I wondered if the key to connecting to my dragon was in part to do with my wolf. I had no doubts that my wolf would go at the barrier until she got through. Had the answer been in front of me the entire time and I had been ignoring it, thinking that my wolf and dragon wouldn't be able to exist within the same space? Maybe it was time to bring the mingle.

I opened my wolf's cage enough to let her prowl free, but stopped the change from sweeping over me. This release had to happen on the inside. The shine of black coat flashed across my inner mind as the spirit of my wolf leapt out. Gods, she was so beautiful, so absolutely regal. I was blessed to have her with me.

Go! I urged her toward the dragon cage. She briefly hesitated, unsure about the situation into which she was walking. Keen intelligence was one of her strongest traits, and a survival instinct like no other. Curiosity won out in the end, as she slowly prowled toward her roommate of the past twenty-two years. The dragon rose, smoke brewing from her scaled nostrils. The two paused on either side from the other, just staring. Then my wolf threw back her head and howled, long and loud, a full moon, joyful howl. The dragon followed suit with a bellow of her own.

Jacob's ring of fire was starting to flicker around us, and I could see the strain and fatigue on his handsome face. I was running out of time. We needed the dragon now. As if she sensed my urgency, the wolf threw herself at the dragon cage, scratching and pummeling against it. The dragon mimicked her actions from the other side. Instead of just smashing against the cage, she was using her claws, learning from the wolf.

Because I'd never properly connected with my dragon, it was almost like she was a newborn pup. Or whatever the dragon equivalent was. Cub? Dragonling? Anyway, she was learning from my wolf, and together they were doing what my dragon and I couldn't manage alone. They were cracking the wall.

Come on, guys! I was mentally cheering them on, and at the same time I reached out and hugged myself to Jacob's side, offering some of my energy to keep the fire burning.

I felt the slightest drain on my being then, not enough to leave me vulnerable, but hopefully enough to keep the thousands of creatures at bay long enough for my dragon to break free. The fiery ring flared brighter, the width increasing just slightly, pushing back on the masses which still seemed to be multiplying around us.

The growls and bellows increased within and I could sense it was close now. Deep fissures appeared in the wall between them; the magic of the dragon was seeping out. I recognized it from my many years with Braxton, and the few times I had touched my own dragon. It was wild, fierce, ancient, like nothing I'd ever felt before or would feel from any other creature, not something you could hold or contain, despite the fact that she had lived within my soul for many years. The dragon magic was wild and free. I sensed that it belonged to no one and that the only reason supes were blessed enough to experience it was through the dragon's choice. The fact that my dragon chose me to share her essence with, well, it was one of the few things which truly humbled me.

With one final lunge the dragon's bulk smashed through the wall holding her captive, and as it fell, a fracturing of some sort started in my chest. For a second my vision flashed in black and white before returning to regular.

I knew there was no reinstating that wall. The dragon was free and the barrier between us would never exist again. A wash of dragon and shifter magic swept through me, and in a rush of panic I ushered – maybe even shoved – my wolf back to her section. I didn't want to end up as some sort of literal half wolf dragon – a fluffy dragon was bad enough.

"Jacob, get away from me!" I screamed as the change started to shake my body. The fey dived to the side, somehow still maintaining the elemental ring around us. I had no time to admire his move though, I was about to become a dragon.

Every muscle and nerve in my body was quivering as power and adrenalin flooded through me. The magic engulfed my mind, and unlike the other times I had shifted, I was aware enough to feel everything. The swelling of my heart as it enlarged into an organ five times the size, big enough to fill the massive chest of my dragon, this heart was filled with fire and heat. At the center of the beast was an inferno which burned hotter than lava. My bones cracked and popped, but the magic prevented the pain from being too intense. It was worse than with my wolf, but nothing I couldn't handle.

The shift was fast, and at the same time felt like an eternity as my limbs lengthened, tearing through clothes. My mind was the last thing to shift, the world suddenly filling with the kaleidoscope of colors which dominated the dragon vision.

I blinked a few times, orienting myself to the new body and thought patterns. The dragon was less animalistic than the wolf, more evolved and wise, overflowing with an abundance of magic. Still, there was something extra foreign about my mind now, something which scared me a little and felt disconnected, like the dragon and Jessa brains were not meshing as closely as they should. Probably just another part of the bonding that I needed to work on.

I could sense thousands of life forces around me; the strongest was the fey close to my side. Jacob was awash in shades of turquoise, the energy of his fey power. *Brother.* The dragon knew him, trusted him. He was one of her guarded treasures, her family. The rest of the creatures who sought to harm us were another story. They would flee or die. There was no other option in the dragon's mind.

I threw back my head and let out a roar. It bellowed deep from within my thick chest and echoed out into the darkness of the world. Strangely, the labyrinth seemed to be even more shadowed and ominous right now, as if it were reacting to the dragon's presence and upping its scariness. It wished it was as scary as me.

The burning heat in my chest increased; flames followed the bellow, courtesy of the lava in my center. The impressive plume shot out into the air and was about a zillion times hotter than Jacob's ring of fire, which looked to be on its last legs. Time for my dragon to step in and clear the path.

I lowered my head and nudged at my pack mate. Even with the wash of turquoise, I noticed that his skin was extra pale. He was low on energy. With a flick of my snout, I indicated that he needed to get onto my back. I was getting us out of here, one way or another, and while I knew it wouldn't be as simple as just flying away – the labyrinth would not let me go that easily – I could at least clear a path.

His eyes flashed as he climbed on, his almost non-existent weight settling in behind my wing joints. I flapped a few times to ensure I had enough movement.

"I need to drop the elemental ring now, Jessa babe." His low words were easy for the dragon to hear. "I want to have enough energy to keep your back protected."

I nodded my head at him, letting him know I was ready. It was time.

The fire winked out in a final flash of heat and light and the noise seemed to increase then, as if Jacob and I had been in our own personal bubble. My powerful limbs surged forward and the instincts of the dragon kicked in. Which was good, because the Jessa part of me had no idea how to utilize this weapon which was my beast.

My tail whipped around in an arc, clearing out the enemies sneaking in behind, and with two hard thrusts of my wings I was up off the ground, about six-feet high, which allowed me to use my four powerful claws as weapons. Creatures threw themselves forward and I wiped through them like they were nothing. A lick of heat grazed my right side, and I glanced down to see that a bunch of the fire slugs had morphed together and were trying to blast through my scales and fur. I wanted to chuckle. I was a dragon, fire was my friend. It almost felt rejuvenating, as if I was sucking in some of the element and strengthening myself, slices of heat flickering through my blood and into my muscles and organs.

I roared again and my own flames shot out, incinerating everything in the path, flames of the brightest red and orange, with shimmers of blue, almost like the blue flame which surrounded Braxton when he went into raging maniac mode.

Braxton.

On the outside we were still fighting, flames and claws making light work of the creatures who had made the mistake of taking on a dragon. Jacob on my back was helping too. I could see flashes of his elemental magic in the dim light. Yep, on the outside we were all badass, but on the inside my dragon was making a sad, mourning cry. It hurt my heart, like someone had just reached into my chest and was squeezing it tightly. I realized I was mourning too.

Mate, we both said in a whisper to the other. I understood her emotions; she had accepted Braxton as the mate for me, and we both missed him and his dragon.

I pushed down my ache for the moment. I needed to focus. So far the labyrinth had only thrown evil little critters at us, no match for the dragon. None of them had an attack which could hurt me. But I sensed something more lurked in the shadows.

"Move, Jessa!" Jacob's shout spurred me into action, and my wings, which had been in a glide position, started to flap and push us forward. My flames cleared the path, and finally a few of the small annoyances must have grown a brain, because they were fleeing back into the bushy hedges around us.

The darkness was no problem for the dragon. The world was awash in a medley of colors, everything tinted with light so I could see clearly. Within a few seconds we were well past the chipmunks and friends, but I knew there was a reason Jacob had warned me to move. Something was stalking us, something big.

I heard a tense chuckle from my fey pack mate. "I love the way you could have taken off immediately and flown above their heads, but instead you stayed and showed them their mistake in attacking us."

Hell yes I did. Next time they would think twice about it. I was dragon and wolf. We did not run from a fight; we were dominant and needed them to know it. Plus, it was fun to let free some of my frustrated anger. I hated the path my life had taken lately: the dragon mark, the Four, Larky. And most especially that my bond with Braxton had not formed properly. If it wasn't for the fact that I had found my twin – who had some decent groveling to do the next time I saw her so I wouldn't kick her ass – and I had freed my dragon, I'd think that the fates kind of hated me.

Bitches.

Okay, they did give me Braxton as a mate, sort of, so I couldn't really hate on them too much.

Still, it wasn't like I'd had any time to actually enjoy or appreciate this gift. Sooooo ... I was right back to wanting to kick the fates in their faces. Their stupid, smug faces.

"Jess, you need to move faster. Death stalks us on swift winds. The evil is so infiltrated in this area I can't even tell where it's coming from."

I realized I had slipped easily into my Jessa mind then. The dragon and I were coexisting so much more independently than me and my wolf, like there were two separate brains inside my head. I worried about that. Shouldn't there be more melding between us?

My chest started rumbling then, and I knew the dragon was feeling the same evil as Jacob. I let my mind go, let her take control again, and the world was once more flashing at me in so many different stimuli. The wind whipped around us, and in the air currents I scented the shadow stalking us. It was strong and dark, familiar, but also smoke-like. Every time I got a decent feel for what was after us, the sense slipped through my fingers.

My wings flapped harder, the cool air whooshing by. I barely felt the chill, but something told me it was almost freezing. I hoped Jacob was doing okay back there. His magical bond with the elements should keep him warm. The labyrinth, which was actually not a labyrinth at all since there was nothing maze-like to this path, seemed to be changing as we progressed further through it.

The unease was creeping closer, my scaly hide growing extra sensitive to the currents around me. That ache which had started in my lower back when we were first attacked was still present, even while in dragon form. Which was odd – shifting usually healed minor wounds.

A shadow closed over us and I knew an attack was imminent. I mentally urged Jacob to hold on as my dragon went into stealth mode. I dived lower, whipping in and out of the shadows, pulling my wings in tight so my large dragon body moved as swiftly as a bullet.

I risked a glance backwards, and the flash of black, red, and orange caught my gaze. *Motherfucker*. Larky had finally caught up with us; that bastard just did not give up. I kicked up my speed. I could not risk Jacob. I wasn't sure what the king would do if he got his hands on him, and my best friend was vulnerable without his brothers.

The greenery around us changed again, thinning out and giving the general vibe that we were coming to the end of this journey. I spread my wings again and flapped a few more times, my brain screaming for us to go faster, although my dragon remained calm as she kept one eye on our surroundings and one on Larky. I dived lower, my claws almost scraping the rough ground. There were no creatures to avoid here, just the giant shadow tailing me at a rapid rate.

I heard Jacob give an excited yell and I focused forward. *Yes!* We were nearing the end of the path, a trail which would have been very long and difficult to traverse without the help of my dragon. Of course, I wasn't sure if all those tiny asshole critters were courtesy of the jinn; those ancient fuckers kept trying to passively kill me. Even if the "ass eaters" were just a special gift for me alone, the sheer length of this path could have any person wandering for weeks.

The dragon cut through the distance with a speed that would be impossible for any other supernatural. Freedom was so close I could practically smell the fresh air, or at least new air from whatever lay on the other side. The damp, decaying scents were lessening, and I had a sense of sunshine and crystal clear waters. Something beautiful was on the other side.

The shadow was close. It would be a race to see which of us would make it there first. The steel trap of my dragon mind forced me to focus on the end of our maze, to push our wings harder, to dip and dive through the air currents, seeking the fastest route. I'd had no idea that dragons could actually use the elements to increase their speed. My beast showed me differently.

Even though shifters used magic to shift, my wolf was still animal, bound by the laws of her species. I was starting to think dragons had no laws, which was just fantastic when I had another crazy-ass dragon chasing me, one with a god complex and delusions of grandeur.

The space between the hedges was widening. I could actually spread my wings their full width, which had to be well over fifteen feet. Jacob pressed himself more firmly against me, and at the same time leaned back to give me a chance to really flap hard.

"Fuck!" My fey quad's curse was low and menacing, and I knew our time for running was up.

In a flash, I flipped myself over into a complete tumble, which somehow let the dragon body snake around and face back the way we'd just come from.

Holy flaming shitballs. How the hell had that even been possible?

Especially considering we'd been flying fast, like a freaking bullet fast. That was a wicked move. I needed to learn what the dragon was capable of. Both of us were pretty clueless. Thankfully, she had millions of years of instinct guiding her.

As the dragon focused back into the darkened labyrinth, the shadow was no longer just a shadow.

It was a massive sunset-colored dragon, at least twice the size of me, the stuff of horror and legend. The breadth of its black wings, tipped in red points, were well over twenty-five feet, Larky's four heavily-muscled legs tucked-up beneath. He had managed to change his own trajectory and was now hovering about a hundred yards from us.

My dragon had mixed emotions about this magnificent creature. She seemed both in awe and annoyed. I understood this. Larky was pretty magnetic, and his beast was damn impressive. From this angle his dragon looked even larger than Braxton's and that was saying something. Still, neither of us particularly liked that he kept chasing us and trying to lock us up like a friggin' circus sideshow.

Jacob slid himself off to the side, hanging close to my head. "I'll distract him, Jessa babe, you get out of here. Get to the boys so they can help you fight. You and I can't take him right now. He's too powerful and we can*not* let him get a hold of you. Whatever plans he has, they're not happening." The fey practically hung mid-air on my right flank, his air element assisting him to stay aloft.

A growl rumbled my chest. He was as crazy as donkey balls if he thought I was going to leave him here to the mercy of Larky. I knew for a fact I wasn't going to die today. King dickhead needed me for something, but Jacob did not have any protection against his treachery. And if he died, my world would cease to exist.

I lunged out to snap at his shirt. Once he was in my teeth I'd be hauling him back onto my back, but he had already let go of me. He fell thirty feet to the ground, in a rapid but controlled drop.

Bastard. Jacob didn't have to worry about Larky, I was going to beat his ass when I got to him. Ignoring his orders from before, I followed his path, the flash of blond hair easy enough to track in the darkness. He was heading straight for the other dragon.

"Jessa babe, go the other fucking way," I heard him yell, but he didn't stop, and I wasn't stopping either. Larky was still hovering, his orange-tinted eyes observing us as we both barreled toward him.

"Braxton is waiting for you, Jess."

Jacob was playing hardball now. My chest actually clenched, even in dragon form. Both of us loved Braxton. But I also loved Jacob and I would never be able to face the rest of my boys if I left one of them behind in here with the dragon king. I would never be able to face myself again.

I covered the distance in seconds, the darkness again closing in as I left the light and freedom which had been so close. I had no hesitation to attack, but I decided not to hit the dragon king head on. In the last possible second I ducked myself beneath the massive form of the sunset dragon, avoiding his claws and coming up behind him. I snaked out and bit down onto his tail, which hung low and heavy, avoiding the three-foot spikes which littered the spine of his body and tail, and crunched into scale and flesh. As my jaws locked on, I ceased flapping, dropping straight down. Larky gave a roar as I took him down with me, but, unfortunately, just as the ground closed in, he flapped those powerful wings and halted our descent.

I will not let you be hurt. You must stop fighting me.

Oh hell to the no! *For the love of all the fey gods, someone tell me Larky is not able to talk in my head!* That was supposed to be something I experienced the first time with Braxton, the way dragons could communicate with each other.

I projected my thoughts back as loudly as I could.

Go. Fuck. Yourself.

A low, rich and kind of creepy laugh echoed in my mind. *I would much rather you did that for me.*

Well, shit. I kind of walked right into that one.

Larky continued to hold both of our weights with no effort, the air around us whooshing as his wings beat rhythmically. I had no idea how to stop him or escape. I couldn't see Jacob any longer, and I really hoped he was somewhere safe now.

In a desperate move, I opened my jaws and let myself drop very close to the ground. The hedges were narrow in this section. As fast as I could move, Larky would not be able to follow me. I was determined to lead him away from Jacob.

I zoomed along with the currents, enjoying the whip of icy wind on my snout. The large dragon shadow fell in behind me, which sucked, but at least he was following me, which is what I wanted. Except the closer we got to the end of this maze, the easier it would be for him to spread those massive wings and catch me. I hadn't forgotten Rose's words though. Larky was not welcome on the isle of the shining ones. The gods hated him too, so if I could just make it through to there, I'd be safe.

And if Jacob wasn't on the other side when I got there, I was gonna be pissed. I flapped harder, an ache developing in the joints of my wing. I wasn't used to using these muscles. My poor dragon had spent too much of her life trapped inside of me.

There I went again, acting like she was a separate entity from me. I'd never heard Braxton express this sort of feeling for his beast. I'd just never expected her to be so independent, unique, and strong of personality. I was actually sad that she was not free, that she was under my control. Why didn't it feel like that with my wolf?

The light was bright again. I'd made good distance, but now would be the true part of the race. I heard a roar, and felt flames licking at my tail. Larky was gaining on me, but I had sheer desperation on my side. I flapped harder, the pain in my wings and back fading out to almost nothing as my adrenalin skyrocketed.

The shadow was closer now, so close I could smell the wild magic of his dragon. With my own bellowing roar I pushed myself further, praying for strength to make it to the end. I was losing momentum, the adrenalin only able to sustain me for so long. I wasn't going to make it.

Claws attached to the spiked crown which ran down my spine, and I was jerked back, painfully, as a handful of hair caught in that hold and ripped out in chunks.

I flipped over, flinching as more flesh and hair tore from my body, but I didn't let that stop me from clawing out. I was too close to freedom to give up now. The light was at its brightest about twenty yards from where we fought. My dragon could cross that in seconds. I just needed a distraction or something.

My claws dug in deeply. The belly was about the only soft place on the crimson beast, and I didn't hesitate to tear free masses of flesh. Blood rained across me. Larky bellowed again, but didn't fight. He was only trying to contain me.

Maybe that was my advantage.

I lunged for his throat, my claws again finding traction in the soft belly, my teeth slicing through scales to rip into his flesh. The dragon king could do nothing but hold me. I was too close to his body for him to defend against my attack. He was bellowing, feeling the pain, but not enough for his grip to loosen. I clamped my jaws harder and tore in a clean jerk. Bone crunched, flesh tore, a rain of deep, rich blood almost black in color washed across me.

Larky swayed then, and I knew that this time I'd hurt him. He wouldn't die, but maybe it was enough to escape. His hold on me felt precarious, and even though I knew it was going to hurt like hell when I tore myself from him, I didn't hesitate. I thrust my wings sideways and propelled myself away. Sure enough, pain cut through me like a knife, sharp and burning, rending away chunks of hair and flesh, one or two of those large spines ripping from my body.

The pain was excruciating, but I'd been hurt before – I could do this. I continued flapping, my rainbow vision growing tunnel-like. My movements were like a swimmer trying to backpedal in a lake to escape an alligator, desperate and uncoordinated, but I was making distance. I heard movement behind and knew Larky had started to recover, his dragon body repairing. His beast was damn strong.

But I was almost free.

Black dots danced in my vision. I managed to hold on until the light was so blinding that it was impossible to see anything else but the white of the land. As my mind went all gray, the world blurring, I realized I'd made it. I was out of the labyrinth.

With that thought the world went dark.

Chapter 6

The first thing that registered through my haze was the snarling. A multitude of angry howls seemed to be shaking the land on which I lay. I had no problem recalling the last few moments before the blackout. I'd been trying to escape, hoping to lead the dragon king from Jacob...

"Jessa babe..."

The low, harshly-uttered words wrapped around me. Familiar. Safe. Family and pack all in one.

"You better fucking repair every ounce of damage, Louis, or I'm going to enjoy the taste of sorcerer blood."

The guttural nature of Maximus's voice deepened and my heart started this strange pitter-pattering, even though I was struggling to rise from the last of my unconscious. Pain was there, in these wave-like jabs, but much of that was dulled in my half-aware state.

"I *am* fixing her. I'm starting to find it less amusing the way you Compasses continue to threaten me when you know very well that I love

Jessa too. I'm a goddamn level ten sorcerer. I have entire supernatural races cowering at my feet, but not you four hotheads."

"Yeah, yeah, we get it. You're all amazing and powerful, but you can add dead to that list if you don't start healing her. Oh, and shut the fuck up while you're at it." That was Tyson, my wizard quad. They were all here with me. My heart swelled and the pattering increased to some sort of gallop.

The boys' advanced hearing would be picking that up, hopefully reassuring them that I was okay.

As much as I was ecstatic to be with my pack, where the heck was Braxton? Of any of them, he would have been the first at my side, so something must be wrong. It was this thought, teamed with another ground-shaking roar, that gave my body the kick-start it needed to clear the last of the fogginess. The pain hit me harder, sharp and biting, no longer dulled by my mental state. I was hurting – not the worst I'd had, but enough to give me more than a moment's pause.

My eyes fluttered open. The brightness of the world overwhelmed me and I was blinded for a few seconds. Heat washed over me. I'd been healed enough times to recognize the sensation.

"Holy shit, thank the freakin' gods," Tyson said as his strong arms wrapped under me and lifted me into his body. "Dammit it, Jess, I'm starting to think Maximus was right all those years ago."

"I'm always right," Maximus said from somewhere to the side, "but for the record, if you're talking about not being friends with girls, I might make an exception for Jessa. Life wouldn't be quite the same without her."

I shook my head against the hard shoulder it was pressed to. Wrapped in Tyson's arms, my body started to relax, and I barely noticed as Louis finished the last of his healing. I could see the handsome, aristocratic features of the sorcerer from the corner of my eye. He gave me a wink, and I flipped up the edge of my lips in a semblance of a smile. A quick glance down assured me that not only was Louis healing the holes in my body, but he'd also clothed me in jeans, a tank and nice ass-kicking boots. I loved magic – except when it was used against me, then I hated it. It was a complicated relationship.

I finally pulled back to see Tyson clearly. His auburn hair was quite short at the moment, spiked up in a mini-mohawk style. I'd never seen it like that, and for a second something hurt inside of me. Okay, it was a stupid thing to get upset about after everything that had happened in the past month, but to feel that even a small part of these boys was unfamiliar to me, well, it was a slippery slope to a division in our pack. I would never accept that. Never.

His honeysuckle eyes, which had just the slightest threads of gold through them, brightened as we continued to stare, memorizing each other. I desperately wanted to ask where Braxton was but I was afraid to hear the answer. I could see nothing in the vicinity around me, though those roars had come from somewhere.

"My turn," Maximus demanded, shoving his brother to the side and wrenching me into him. The vampire Compass's strong body trembled as he held me, and I found myself wrapping my arms as tightly around him as I could, offering comfort, warmth, and the knowledge that I was here. I was safe. They had finally found me.

Eventually, I couldn't wait any longer. "Did Jacob make it out? And where is Brax?"

Maximus set me on my feet, and after a quick hug from Louis, I was soon in the center of a man sandwich. The three massive males made me look positively petite, which I freaking hated. Someone get me a goddamn ladder, I was getting out alpha'd here by a stupid quirk of genetics.

"We haven't seen Jake since he followed you into the labyrinth." Maximus looked more than a little worried about his fey brother.

"I left him in there after I made sure Larky followed me," I said in a hurry. "I'm going to kick his scrawny ass so bad. When the dragon dick attacked us, he decided to be a freaking sacrifice and took off."

My attitude came out in full force when I was freaked out. Jacob better be okay.

"Who the hell are you calling scrawny?"

A surge of relief just about dropped me to my knees. I swung around to find Jacob and Jonathon, my father, striding out of the darkness near the end of the maze. My feet started to move then and I sprinted to reach them. I threw myself at Jonathon. He caught me with ease. We hugged for a long time before eventually I pulled back to stare into his comforting face.

His blond hair was extra bright here, but I was surprised to see that his eyes, dark blue like my own, were sunken, with some very fine lines visible around them. My father was not old for a shifter, only a few hundred years, so he still looked early thirties, but clearly the stress of recent times had taken its toll. I had a brief worry that maybe something else back home had happened. I really hoped Lienda and Mischa were okay.

My twin was never far from my thoughts; I could always feel her in my head and heart. We had been bonded from the moment she'd unlocked her powers; a part of me was irrevocably linked to her, very faint now with the distance between us, but I believed I'd know if there was anything serious going on with her.

Jonathon's strong hands remained on my biceps, holding me in place. "I'm so glad you're okay, Jess. It's been hell the last few weeks, absolute hell, and I know that it's not over yet, but with all of us back together I believe we can beat him. We can finish this. There is no other choice."

I had so much to tell them, all the things I'd learned in the castle, but that would have to wait until I found my mate.

I swiveled a glare on Jacob. He opened his mouth but I cut him right off. "Don't say a mutha-effing word. I will deal with you later. For now we have bigger problems."

The asshat didn't even have the decency to look worried. If anything, his eyes were sparkling as he tried not to laugh.

"Hey, Jess, Jake, Jonathon..." shouted Maximus. "Come on, we have to help Brax."

Spinning around I saw that the other boys had not followed me across to my father. I spotted their backs before they disappeared into the brightness.

Braxton needing help had my feet scrambling and my heart racing. I headed in their direction even though I couldn't see them any longer. Jacob and

Jonathon caught up to me within a few strides, and we moved in a single-file line across this land of white and light. I guessed this was the center of Faerie, the place that would lead us to the Isle of the Gods.

I was trying to remember what Rose had said about this area. Could Larky have followed me here? I was pretty sure Rose had told me he was able to be in this center place. With Braxton? *Holy shit!*

My feet were slamming against the white ground, my eyes cataloguing everything. There were no defining features here, just the darkness of the labyrinth behind us and the blinding white in front. I couldn't really see more than about five feet in front of me.

As we ran Jonathon reached out to take my hand, giving it a squeeze. "I've dreamed about hearing your voice again, Jess. I really missed your snark. Your mom and sister have been beside themselves with worry. Mischa especially. Your sister is fading away without you. We need to let them know you're safe as soon as possible."

"Hopefully we'll be back with them soon," I said, giving my father a smile, relieved to hear that my family had been alive and well the last time he saw them. I wanted to ask him more, but now just wasn't the time. I needed to focus on this place, and Braxton.

From what Rose had said, this was the center of Faerie, the area where we would find the path to the Isle of the Gods, but it was almost a nothing space. Just as I was wondering if we'd be lost in this land of white forever, I realized the landscape was changing. As if a fog were lifting from the space beyond us, I could now make out some mountainous shapes. Very odd mountains. They almost looked like large mounds of coral, the sort of coral which was dead, leached of all life.

"What the hell is this place?" I murmured as my boots crunched on the coral pieces littering the path. I was starting to really panic about the fact that Larky had most probably followed me out of the labyrinth. I'd been trying to protect Jacob, and had instead put the rest of my pack in danger. Especially Braxton.

"Brax…" I breathed, having a very good idea now of what that thumping and bellowing had been when I first awoke.

I ran harder, a scattering of white raining around us as I scrabbled through the now-rocky terrain. We were climbing higher, and something told me at the top of the coral hill I'd find not only the doorway to the four lands, but also my mate battling against the supe who had taken me from him. I never had any doubt that I belonged to Braxton, just the same as he belonged to me. That was how true mateship worked. You didn't own the other. No, that was for cars and houses. It was more that you couldn't exist without the other. In the same way that my heart and lungs belonged to me, were part of me, were essential to my survival, Braxton was that and more. He was my soul.

Something shifted in my body, heat licking along me, and that sensation which always sat at the nape of my neck when Braxton was near started to increase. Another piece of our bond had sealed, but still a dissension remained. Whatever choice I still had to make was keeping the bond from completing. The fates had told me that I would face a choice, a sacrifice, one that might cost the supernatural world everything. I was starting to see that for Braxton I just might not give a shit about the rest of the world.

My frantic pace had separated me from Jonathon and Jacob, but the steepness of the terrain soon slowed me and they caught up. Together the three of us managed to keep balance as we climbed. My dragon lifted her head a few times, asking if I needed her help, but I gave her a quick pat and she soon settled. It was nice to know she was there now if I needed her, easily in reach, no barrier between us.

As I leaned over to stabilize myself on the very steep incline, I was hit with that dull ache in my back again. It gave me a moment's pause as I recalled the chipmunk attack in the labyrinth.

Jonathon must have noticed my expression; he reached out and captured my forearm.

"Is everything okay, Jess?"

I swallowed, wiggling my lower half to try and relieve the pain. "I got hurt when we were fighting in the labyrinth, and every now and then I'm hit with this dull spasm of pain across my lower back."

Jacob's hand pressed against my lumbar area then, gently, in a light massage of sorts. "You shouldn't still be in pain," he said. "Not only did you shift, but Louis healed you, and he would never miss an injury."

I shrugged, before sort of arching away from Jacob's hand. The fey looked confused and then worried, his brows drawing together as he examined me closer. Generally, I loved massages. I was the queen of relaxation, and rub downs were the shit, but right now it was not a pleasant sensation.

"It's like my body doesn't want to be touched," I said, feeling my own brows drawing in closer. "It's pain, but it's dull and deep. Maybe I have some sort of internal damage and Louis didn't realize, so it's still healing."

I was clutching at straws here. We all knew that the moment I shifted into my dragon just after the attack, all wounds would have healed. Dammit, we had enough to deal with without me having some kind of body breakdown.

"Well, just take it easy until we can get you checked out, Jess." Jonathon's hug was very gentle, as if he sensed how much I didn't want to be touched. Odd, considering that I was a pack animal; we loved hugs and touching, and all the men had hugged me just before and it hadn't bothered me. Maybe it wasn't a body breakdown. Maybe it was mental.

We continued our trek, both men shooting me worried glances, but no one said anything, and thankfully they didn't offer to carry me the rest of the way or something. I was lucky it was Jonathon and Jacob, the least pushy of our pack. Even though my father was an alpha, he was always content to let me be my own alpha chick. Maximus and Braxton wouldn't even have given me a choice. I'd be getting carried up this mountain whether I liked it or not.

"Almost there," Jacob said, not an ounce of fatigue in his voice, even though I knew he had to be as tired as I was. He'd expelled all that elemental energy in the labyrinth. "I can see the peak of this mountain, and there looks to be blue sky above."

Wow. About freaking time color showed its face.

I'd just started catching flashes of this blue when a rumbling thump hit the land close to us. It shook the entire side of our range, and if we hadn't dived to the ground, all of us would have fallen off the side. I decided to crawl the rest of the way; the aftershocks were too strong for us to stand yet, but I was getting up there one way or another.

The dead coral bit into my skin, but the cuts soon healed. Finally, the spark of blue sky came into full effect. The whiteness around us receded and I was able to see the true scope of our surroundings. Unlike the last time we'd been in Faerie, where the sky had been green, it was now the brightest of blue I had ever seen, a true sapphire color.

"Your eyes look incredible, Jess." Jacob was at my right shoulder, both of us still half crouch-climbing, trying to make it onto the peak. "They're a perfect match to the sky. I wish you could see the way the reflection enhances their shine and color."

My reply was cut off by another rocking thud into the side of the mountain. More crumbling trails of stone littered around us. With all three of us helping each other, we found enough foot and handholds to haul ourselves safely to the top.

I had to blink a few times to truly comprehend what lay before me.

The land of white coral was gone, replaced by fields of green, the lush grasses bordered on one side by sparkling water. Yep, this was what I scented in the labyrinth: sunshine, beauty, nature.

To top off this splendor, on the far side of the meadow were four golden bridges, long and ornate, glittering in the light sparkling across the sapphire sky. There was no visible sun, but just like the last time in Faerie, everything was lit by a magical light. The majesty of those bridges held me captive as I got to my feet – the gateways of Faerie. Even from this distance I could see they were ancient, hand-built, each section lovingly crafted by the most skilled of artist, heavily inlaid with swirling arcs on each side, lavishly tapering down to a paved road wide enough only for single file foot traffic.

The bridges spanned off into the open sky, cut off by some sort of smoky ash hovering in the distance, a deep rich charcoal color that hid everything below the bridge. I wondered if anybody had ever fallen into those depths. What lay below?

Another roar shook the land and I tore my eyes from the paths to focus on my pack, and then, without hesitation, I ran toward the broad, muscled backs which were across the meadow, my boots crushing the beautiful flowers and grass. There were more shouts and roars, and as I closed in on the group I counted five massive figures. Larky was no longer in dragon form.

I ran like hellhounds were on my tail. My pack was actually pretty close to the four bridges. The heat in my chest and neck kicked in harder as I neared my mate. I never slowed or hesitated, but at the last moment before I was about to launch myself into the middle of the group, Maximus reached out and caught me.

"You don't want to go in there, Jessa babe," he said as he tucked me in under his arm.

My heart was beating so hard, the back of my neck burning hot. This burn seemed to be increasing the intensity of the dull ache in my lower back. Everything in me was straining to get to my mate.

My absolutely stunning and furious mate.

I was greedy in those first few moments of seeing Braxton – standing legs set, arms held out to the side as he prepared to attack. He looked massive, bigger than I even remembered. He was six and a half feet of muscled badassness.

His eyes locked in on me, the blue intense and shining, and there was almost nothing human left in that gaze. He was animal. He was predator. He was a lethal killing machine and I had no doubt he'd made a very good attempt at destroying the world to find me.

Maximus was the only thing stopping me from going to him, my need to touch Braxton so strong it was choking the breath from my lungs. My eyes frantically worked to examine every part of him. Had he always been so freakin hot? He was the sort of male that statues were carved from, with an ancient and timeless beauty and strength. Like the dragon itself, there would never be an equal to my mate.

Although, the douchebucket across from him, Larky, was almost a close second. Both of them had death in their eyes, both filled with dragon magic, but only one of them was mine, and I would not let anyone take him from me.

King dick growled then. He didn't appreciate the intense and emotional moment between me and Braxton. Without warning, Larky attacked, moving so quickly he was a blur as he smashed out with a long-bladed sword. *Where the hell had he gotten that from?* Supernaturals are kind of old-fashioned; we don't trust modern weapons, and for a lot of us they don't even work. The human-made materials are not compatible with our magic.

But swords, they always work, especially those forged in dragon's blood and with a bone of our beasts used as a blade. Which was what Larky had somehow pulled from his ass. These swords were rare, and highly prized, and my heart almost stopped as Braxton spun to defend himself against the king's attack. I wanted to scream a warning as Larky swung the razor sharp blade in a broad stroke, but Braxton was already moving, his hands partially shifted into dragon claws, which allowed him to deflect the strike.

My heartbeats continued in an erratic rhythm as I watched, Maximus' strong arms offering limited comfort. I'd never had to fear for Braxton's safety before; there were very few creatures in the world which could best a dragon. But I knew Larky was old, powerful, and allegedly had sorcery at his disposal.

Braxton showed not an ounce of concern, moving aggressively, his claws cutting through the air and smashing with sickening clashes against Larky's sword. The king was skilled with the weapon, but for now Braxton was holding his own. My mate fought with a cold fury, his movements methodical but deadly, aiming to not only hurt, but kill. I'd never seen him lose his shell of humanity before, to become nothing more than a base instinct of kill, protect, love. Those fundamental elements had risen inside of my dragon quad, squashing down everything else. He'd never looked more the ancient warrior than right in this moment.

A hand snaked out and grasped mine. I looked down to find Tyson now helping Maximus hold me back. Unconsciously I was still straining to reach Braxton. Sure, logic told me I'd be a bloody mess if I threw myself into this fight. But logic could kiss my ass.

The dragon king swiveled in a complicated motion and slashed across Braxton's arm. My mate's blood shot off in an arc, before dribbling down his tawny skin. A growling rumble rocked my chest. I was not okay with him being hurt.

Larky's stormy gray eyes narrowed on me, as if he'd heard my inner thoughts. Braxton used this distraction to his advantage, stepping into Larky's body and clipping the king in the jaw with an uppercut. As the lines of fury deepened on Braxton's face, I sensed his need to hurt the dragon king. He wanted to draw it out and make Larky pay for what he had done.

I was damned impressed, especially against a dragon blade, to see how much injury Braxton was inflicting. He did suffer some return wounds, but nothing to slow him. Yet. With Larky's invincibility, eventually he would gain the advantage, so we had to figure out a way to incapacitate him long enough to get to the island.

The dragon quad started to hit the king in a rapid succession of jabs, upper cuts, and slamming hooks. Blood and bruises blossomed across the king's face, no time for him to heal with all of the damage inflicted under Braxton's heavy fists. Larky swung out a few times and managed to slice some deep cuts across Braxton's chest. *Bastard!* My mate roared then, and ran full force at the king, managing to side-step the blade. He must have realized he wasn't going to win like this, and had changed tactics.

The two large bodies slammed together, the force shaking the ground. Braxton let more of the partial shift wash over him, blue flames licking across his skin, and as his body morphed into that huge fusion-shift state, he started to gain traction on Larky. Pushing him back toward the edge of the cliff.

Yes! Great plan. The struggle continued, and my worry increased as more blood poured from my mate's wounds. The king gave an extra loud roar, his own hands partially shifted, but he wasn't in a fusion state. Could he not achieve that? Or was he just so arrogant he didn't think he needed it to beat Braxton?

I was pretty much breathless now as I watched the deadly struggle, both massive males teetering on the edge of this land. There was no way to tell what lay below us, the black ash was all encompassing, so Braxton could very well disappear forever if he fell.

Energy washed along my body and I realized that the quads were adding power to their brother, giving him the advantage he needed to dig both clawed hands into the king's biceps and launch him off the cliff edge. In the split second before Larky tumbled away his stormy gray eyes found mine, and I really didn't like the calculating smile he bestowed on me before he disappeared into the abyss.

Chapter 7

Braxton remained at the edge of the cliff, not moving, staring out into the emptiness as he fought for control. He needed me. I knew it, and so did the boys. But they were still holding on, as if they wanted to be sure of their brother's mood before freeing me.

"Let me go," I hissed, elbowing out with both arms, trying my best to dislodge the two hulking males. They had pulled their spandex on again, channeling superman. But it was Braxton. He would never hurt me.

His head whipped up then, face still filled with fury, blue eyes lit with fire as he locked the three of us in his gaze. He took a graceful stalking step in our direction. I knew Maximus and Tyson sensed the danger they were suddenly in. Nevertheless, they remained in their protective pose.

Maximus had his calm-the-fucking-psycho voice on. "Brax … brother, are you back with us, or is the dragon in control?"

"I would never hurt my mate." Braxton's words vibrated across the clearing, deep like they had been struck from a bass.

Truth.

The pair let me go and I lurched through them, stumbling a couple of times, crossing the distance between us as fast as I could. Something in Braxton's hard features softened as my teary gaze met his. I didn't have to go the entire way. He moved in his preternatural way and demolished the last of the distance between us. Our bodies smashed together and I was up off the ground and in his arms before I could even blink. My entire body clenched as need burst to life inside of me, both emotional and sexual in nature. Shifters were hot blooded, and sex was a large part of our society. It was bonding, it was beautiful, and it was damn enjoyable, especially when it came to someone as skilled as Braxton.

Right now was not the time for that. We had an audience, and a job to do. But there was no way I could wait another second to kiss him, and he obviously felt the same. Our lips crashed against each other, soft yet firm, the kiss deep and hypnotic. His tongue swept across mine before sliding deliciously into my mouth. I was drowning in sensations, the taste, the feel, the scent, the warmth.

Being wrapped in Braxton's big body was like being home. It was everything.

The kiss went forever, and yet it was still far too short. With great reluctance, our lips finally parted, and Braxton rested his forehead against mine. We didn't speak, there were no words needed, but I could feel him in my head and my heart. Our bond was deepening, our connection as hot and rich as anything I'd ever felt before.

We stayed like that for many moments, foreheads pressed together, Braxton's strong arms wrapped around me as he held me up at his height. Images of the fight crossed my mind, and as I finally lifted my head up, I couldn't help the smile which spanned my face. Braxton raised an eyebrow at me. "You held your own with the dragon king," I said. "Weren't you a little afraid? He's like the scary boogieman of our world."

Braxton shrugged, his own smile playing across his lips.

Jacob's voice was filled with laughter. "Welcome to the new and improved 'I don't give a fuck' Braxton."

"It's been both amusing and scary as hell to watch," Tyson said.

Jonathon and Louis both groaned at the same time. As the shifter alpha and council leader, my father would have to deal with whatever mess

Braxton left in his wake. Hopefully, he hadn't done anything bad enough to end up back in Vanguard. Not that any of us would let that happen again.

"We've managed to keep his very effective form of information gathering under wraps," Louis said, clearly noticing the stress on my face. "The fruit twins didn't make it, along with a few of the dragon king's other minions. But since they all deserved what they got, it was my pleasure to dispose of the evidence."

I let out a relieved sigh. This wasn't the first time Braxton or the quads had killed for me, and it wouldn't be the last. It didn't bother me in the slightest. We didn't go looking for trouble, but if you messed with our pack, we put you down.

"My information gathering was not that effective," Braxton said. "His castle location was a secret, even from his daughters."

I could tell that had eaten away at Braxton, the fact that he didn't know where I was, or what was happening to me. If the roles had been reversed, I'd have been just as crazy.

It was going to take more than a few minutes of us being back together for him to let go of the rigid anger which was riding his entire demeanor. I'm sure that rage was the driving force behind his actions for the past few weeks. It might have only been a few days' separation for me, but for him it had been a lot longer than that.

The rest of the quads must have decided that their brother and I had had enough one-on-one time, they moved closer, stepping in to join us. The five of us were feeling the pull on our pack bond, we needed skin on skin contact, a moment to reinforce our pack ties. Jacob was on my right, Tyson on my left and Maximus at my back. Strength flooded through me, and the weird niggling of not-wanting-to-be-touched faded away. I closed my eyes, just breathing it all in.

Eventually Jonathon pulled his alpha voice out. "I know you guys need this, but Larkspur could return at any moment. We should start moving. We don't know if next time he'll call on the power of the marked to detain us."

"We really have no idea what Larkspur is capable of," Louis said from behind me. "When he was alive rumor had him displaying skills equal to a level six sorcerer. And yet, just now I got no magic vibe from him ... which is odd. Still, we can't forget that he has an army at his disposal. It was pure arrogance today which led him to believe he could take you all on with just his sword and dragon. He'll not make that mistake again."

With obvious reluctance the quads pulled back from me, all except for Braxton who kept me close to his side. Something told me I was going to be spending a lot of time in his arms in the coming days. Boy had been possessive before, now he was going to be downright annoying. Still, I was not complaining. His arms were my home, and I could stay there forever, no worries.

One of his large hands settled on my lower back and he started rubbing gently. Had he somehow sensed the dull ache which had been plaguing me there? As always, his hands were the most skilled of any I knew – oh, and his massages were pretty great also.

I was relieved to see that the gashes across his tawny skin were already healing, and a few muttered words from Tyson took care of the spatters of blood and damage to his clothes.

Right now I wanted nothing more than endless time with my quads, but alas, dragon dick was ruining my life again; we had to get to the Isle of the Gods.

I sighed. "Dad's right we need to move. We have to go to the land of the shining ones. I believe they're our best chance at finding a weapon which can take down the dragon king."

A multitude of expressions crossed the men's faces. I hurried to explain further. "The reason the king can't be killed is because of the connection between him and the dragon marked. We have to find a way to break those ties, and since it appears this curse originated with the fey gods …"

I trailed off, and since no one looked surprised, I figured this wasn't the first time they had heard of this. As a group we turned to face the four bridges. They spanned as far as the eye could see.

"How do we know which one leads to the Isle of the Gods?" I hoped one of the others would know.

"You ask them." Power dripped from Louis' words. "They're an illusion. There's only one true road from here. You have to make the choice. Tell them which path you need."

I used my free arm to give him a hug. "I've missed you, big brother," I said, my grin actually lifting into something real. Probably one of the first true smiles to cross my lips in some time.

"I missed you too, Jess. Please don't get kidnapped again. It was stressful and worrying, and I had to deal with not only your guard lizard, but the rest of your men."

Braxton grinned, probably impressed with his ability to piss off the sorcerer. My heart clenched tightly then, and it was as if I could finally feel the true depth of my heartache during my separation from the boys. I'd been numb during my time with Larky, too numb to really feel the pain, because the cut had been so deep. I couldn't let that happen again, I could not lose any of my pack. I would not survive it.

We were already close to the edge of the land, I gave Louis a side look and he nodded, so taking a deep breath I stepped up to the first of the four bridges and yelled: "Isle of the Gods ... the shining ones." I felt a bit like an idiot shouting at a bridge, but I trusted Louis knew what he was talking about. He seemed to be a Faerie expert.

A shimmer of light beamed through the golden side arches and I was blinded for a second. By the time my sight cleared, the four-bridge illusion was gone and in its place was one massive structure. This single bridge was at least sixty feet wide, spanning off into the distance. I knew it would stretch for as long as it needed to reach our destination.

"Jess…" Jonathon's voice stopped me right before I was about to step out onto the wide, glowing wooden planks. "I've stayed as long as I can, but now that I know you're reasonably safe, I'm going to head back to Stratford. The town is falling apart. There's no leadership, and if I don't get this under control, the human world will soon be more than aware of our supernatural communities. I know you have your boys with you, you'll be fine, but your sister and Lienda are alone."

I didn't need his explanations, I understood completely. I actually loved that he had so much trust and faith in mine and the pack's abilities to take control of this situation.

"Totally fine, Dad. You have responsibilities. I'll be happier knowing you're there to keep everyone safe. We'll meet you back home as soon as we figure out what the hell is on the Isle of the Gods which might help us defeat the king."

"I'll take him back," Louis said. "I'll find you on the island. It might take me a while, but if you need me, just call. I'll always come."

Louis kissed me on the cheek, ignoring Braxton's growls – though the sorcerer definitely got out of my personal space quickly. I gave my father a hard hug, trying to squeeze another few more precious memories from this moment. Some daughters might freak and feel abandoned by Jonathon, but I understood. My father had always had responsibilities outside of me.

I took a few, deep, steadying breaths as the pair disappeared through Louis' step through. That was all the unease I allowed myself. The entire supernatural world was depending on us.

As I took that first step out onto the golden path, quads by my side, my wolf and dragon went into high alert. When nothing crazy jumped out in the first few feet, I relaxed and the five of us hurried our pace. It was wide enough for us to walk side by side.

There was no casual conversation. Our goal was to get over this bridge in record time. Still, sensing a gaze on me, I found a pair of burning blues locked on me.

"Are you really okay, Jess?" Braxton's voice was not a whisper; he didn't bother to hide his fears from his brothers. "What happened while you were gone?"

I rubbed a hand over my face, trying to decide what to tell them. I wouldn't lie, but maybe there was some things to skim over so that they didn't completely lose their minds. *Ah, screw that.* This was my pack and they deserved the full truth.

I started at the beginning, explaining Larky's castle and the illusions, then moved on to Rose and my escape attempts, which was what ultimately led them to me.

"So he never laid a hand on you? He was trying to ... seduce you? Romance our Jessa?" Tyson's eyes had those streaks of gold through them. He wasn't too happy.

"Next time I'm going to make sure I hurt him just a little more." Braxton was all growls and rumbling chest right now. My boy had pretty much been one big growl since we'd found each other again.

Tyson interrupted. "What's his ultimate game? I don't understand why he hasn't pulled the army in and started training them. Why are the marked still just hanging around?"

I had no idea, and that was more worrying than anything. Before Larky had come back from the dead, I always thought his first act would be to gather his army and then wage a massive war. So far, though, he'd been more interested in me.

Our pace along the bridge was just short of sprinting, my energy holding steady, but if I didn't get food and sleep soon I'd be completely useless. Food was a dream that I'd hold close to my heart, the sort of dream that I'd bring out and examine when I needed some beauty in my life. *My precious one.*

Stretching my muscles as I jogged, I winced as that low pain rocked through me again, my hand instinctively reaching back to press against it.

Braxton never missed a thing, and I should have known he would jump all over me now. "What's wrong, Jess? Are you injured?" His pace slowed, and I knew I was about eight seconds from being scooped into his arms.

Jacob opened his big mouth and dumped me right into the shit. "Her back has been hurting since we were attacked in the maze, but she should be healed. I don't know what's wrong."

Concern etched across all of the quads' faces, and the others slowed their pace, forcing me to stop.

"Spill, Jessa." Four sets of eyes locked on me, eight muscled arms crossed across broad chests. They were so alike that I actually had to stop myself from kicking them. They were doing that stupid thing like the Four, where they were carbon copy robots. I wanted my individual boys back, right now.

Knowing they were as stubborn as me, and that we could be in a standoff all day, I spoke quickly. "I've been having this lower back pain. At first I thought it was just from when a critter dug his claws into me, but Jake is right, I should be healed by now."

Braxton's hands reached around me to gently massage my back, his warmth and energy soothing not only my pain but my soul.

"I sensed you had some discomfort there, but I didn't realize it was actual pain. Why didn't you tell Louis while he was here? He's the best we have to heal anything complex."

The shifter in Braxton was rising up with the need to protect and care for his mate. I'd been thinking about the pain a bit, and I actually had an idea about what it might be. The timing wasn't exactly right, but maybe with my journeying in and out of Faerie, the timeline was all messed up.

"It's possible I'm coming into my fertile period," I said. Generally I had very distinct symptoms a few days before it was to begin, symptoms which I hadn't had, but this was also the first time I'd been fertile since the release of my dragon mark. And none of us knew what that might have done to my body and hormones.

Fears crossed my mind. "Do you think Larky did something to me? Brought on my fertility early? We all know he wants something from me. What if that something is a baby?"

As the thoughts continued to pour from me, my voice sounded a tad hysterical, which was another thing that occurred during my fertile period – heightened emotions. I felt Braxton's arms tighten around me, and before I could blink my feet were off the ground. The dragon shifter had his arms tightly wound around me and I could feel the heat pouring off him – the rage and fear.

I kept my voice low and calm. "He never touched me, Brax. There's no way I could be pregnant with any little dragon babies, unless he used osmosis."

It didn't work. The thought that I might be pregnant to someone else had pushed my mate over the edge. He was not listening to me now, and the moment any of the quads moved near us, growls ripped from him. I wriggled closer, managing to free my arms before lifting my hands to cradle his face.

"Braxton Compass..." I was relentless, forcing him to focus on me, holding his head firmly. "He never touched me. I would never touch another male. You're it for me. I made my choice and you're never getting rid of me."

We stayed like that for a few moments, and finally some of the feral faded out of those tumultuous eyes.

"Why would he want a baby with you?" Each word was ripped from his throat, sounding gravelly and pissed. "Why is he trying to create a dragon heir? There's a larger plan here, and it's part of the reason why he's been lax in using his army of marked."

I would have gasped deeply but I wasn't able to breathe too much. Braxton was right. His keen intelligence had risen to the surface as soon as he pushed enough of the predator down.

"That makes perfect sense. That's why he was trying to seduce me. He wants an heir. He must have been waiting until my fertile time. Maybe the fact that I was in Faerie has brought it on early."

Either Faerie or Larky himself had done something to bring it on early. I had eaten the food from Rose; there could have been some sort of elixir or spell in them. My wolf usually detected such things, but not always. Rose had seemed legit, but right now I trusted no one but my pack and family.

Despite the unease which hung amongst us, we couldn't delay on the bridge forever. Braxton held me close for an extra few moments before eventually dropping me back on my feet, his touch soothing as he ran his hand across my back, over and over, in this gentle circular formation.

Generally, when I came into my fertile period, it started with lethargy for a few days, and then this massive high of energy. My wolf would become very agitated, unease stirring her – I always knew at that point it was time. Even though it was only a week of discomfort, shifters could get pregnant from as early as the first signs of fatigue, so we had to be careful. I was generally careful for the entire month of my fertile time, even though there was no more than a two-week window to conceive a pup.

This sort of lower back ache had never happened, certainly not this early out. It felt like magic, like something trying to force my body into a state it was not ready for. I was half tempted to march back along the bridge and find the king's body so I could kick the shit out of him. That stupid asshat. What had he done to me?

Chapter 8

The bridge remained unchanging, glowing, and spanning into the distance as we walked. None of us knew if the end would just pop up out of nowhere or if we'd see it coming. Nerves and worries still crossed my mind, and needing a distraction from the fears, I said: "I think you boys better tell me exactly what's been happening while I was gone. How much time passed on Earth?"

Jacob and I had started this conversation, but a lot had been left unsaid.

Tyson jumped in first. He liked to talk and liked being the center of attention. Unlike Maximus and Braxton who just preferred to kill shit in the background.

"The moment you were taken in Krakov, Braxton pretty much lost his shit. He was mindlessly smashing anything that walked into his path, which unfortunately for one of the fruit twins, was her head."

I heard Braxton give a bit of a snort, trying not to laugh at his idiot brother. "Yep, you could say I was a little upset."

I heard the absolute chasm of emotion in his monotonous words, which might seem like an oxymoron, but Braxton was at his scariest when his voice and tone was dead. If he was showing no emotion, then you knew for damn sure he was feeling everything.

Tyson continued: "So Braxton had just killed one of the twins. Everything was in chaos, and I was helping Grace while she worked on keeping your sister alive." The wizard's voice lowered when he said the healer witch's name.

Grace used to be a little in love with him when they were younger, and he'd rejected her without much thought. Now, though, it seemed that careless action had turned back on him. He wanted to explore how he felt and Grace was refusing to let herself be hurt by him again. It was complicated, and with all the drama there was no time for these sort of personal worries. I had faith that it would all work out for them though. They were both awesome supes, and I'd love to see some happiness in their lives. As long as Grace didn't mess with our pack dynamics, she was okay with me. Cardia, on the other hand … I still wasn't sure how I felt about

Maximus' mate. I just knew we were going to have trouble with her.

Our pace picked up to a run again as Tyson continued his story. "We took the other twin back to the sanctuary. Louis wanted to make sure his brother was okay, and that the dragon marked weren't going to immediately rise up and form some sort of crazy army."

"Where are Quale and the rest of the mystics now?" The strange silver-haired supernaturals were the council for the dragon king, but it had never seemed as if Louis' brother was really on board with that.

Since none of the mystics had met the king, they were the descendants of his original council. I wondered how they'd all reacted when he'd popped back into existence. Bet they were at least a little worried; his last council had lost their heads, which wasn't the nicest legacy to live up to.

Maximus shifted his arm, hugging me to his side. "They're still in the sanctuary," he said. "The last time we saw them they had received no orders from the king, and were still just going about their everyday lives. The knowledge that he's free is being kept quiet around the supernatural communities. The councils are hoping we can sort it out before mass panic ensues."

I was pretty sure the councils were shit out of luck. Larky had lost me, his prize, he was going to be very angry and totally come out with guns blazing. Jonathon had a legit reason to worry that this was all going to spill out into the human world.

"So both twins died, and you still had no idea where I was. What did you do then?" Our pace had increased, and something was glimmering on the horizon.

Braxton's voice was monotone again. "No one knew anything. Larkspur literally appeared on this plane, snatched you up and disappeared to Faerie. There was no time for even his closest followers to be aware of his actions."

Jacob snorted. "Yep, Brax learned the hard way that no matter how hard you beat someone, they cannot give you information they don't possess."

My mate chuckled, some of his old humor returning. "It was kind of therapeutic, hunting down and questioning those who had ties to the king. Gave me a distraction from my need to kill every single member of our councils. Useless assholes were far too slow in their reactions."

He stated this as fact, and none of us doubted that it had been a fine line of control which stopped him going on a mass killing spree which would have made the time of the dragon king seem like Sunday brunch in the park.

"Well, we're all back together now, and I for one am not letting anyone else get their scaly claws on me." I could reach my dragon now, and we would fight those fuckers all the way to our death.

Jacob spoke up then, he must have been following the same train of thought. "Has Jess mentioned that she saved our asses in the maze by learning how to call on her dragon?" He was all proud of me and shit.

The rumble in Braxton's chest increased. "You figured out how to shift on command?" It was sort of a question, but mostly he sounded proud too.

"Yep, we broke down the wall. Now there's no more barrier."

Tyson reached across his brother to drop a large hand on my shoulder, which was quite the dexterous feat with our current pace. "Never doubted that you could do it, Jessa babe. Damn, I missed you. I don't think any of us realized the true depth of our pack bond until you were gone. We were fucking lost … a mess … a bunch of idiot males wandering around beating the shit out of people. We're nothing without you, Jess, so don't disappear on us again. I'm not sure any of us would survive."

I had to swallow a few times. There was this stupid huge lump in my throat. Maybe it was the fierce and loving looks the boys were bestowing on me, or the emotion rocking their voices, but I was feeling every single way they had suffered without me. As much as I had hurt, it had been much longer and worse for the quads. They had not known if I was being tortured or other horrible shit. Larky was the big-scary in our world, and I'd been his captive.

I reached up and squeezed Tyson's hand. "I felt the same pain, like I was missing an essential part of my soul, and for me it was only a few days that we were all separated."

"It was a month for us," Braxton said. "The longest damned month of my life. How do you feel about handcuffs?"

I snorted. "As long as it involves whips and chains, then I'm down, but if you're talking about leashing me to you for life, not a chance, buddy. I can fight plenty fine on my own. Larky took me by surprise in that first meeting, but I've been fighting him ever since."

Maximus skipped back to our previous conversation. "Tell us more about this Rose."

"She's the first marked, and apparently Larky's wife. Like I said before, she's human, but there's something important about her blood. It's tied to the marked curse. The fact that her family line is descended from the shining ones allowed him to use it to bond the supes to him."

The boys were silent for a beat before Jacob said, "If we kill her, will it break the curse?"

I scrunched up my forehead, trying not to think too hard about that. "I doubt it. Firstly, there's no way to truly know, and I'd hate to think she'd die for nothing. And secondly, Larky is very protective of her. We'd never get close enough to hurt her. She's a victim in all of this. Killing her should be the absolute last resort."

No one answered straight away and I knew what they were all thinking. If it came down to me or her, Rose was fucked. They would not hesitate for even a second before ripping her head off. I had to make sure that didn't happen. We had to find something on the Isle of the Gods.

I changed the subject from the killing of Rose to Faerie gods. "Do you think we're getting close to the ... the destination now? What dangers are we facing there?"

Surprisingly enough, Jacob answered, and with none of his usual reticence of sharing about Faerie.

"A long time ago Faerie used to be ruled by two powerful groups: the shining ones and the shadow spawn, two factions who lived on opposite sides of our world. The Isle of the Gods was home to the shining ones, and the Land of the Dying was where the shadow spawn existed. The shadows are a dark spirit, they care very little for anything other than power and feeding. The shining ones were pure of spirit ... or so they would have you believe, but like all powerful beings, were never to be trusted. They always have their own agenda."

"So what happened?" I asked. "You said *used* to be ruled."

"I wasn't born of course, so this is a folk tale passed down through the generations of fey. There was a war. The shadow spawn rose up against the shining ones, they wanted the Isle of the Gods, for it was there that the most abundant of magic existed, the Gold. You know the essence they teach us about in magic classes. The base of all supernatural creatures. If they had gained control of this wild and ancient power … shit, it would have been bad. End of world bad."

Echoes of something flickered across Jacob's green eyes. He might not have lived there, but he felt the pain of that time quite acutely.

"The battle raged for countless years, thousands of years in Earth time. So much of Faerie was destroyed, but still there was never to be an end. The shining ones and the shadow spawn were the balance of each other. Neither could ever truly be destroyed."

This was not sounding great. No wonder the fey had started to flee.

"In the end, the shining ones managed to trap the shadows, placing the demons into a deep slumber, and then they removed themselves from actively policing Faerie, focusing on keeping the shadows locked away. Faerie has fallen into a land of ruin and fear ever since. Without the shining ones influencing the Gold, the world was no longer safe for the fey, so some of our ancestors left."

"Do the shining ones still live on the Isle of the Gods?" Braxton asked his brother. "Will we have a fight on our hands when we get there?"

I knew the boys wouldn't care either way. We had no choice here. But it was always good to be prepared.

Jacob shrugged his broad shoulders. "I don't know, Brax, I've never been to the island, and I don't know a single fey or demi-fey who has either. The shining ones abandoned our land. Maybe they're slumbering too."

I was reminded again of Louis saying that he hoped "they" wouldn't wake. *Shit.* Right about now I needed that damn sorcerer here so I could ask him if he was talking about the shadow spawn or the shining ones. It would be nice to know what we were walking into, and who we didn't want to wake.

"Where do the shadow spawn sleep?" I wondered out loud.

Creases formed around Jacob's fey eyes. "The location of the shadows has been lost through history, either deliberately or by chance. I don't think any fey know where the shining ones stashed them."

Great, so they could be anywhere. We were so screwed.

During this conversation our speed had continued to increase; we were running now, and the length of bridge behind us was increasing dramatically. It also seemed as if the length in front was shorter. I still couldn't see our destination, but it looked brighter across the horizon.

Why is Larky not welcome on the Isle of the Gods any longer?

This information had been niggling away at me. What had he done all those years ago? What had he asked for and promised in return? Creating an army of marked required a massive level of power. A spell like that was multi-layered, intricate, and extremely difficult to cast and maintain. We were talking about thousands of supernatural creatures, all now tied to the king. The shining ones would not have done this for him unless he'd promised something huge.

A heaviness settled into my gut, joining the dull aching pain in my back. I knew his plan had everything to do with me, with the massive dragon mark spanning the side of my body. I was different to the others, but why? What had Larky done?

The bridge started to descend in a gentle slope and the brightness at the end increased. We were close now. I forced myself to focus on simply getting in and out of the island without some god screwing us hard. Because even in my sexually-deprived state, that did not sound enjoyable. Plus, I was only going to drive myself insane trying to put together a puzzle that was missing so many pieces.

I reached out and Braxton met me halfway, fingers interlocking. Somehow he knew I needed something to keep me from drifting away. Or maybe he'd needed the comfort too. I was used to being strong, never letting shit bother me, but I'd been thrust into this massive battle and I had no clue what I was supposed to do.

None of us slowed even as the brightness became intense enough to blind. I could tell by their rigid jaws and lack of comment that the boys were not exactly happy to be running into an unknown danger, but when you have no choices left ... yep, this shit sucked balls.

At the very last moment, when the piercing brightness was causing actual shooting pain in my head, I closed my eyes. The wooden planks disappeared from underneath us and the ground softened. I stumbled as voices rang out, a chorus that was so familiar. Braxton's firm grip on my hand was the only thing which kept me standing.

I blinked rapidly, trying to clear the black dots and blurry vision. The moment I could see, I spun in a circle, taking in everything, trying to catalogue it all so my poor brain could catch up with what my eyes observed.

The bridge, voices and ashy mist were gone. We were on a very large island, surrounded by water so clear I swear I could see the sandy bottom for miles out. The sky was a peach color, and I couldn't tell if that was because of the time of day, or if this soft shade was simply native to this part of Faerie. The waters held me mesmerized for some time. They were magical in nature, sparkling unnaturally, brighter than any green I'd seen before, so many shades of aqua and turquoise that there was no true way to describe it. Its beauty was literally breathtaking. I was having trouble taking it all in.

My wolf and dragon slowed their pacing inside and stared with me, all of us finding a sense of peace and tranquility. I could have stood there staring out into the waters for an eternity and that still wouldn't have been long enough.

I'm not sure exactly what snapped me out of the daze, but by the time a sense of clarity started to filter in, there was a strange tingling sensation running up and down my side. I lifted my shirt to see what was happening to me.

Braxton ran a warm hand along my body. "Your mark is changing, Jess." His voice was low and rumbly as his hand continued to glide across my side. "It's moving, swirling. It almost looks as if your dragon is flying. It likes this island."

I could see it now, the red and black moving, dancing across my skin. The entire mark seemed to have shifted at least three inches lower. The rest of the quads gathered around me, shaking their heads as they stared.

The mark eventually stopped its weird little dance and I dropped my shirt back down. The five of us turned to the island, which was as captivating as the water, possessing a beauty beyond compare – golden sands, greenery that was so bright it looked unnatural, sparkling waterfalls, picturesque ponds, the lightest of breezes and the sweetest of animal sounds.

Take every clichéd image of a tropical paradise, mesh them all together, polish it off with some magical dust and throw sparkles into the air … you had this island.

Tyson lifted his face, tawny skin glowing in the soft light. "I sort of think we should just forget about the king and live here. We'll get the rest of our people and just chill here in the land of shiny shit forever."

I had to chuckle. He sounded half serious, and I couldn't blame him.

Maximus slapped his brother on the shoulder. "What have I always told you about pretty things? Often they hide the most darkness inside. That's why I said you couldn't trust beautiful women, they're treacherous." He gave me a wink. "Except for our Jessa babe. But then again, she can be a little evil if you interrupt her sleep or steal her food."

I groaned then, my hands instinctively clutching at my stomach. "Gods, don't mention food. I'm so hungry."

A faint nausea was fighting for control of my stomach. I was starving, but the actual thought of eating anything made me feel queasy. It had been too long between decent meals. Rose's sad little – possibly magically tainted – sandwich most definitely did not count.

"We'll find you some cake soon," Braxton promised, and I actually bounced a little on the spot.

"I love you," I pretty much squealed. "You're the best mate ever."

Braxton's blue eyes were piercing then. They locked me into place, and all of a sudden it was hard to breathe.

"I love you too, Jess. I always have." His words were low and serious as he stepped closer. Hot flashes started rocking through me. I wanted him so badly it was painful. "I'll find you an entire cake. A goddamn truck filled to the brim with cakes."

The moment between us was intense. He'd just told me he loved me – not in the normal way we'd always said it – and I wasn't sure I'd ever recover. None of the other Compasses blinked an eye at our emotional leakage. They all looked really happy for us, like any true pack members would be. I wondered if Braxton could feel the epic scale of my emotions right now. They were vast and strong. Way fucking strong. I wasn't even sure I had the capability to process them.

I had never been in love before – I loved the Compasses with every cell in my body, and knew I couldn't live in a world without them in it – but *in* love was totally different. Braxton just had to go and up my emotions by a few million steps.

Damn him and his damn dimples. Not to mention that unwavering loyalty. He had waited a long time for me to wake up to our inevitability. I had no idea what I'd done right to deserve Braxton as my true mate.

The dragon shifter's eyes twinkled then. "As long as we're clear that I'm the alpha ninety percent of the time, I'll try my best not to challenge you for the other ten percent."

All of my loved-up emotions morphed into the urge to punch him in his smug face. "Dream on, buddy. We're just going to have to share alpha. I ain't giving that up for anybody, not even *the* Braxton Compass."

The twinkle deepened. "Wouldn't have it any other way, Jess." He yanked me hard into his body and wrapped his arms around me. Against my better judgement I sank into him. The boy already possessed the ability to totally enchant my mind and body. I was in trouble.

"Anytime today, lovebirds. Don't you think we should get our ass– "

Braxton's growl interrupted Jacob mid-sentence.

"Never mind," the fey mumbled, and took a long step backwards.

I patted my dragon shifter on his chest a few times. It took nothing for him to morph into that possessive dragon mode. "He's got a point, Brax. Time to get this all-inclusive Isle-of-the-Gods-tour started."

Focus descended across the quads in an instant. It was odd seeing it happen, almost like the fun-loving side of them got tucked away behind the warrior. And their warrior sides were quite scary. They took point around me, two on either side, and together we started to move further into this beautiful land with its undercurrents of scary.

The boys fell in sync, walking with the same long strides, doing their quad thing, which reminded me of the time they joined their powers in the sanctuary. My eyes flicked between them.

"Has anything changed between you four since you received your calling?"

I hadn't fully shrugged off the worry that I would lose them, their individual traits bleeding together. The original Four were total freaks, identical looks, identical creeptastic asshole tendencies – like locking away babies and shit. For now my boys still seemed the same as ever, but I needed to stay on top of that. I worried that the more time they spent joined, the worse it would get.

Maximus answered me. "We're more tuned into each other. I can sense them in my head, even though we don't really share thoughts unless we're actually joined. The calling does run through us, wanting us to join, to go back to Larkspur and finish what Braxton started, but we're strong enough to resist it."

Tyson joined in. "Yep, especially since we know there's no way to kill him yet."

"I feel stronger," Jacob said. "The elements respond almost without any expulsion of power. The fire burns more intensely in my chest."

Braxton shifted at my side. "Same. My beast is stronger, my urges too. Joining together has heightened our natural supernatural abilities. We're evolving. Hopefully the strength is enough to help with the coming battle."

"You know, I didn't think much on it, but I haven't had blood for days," Maximus said. "And I'm not as weakened as I normally would be."

The vampire members of our supernatural world were not bound by most of the lore of their kind, but the drinking of blood was one thing that humans did get right. For some reason vampires had a very high blood cell turnover. Blood cell death took about sixty days for most of us, but for vamps it was twenty. The rapid regeneration was too much for their bodies to maintain, so a little help was required. This regeneration did allow them to be resistant to injury, as rapid as a bullet, and a plethora of other coolness. So it wasn't a bad tradeoff.

"Speaking of quads, we ran into the Four while we were looking for you." Jacob said this all casual-like, the same way he might have said he'd had some eggs for breakfast, or punched a dude in the face.

Meanwhile my mouth was hanging open and a sort of red haze had descended across my vision. I'd like to think I was mature enough to accept some of what the Four had done. They'd had a job to do, and the way they treated marked was not personal, but reality was I hated their ugly, robo-cop asses, hated them enough that if Jacob had said they were dead, their heads stuck on spikes and mounted around the borders of Stratford as decoration, I'd be okay with that. I'd even ask for photos so I could put them up on my wall.

Jacob, noticing my expression, hurried along. "We had no real choice, Jessa. We need their help. We reached a tentative agreement: if the king teams up with the marked, the Four will fight with us. They can use their energy to hold dragon marked at bay, giving us a shot to take out the king."

Maximus snorted. "Yep, we reached this agreement right after Braxton smashed two of them in the face. A little payback for when they tried to take you from Stratford. FYI their calling power does not work on dragons."

I tilted my head back to see Braxton. He was focused on our surroundings, no expression across his face, but there was that look in his eye. He didn't like the Four any more than I did, and trusted them even less. He wouldn't be letting his guard down.

I freaking hated that they'd made this deal, but there wasn't much I could do about it now. I had to focus on finding some sort of weapon to defeat the king. This was the key to bringing control back to the supernatural world, to making sure that supes like the Four never came into our lives again.

I focused on our surroundings. Rose had said the answers were here, but where? Would a weapon or god just jump out at us, or would we need to search? From her tone I'd certainly expected a level of danger on this island, but so far there was nothing scary.

Of course, just like the last time I'd thought shit in Faerie, the damn land decided to bring it to life. A rumble rocked the ground beneath our feet. My dragon and wolf jumped to attention as electricity filled the air. *Holy freaking ogre balls*. Damn my random thoughts. The next time I thought of something here, it would be cake shops and naked Braxton.

The peachy sky darkened and we were looking at a world of twilight. A sense of danger filtered through to us and we closed ranks. Before any of us could react, a schism split the grassy land, opening a massive crater beneath our feet, so fast and wide that there was no way for us to avoid the fall. The five of us plunged straight down into whatever waited below.

Chapter 9

The space we fell through was not large enough for Braxton or me to call on our dragons. We'd definitely kill the other quads by dragon-bulk-into-rocks. But we might also all die by plunging into the ground below, so ... hard choices. The darkness of this chasm, beneath the beautiful island, was all encompassing, no way to know what we were heading for, or how long until we were pancakes. Braxton was close by and I knew he'd be tapping into dragon sight, trying to see if there was enough space to shift and grab us all. He would only need a few seconds to save us all.

The air started to cool as the space between the rocky walls narrowed. Maximus was plastered to my front, Braxton was at my back, both of them probably trying to keep me safe. I mean, I did love me some Compass sandwich, but these circumstances kind of sucked the big one.

My dragon roared, sensing something below, but before I could freak out, iciness encased my legs as we plunged into a dark watery abyss. In the last second before going under, I managed to take a massive breath.

Confession time: I hate swimming when I can't see what's in the water. The deep darkness hides many a thing. We dropped for a long time through the blackness, the water eventually slowing our descent. I kicked out, forcing my body back to the surface. It was hard not to lose my direction. It was so dark that if I turned myself around, I'd find myself swimming to my death.

The boys were close by. I could feel their ripples of energy, and thankfully one of them – Tyson I'd guess, because Jacob's fire was not going to work down here – produced a magic light that filtered through the water.

I was starting to get a little lightheaded. Lack of oxygen would become a problem sooner or later. Strong bands gripped my biceps and I jerked before realizing it was Braxton. He made a few military style gestures at me, trying to tell me something but I had no idea what it was, eventually he just held me close and powered upwards. Swirls of water churned below us – Jacob was using his affinity for water to speed our trajectory. The pressure around me started to lessen.

As my head broke above the surface I gasped, trying to suck in as much air as I could in those first few seconds. Braxton's chest heaved beside me, but he was mostly silent as he held me, keeping us both afloat. The other Compasses were up now also, all of them breathing hard and trying to figure out what the hell we'd just stumbled into.

Braxton wrapped one of his hands around the back of my neck, threading his fingers into my long dark hair and tipping my head back. "You ever plunge into water like that again," he said, his low voice echoing around the cavern, "shift into your dragon. She has a much larger lung capacity, loves the water, and will always know which way is to freedom. We can feel the call of the sky."

I coughed a few times before managing to answer: "That's what you were trying to tell me. Man, I wish you could talk in my head like king dragon dickhead did. Would make things that much easier."

Braxton's grip tightened and silence descended across the darkness, all-encompassing like a vacuum had been fitted to this underground cavern. I didn't have to guess about what had caused the soundless and angry vibrations from my mate. I had just noticed that the icy water was getting warm when Braxton thrust me toward Maximus. The vamp caught me as blue flames licked across the shifter's skin.

"He was in your head! Like a mate bond?" The words ripped through the shifter's teeth, a definite snarl on the end of each one.

I was enthralled by Braxton, his hair so black, slicked back from his perfect features, blue flames highlighting every facet of his dark beauty. But then I registered his words.

"No," I shouted. "No way! There's no mate bond between me and Larky! It was just that we were both in dragon form. You said we could communicate in dragon form, right?"

Water swished as he moved closer, the flames dying down until they were no more than a fine tendril coating his skin. "Yes, that's right, but he should never be allowed in your head. I need to teach you how to block those you don't want to hear. How to protect your mind. The dragon has natural protections, but if you encounter someone more powerful than you, they'll be able to get in your head."

The more he spoke, the calmer he got. The blue flames were all but gone, and the underground seemed a lot darker than it had been, even with Tyson's light still shining around us.

Speaking of, the wizard had something to say: "Well, I don't know about you all, but I'd like to get the fuck out of this water pit. Who the hell knows what's in here with us, and I'm kind of freezing my balls off."

He made two very good points. If I had balls, mine would be frozen by now. This water was like the freaking Antarctic, and I refused to even consider if there was any creepy shit in here.

"I doubt they'll want to mess with two dragons. They'll leave us alone." Braxton was confident as he reached out and captured my hand, pulling me from Maximus. He then threw me up onto his back. The total hotness of that was sort of dimmed by the implications of what he had said.

What things are in the water?

Before I could freak out and start trying to see into the depths below, we were moving, swimming rapidly across the chilly water. I wasn't sure what landmark they were using for direction, but I hoped it wouldn't be too long before we were on land and dry. The heat which was a natural part of Braxton's body was keeping me warm enough, but I still had that urge to get out and shake the water from my fur – metaphorical fur, but still the same sensation as when I was wolf.

"Hey, Brax!" yelled Jacob. "Not sure they got the 'won't mess with dragons' memo."

I scanned back and forth in rapid jerks of my head, but still couldn't see anything.

Braxton still wasn't worried. "If they come any closer, I'll shift into my dragon. I think for now they're just curious."

My voice got all shrill: "You asshats have two seconds to tell me what's in the water with us or I'm going to start punching the shit out of you." I didn't get scared much, not that true fear which starts heavy in your gut and rises up to choke you out, where you can't swallow or breathe. Surrounded by the quads, my fear was manageable, but water was not my thing, and dark underground holes in the world of Faerie added an extra dash of creep to it.

"Look for yourself, Jessa babe," Jacob said from my left. "Knowing you, you'll probably want to keep it as a pet."

I snorted. "Speak for yourself, you were the one always collecting animals and bugs." Tyson and Jacob both. Their affinity for nature resulted in an unnatural attraction to everything in the great circle of life.

I was the one who got all soft-hearted when animals were hurt or treated cruelly. Humans were often on my shit list for the way they disregarded the rights of their animals. Pets. Those to be eaten. Don't get me wrong, I ate meat – my wolf was definitely no vegetarian. But I expected that we not only ate the meat, we used the bone, the skin, the fur … everything. And we did not kill them without mercy or waste what we took. The circle of life. It was there for a reason, and I hated people screwing with it.

Since the boys seemed to expect I'd be able to see whatever was in the water with us, I stopped trying to see below and stared instead into the darkness behind. I caught a flash in the dull lighting.

Holy shut the eff up!

I had to be dreaming ... or hallucinating. Maybe I had drowned and was floating at the bottom of this lake, because there was no freaking way that the Loch Ness Monster was following us right now.

As it closed the distance, I could better see the way its head rose above the water and the rest of the snake-like body curled behind. The flickers of light painted it in shades of silver and turquoise, pretty and magical even as it glided silently through the water.

"How many are there?" I asked as ripples of water washed out around the large serpent.

"Five, I think." Maximus looked like he was out for a casual Sunday swim, his strokes smooth as they cut through the water. "They're demi-fey, ones who for the most part remained on Faerie. One did manage to slip through a water portal into the human realm many years ago."

Of course, why the hell not? Most of the myths and legends in the human world were creatures from our world, mostly demi-fey. They weren't very good at blending in.

"They're associated with the gods," Jacob said. His musical tones sounded extra songlike in this echoey abyss. "They were always in the lakes surrounding their land, acting as guards and guides. They must have been relegated down here for some reason."

Jacob's Faerie knowledge was finally coming in handy.

A second head rose above the water to join the first. "I don't think they'll be scared of dragons," I said, wiggling closer to Braxton's head. "They're pretty much dragons of the water themselves."

"Don't stress, Jess. Everything is afraid of dragons."

Braxton was doing that confident, cocky thing again. Dragons were badass, but something told me that the guards of gods were pretty damn badass themselves.

A thought occurred to me. "Anyone stop and think that maybe they aren't following us so much as herding us?"

Why the hell was my voice doing some weird high-pitched screechy thing? I was a damned wolf-dragon dual shifter. I should not be freaking out like this.

"Oh they're herding us, but since it happens to be in the direction we're already going, no big deal." Braxton's confidence was starting to shit me off – not enough to jump off his back or anything. I was annoyed, not stupid.

"Can you guys see that?"

Jacob had us all focusing, forward this time, although I was definitely keeping an eye on the serpents. It might be a trick of the light, but they looked even closer than before.

"Finally some damned land," Tyson said.

I could see it clearly now. The water was rippling up against long wooden docks. Low beams of light sprinkled across that space, light which was not from any of us.

How the hell was there a dock down here? We'd fallen into the center of Faerie. I wasn't going to complain – anything which got us out of the water and away from the Nessie squad was okay in my books.

A sound startled me, and I swung back around to find five heads no more than ten yards from us now. "Dude! Start freaking swimming. The scaly serpents are closing in."

It was totally unnecessary for the quads to crack up like that. "Why are you not more worried about them? They could crush around us in a heartbeat and drag us down to drown. I'm not sure about the rest of you, but I need to breathe. It's what keeps me alive."

Especially now that the immortality of the marked was lifted.

"Jess, come on. If they wanted to attack us they would have done so the moment we fell into the water. They're about a thousand times faster than we are. We can't outrun them. We'll just have to deal if they suddenly go all lake monster and start trying to chew our faces off."

Jacob was always a jackass.

I conceded that he had made a good point though. But that didn't explain why they were so much closer now. I decided to focus forward, because clearly I wasn't at my best or bravest when I was in the water. I'll stick with land, thank you very much, where strange creatures are visible and not dwelling in murky depths.

I was so thankful to see the wooden pier closing in. I was drained, the icy water sapping my energy at a rapid rate. Braxton must have sensed my need to get out, and with a show of strength that frankly left me jealous as heck, he surged forward and had us at the side of the docks in seconds.

"Okay, that was totally hot," I murmured in his ear, and I loved the sound of his low chuckle. Us being back together was enough for me to feel more like myself. My world was right again.

The docks were quite high off the waterline, at least six feet above our heads, which was going to make our exit from the water difficult. Jacob drifted in next to me, and before I could ask what the plan was, he'd propelled himself out of the water and landed on the wooden decking above. He was just reaching down to hoist me up – I'd risen to my knees on Braxton's shoulders – when a head popped up right beside me.

I'm not going to lie. I might have let out a girl shriek which had my wolf and dragon both shaking their heads at me. Of course, the quads all lost it again, literally pissing themselves with laughter.

"What do you want from me?" I snarled into the large serpentine face that was right beside mine now. Even though Braxton was laughing, his broad shoulders shaking under me, he was still keeping an eye on Nessie, in case it decided to take a bite out of me.

The creature lowered its broad head, and then sort of nudged under my arm, like a puppy when it wants to be patted.

I flinched. Sea animals were not my thing. I liked air and forest. But I couldn't ignore its plea, so I reached out a hand and gave it a gentle scratch along the side of its large jaw. It was scaled and very cool to touch, not as slimy as I expected. In fact there was a rough texture to its skin.

I could see the shadows of the other ones in the background, but they weren't as friendly or needy as this one, who seriously looked like it wanted to climb into my lap and have a sleep.

"Always charming the monsters, Jess." Maximus gave me a wink as he shot up out of the water, and with a hand from his brother, swung onto the docks.

Tyson was next. Braxton gave the wizard a boost from below, and Maximus caught him from the top. Now it was my turn.

I leaned over Braxton's shoulder so I could see his face. "Will you be okay in the water by yourself?"

He responded by brushing his soft lips against mine, sending shooting arcs of heat through my frozen body. "I got this, Jess. Up you go."

His large hands were so gentle as he lifted me. I loved that most of the time the Compasses treated me like one of them. Sure, we didn't have punch-ups or anything, but I also wasn't made of glass to them. But in moments like this, when Braxton was gentle, which was not his usual behavior, I felt like I was precious. No matter how independent a female is – and I liked to think I was pretty tough – every one of us wants to be loved by someone who thinks we're precious, who touches us with reverence. Braxton gave me that and so much more.

I was just reaching up to grip onto Maximus' outstretched hands when I realized another force had joined in lifting me up – Loch Ness. With the help of the serpent, who clearly had the neck strength of an ogre, I was raised up above the docks before stepping easily into the waiting arms of my quads. I swung back around and gave the friendly water lizard another scratch, and even waved a couple of times as it sank back down into the darkness.

I turned to find Jacob watching me closely. "What?"

He shook his head, the stunning white and gold of his hair shifting in the dull lighting. "You're a fascinating creature, Jessa babe. The guards of the gods were not known for this pet-like behavior, but you pretty much had him curling around you and purring."

It was odd, messing-with-my-head odd. "Maybe it's because of my mark. We know it has something to do with the gods."

It was as good a theory as any.

Braxton was up on the dock now, only requiring the briefest of assistance, his massive shifter strength more than enough to power him into the air. The moment we were all standing on the docks, Jacob lifted both of his hands, fingers spread wide, and with a few low, musical words, the water evaporated off us. I let out a deep breath, relieved to be warm again.

"I love that my connection with the elements is so much stronger in Faerie," Jacob remarked. "It feels like home here. If only it was easier to exist between the two worlds. You lose so much Earth time by staying here." He shook his head. "Would never work."

I hated how sad he sounded, but at the same time I would not be happy to lose months of time without him on Earth. He would literally have a day on Faerie and that would be three weeks without him back home. Ouch.

As Tyson crossed my path, I couldn't stop myself from asking him. "Why did you cut your hair?"

Maybe I was some sort of OCD control freak, but he shouldn't have been changing things when I wasn't around to veto it. A few snickers started, and I realized that all of the quads, except the wizard, were stifling their laughter.

"What happened?" I asked, drawing the question out.

Tyson muttered a few times, running his hands through his shorter hair. "Let's just say Grace was not very happy with something I said, and she decided I needed an attitude adjustment. And a hair adjustment to go with it."

I bit my lip, trying really hard not to laugh too. He looked so morose, and I knew that was about so much more than his hair. It was about that healer witch, and how much she was under his skin. They hadn't established a mate-bond or anything yet, and hell, maybe she wouldn't be his true or chosen mate, but either way she was determined to make him pay for his jerk behavior in the past.

I snuggled into his side, offering my comfort. "Want me to beat her up? I'll totally do it for you. Just say the word."

Some of his anger lifted, and I was rewarded with dimples and a true smile. "Thanks for the offer, Jessa babe."

I shrugged. "That's what family is for."

Beating the crap out of people who hurt our pack members. Might not be normal for most, but it was totally normal for us.

He chuckled this time. "Since I've seen both of you fight, and I kind of like Grace's face the way it is, I'll take a pass on that. I deserve a lot of what she's dishing out anyway. Doesn't make it any easier to take."

I patted his arm. "She has to let go of the past. It's not healthy to hold on to shit for so long, and you need to man up and get your girl. You're being a little passive-aggressive. I know you're waiting for her to be ready again … but you need to show her that you're serious about it this time. This is not just about getting into her pants, it's about you caring for her."

Despite my violent offer, I liked Grace. I wouldn't have *enjoyed* beating the shit out of her, but for my boys I'd have done it without hesitation.

Tyson looked contemplative, and I knew he'd mull it over. He was a light-hearted, fun kind of supe, but he was also deep. He could commune with nature and the gods for hours; he had so much going on beneath the face he showed the world. Grace just needed to see that.

The five of us spent the next few moments trying to figure out where the hell we'd ended up. The area was bright enough that Tyson's wizard light was no longer needed, but there was still that dull, underground feel to the illumination. There was also a damp smell, which was not unusual with all the water lapping around us. The docks at least felt sturdy, without any of the rotting planks one would expect.

"Should we just start moving?" Maximus looked wired, like he couldn't stand still. "I'm worried about leaving Cardia on Earth. We have no idea what's going on back there. I never realized that being mated was so … much. I can feel her enough to know she's okay, which is keeping me sane, but we're too far away for any real communication."

New mates could be quite irritating to be around. As the bond worked to establish strong ties, couples were a mess of needs and base instincts. I had no real idea how Maximus continued to leave his mate, but I'd bet she was more than a little annoyed at him right now.

I placed a gentle hand on his shoulder. "Thanks for coming to find me. I know it couldn't have been easy."

He gave me a wink. "Girl, I'll always come for you."

I couldn't tell from his expression whether that was a deliberate choice of words – probably not since he had a mate now. Still, I swung a hand around to Jacob and Tyson.

"Don't say it, either of you, or I will rip your nuts off and feed them to Loch Ness."

Twin grins crossed their faces, but they did still take a step back and remained quiet. Lucky for them. Braxton cleared his throat and suddenly we were all business again. Time to figure out where we'd landed, and how to get back up to the Isle of the Gods. This was the most important thing right now. Finding the answers to how we might defeat Larky.

Chapter 10

The docks made no noise as we stepped across them. I expected swaying, but there was no movement at all. My skin tingled. The magic was as strong down here as it had been above.

"Do you think Louis will be able to find us?" I kept my voice low, not wanting to alert anybody to our presence. "Something tells me we might need him to get back to the surface."

I also liked having him around. He was this weird combination of serious, funny, old-school, and annoyingly clever. I felt safe with him, like my pack.

"I'm sure that damn overachieving sorcerer will have no problems finding us," Tyson muttered.

No love lost there. Tyson was an exceptionally powerful wizard, but he was young. Louis was the big kahuna in the sorcerer world, and somehow made things which should be impossible look utterly effortless. The two magic users had a lot of parallels in their journey – well, so far. Tyson was going to be one of the youngest leaders on the council, just like Louis had been. It was a lot to live up to, and coming second best was not something any of the Compasses did well.

I was starting to see our surroundings more clearly. On the dock it had been like twilight, dull but still visible. Now it was like the first cresting of the sun at dawn, a low, soft light, but with a glow that was bright and almost cheerful.

The docks were slowly fading away and now sandstone pavers lined the floor. There was even some greenery starting to scatter around and ... was that a bird call? How was this possible down here? The further we stepped into this world, the warmer and more appealing it got, and it was for this reason that all of us were suddenly on high alert. We knew better than to trust the world trying to lull us into a false sense of security. It was totally going to drop a bomb on our heads and laugh while we splattered into a million pieces.

The quads spread out around me, two on either side, their usual protective stance. I was probably lucky, with my recent kidnapping and all that, that I wasn't slung over one of their shoulders. Small victories.

The long expanse of pavers was leading to large shapes in the distance. It took a few more yards before I could see that the shapes were buildings, and not any old buildings, but massive castles with lots of intricately designed turrets and ornate marble accents. They looked a lot like sandcastles, with an earthy base color scheme, and then this splash of texture from the marble and stone scattered throughout. There were three of them, one large in the center and two a little smaller on either side. As we closed in on them I could see they were a mile wide at least, and went back really far.

I was whispering again. "Do you think this is the true Isle of the Gods? Like … the land above was some sort of façade, and they really dwelled down here? Hidden. Protected."

No one answered. Like me, they didn't have a freaking clue what we'd fallen into. Braxton took a step closer, the heat of his dragon wrapping around me again. Even when we were walking into the unknown like this, having my pack with me made anything okay.

Our footsteps were silent, the vegetation around us springing to life. We were walking through a landscaped garden complete with large rose bushes and hedges. There was structure to the design, but the plants were also wild, sort of like they had free run but still wanted to be neat about it. Shit. Knowing Faerie, the plants probably did think for themselves here.

The animal noises increased – more bird calls, rustling of bushes and even a few butterfly-cross-bumblebees buzzed past. These odd creatures had a bee body with these massive colorful wings and were at least the size of a small bird.

"It's so strange," I said, "If we hadn't just literally climbed out of that icy water, I would never believe that this was underground."

"Don't trust that we're still underground," Jacob said, his eyes looking even greener than usual here. "Faerie is not a world to easily understand, and there's every chance that we're not where we think we are."

Clear as mud. Thanks.

There was a courtyard in the outer zone of the massive castles. Beyond, large stone blocks rose up to form a barrier. It took us a few minutes of wandering along it before we found an opening, just wide enough for us to duck through, one by one. The path on the other side was perfect, no cracked pavers or weeds littered around, as if this world had a team of gardeners, maintenance mages, and cleaners on staff. And yet it was eerily quiet, like there was no one here at all. It had an abandoned feeling, but this perfect upkeep said otherwise.

"Stop!"

A male voice rang out loudly behind us. We were about halfway along the path which led to the smaller right-side castle. The large outer stone fence blocked us from seeing whomever was the owner of the voice, but we didn't step forward. Better to leave enough space to clearly see what we were up against.

My dragon and wolf roared to their feet, on alert but patiently waiting for my command. I liked knowing that I could shift into either of them, and even though you would assume dragon would be the choice every time, there were some things a dragon just couldn't do, despite Braxton's cocky confidence in his abilities. When stealth and sneaking through small spaces was required, my wolf was the perfect choice.

The moments passed slowly as we waited for the figure to appear. Probably no longer than a minute, but it felt like an hour as the tension ate away at our group. I sensed that the boys were about eight seconds from saying *screw it* and charging down the path, when a shadow crossed over the doorway and a figure stepped through.

"Seriously," I said, breathing out in a great huff. "That was a real shithead move."

I started running back along the path. Louis held out his arms for a hug, but at the last moment I sidestepped and punched him square in the shoulder.

"You're an asshole. Why the hell didn't you say it was you? You should know better than to just shout and scare the shit out of me."

He laughed. "Aw, Jess, always so happy to see me."

I was actually really happy to see him, but he still deserved that punch. Stepping back to his side, I did give him the hug he'd been waiting for, and by that time the Compasses had joined us.

"I couldn't see you, but your pack's energy was close and strong. I wanted to stop you before you made it any further. This is not a world you should step through lightly."

Braxton gave the sorcerer a passive glare, like he wanted to ream him one but knew that we needed his intel right now. "You should probably tell us everything you know about this place," he said. "How did you get down here? And can we get out the same way?"

Louis glanced around, taking in the scenery. "I fell the same as you all did, ending up in the Sea of Tranquility."

The Sea of Tranquility? *What the eff?*

"It's the waters of the gods. They're protective and restorative. They judge all who enter, and if you're not of worthy intentions, you'll never make it out alive."

"Don't forget about the Loch Ness Monsters."

Louis grinned. "They're the guardians of the water. If you don't pass the judgement, they will no longer be the serene creatures you witnessed. They turn into demons of the deep and they're impossible for any to win against. Even a dragon," he said, his eyes twinkling. It was like he'd heard our conversation when we'd first fallen in the water. Braxton didn't bother to reply, but I could see on his face that he thought Louis was wrong.

"They took a real liking to Jess," Jacob said.

Louis' enthralling eyes locked on to me and swirls of something shot through my body. The sorcerer had a way of wrapping his energy around you and infusing it into your every facet. He was scary as shit at times, and I wondered what it would feel like to be mated to someone with that much power and intensity.

Probably a lot like being mated to Braxton, but while dragons had an ancient and wild magic, the sorcerer's was on this whole otherworldly, epic scale. It would take a special sort of magic user to be a true mate to this mage.

"The guardians of the sea are born of the shining ones' dreams. They're pure fantasy. And there's something about Jessa which screams 'power of the gods' as well. It was what captured me when she was a child, and what continues to draw me to her."

I snorted. "Thought it was my charming personality."

He joined the laughter of the quads. "You're actually quite charming, Jess, and your blunt nature is a welcome relief to me. I've spent too many years dealing with lies and deceit. To find people who simply speak truth … well, it's a gift."

I wasn't a particularly sentimental or emotional person, but that kind of hit me right in the gut. I had so many blessings, and Louis definitely made that list now.

"Okay, so do you think my freaky dragon mark is giving me some weird pull? A magical essence which draws creatures to me. Or is it more?"

Thanks to Louis, my mark had been suppressed for most of my life, but now that the energy was free and the king had returned, the power of the mark was burning through me. I was changing – possibly the reason for my sensitive and aching body.

"It could be your mark, or it could be that you have some blood of the gods in you. I know that Jonathon's line is ancient and can be traced back to the time of the first awakening. Either way, Jess, you're special."

Yep, special fucking cupcakes are me.

Louis turned to stare around the castle grounds. "I never believed I would see this world, the true realm of the gods. This is where the shining ones built their power base. The Gold magic is so much stronger here. They protect the true center of Faerie."

"What's at the center of Faerie?" I asked.

"The realm where the shadows are trapped. We don't ever want to find ourselves there. We must never wake the ancient shadow spawn."

I'd always known that we needed Louis' expertise. He had ten times more knowledge than the rest of us. "So where are the shining ones then?"

The place might have been perfect to look at, but it was clear that there were no living beings here. I could feel the emptiness.

Louis shrugged, his white, ribbed long-sleeved shirt rippling across lithe muscles. "I don't know for sure. I believe they abandoned their physical bodies and are simply one with their world now." That could explain the current state of perfection down here. If they were a part of this world, in spirit or power form, they could probably keep the maintenance up.

"I have heard a lot of stories about when they vanished. Apparently one minute they were here, controlling the power of Faerie and existing with their wild brethren, the dragons. They monitored the dragon mating and made sure that balance was kept through the realms. And then … they were gone. Before my time of course, but I've been studying the lands of Faerie for many years. I've gathered a lot of information about the history, because so much of it still affects us on the Earth plane. In truth, though, no one really knows what happened to them."

Both of my hands flew up, palms toward him. "Whoa, hold up. The dragons are their brethren and they monitored dragon mating? What the hell are you saying?" Before he could answer, I spun around to Braxton. "Do you know what he's talking about?"

This was the second time someone had mentioned dragon mating or mated. I had never heard that term before, and I wanted to know what it was. Like right now.

"I have some idea, just very basic information about the way dragon shifters are born." Braxton turned to Louis. "We're never told much of it. Faerie guards their secrets. If you know more, you better start explaining."

I spun around again. "Yes, what he said … start talking, sorcerer." I was fully prepared to beat it out of him, even if he could turn me into a frog with a simple spell. Okay, I was pretty sure it wouldn't be that simple, but I bet Louis could do it.

"We're wasting time standing here," Jacob cut in. "We need to find whatever it is that can break the dragon marked ties. Can we explore and talk at the same time?"

Louis sucked in a deep breath, his eyes flittering across the castles towering over us. "I think we are going to have to venture inside, but I implore you all, stay close, do not wander off. I have no idea which of the ancient powers might be lying dormant in those walls."

I couldn't hold back my snort, which turned into full-blown laughter when Louis turned his sparkling purple peepers on me. "You *implore* us to stay close. No one speaks like you, my friend, no one."

Okay, some of the oldest supes did on occasion lapse into a much more formal style of English, but Louis managed to combine old and new perfectly.

His grin widened. "I'll dumb it down for you next time, shall I?"

I forced my face to go perfectly blank, before reaching up and twirling a strand of hair. "Awesome, that would be like, totally, like just the wickedest thing evers."

I finished that by flipping him off, with both hands. Smartass fucker.

We were silent as we started our journey toward the castles again. This time Louis was leading. He chose the largest, middle castle. The light here felt natural, but we knew it wasn't; there were no shadows, not even a darkening as we stepped up to the doorway. The sandstone building towered above us, its marble accents littered with rubies and sapphires, and the rest looked like a diamond infused membrane. So glittery.

I reached out a hand and placed it onto one of the pillars, which stood tall on either side of the main entrance. Sparks shot through my palm and up my arm, the magic skidding along my body and deep into my veins. I managed to yank myself off the wall before sinking back against Braxton.

"I don't know what the hell that just was," I said breathlessly. "But there's some serious mojo in this castle. It's so infused with magic that I would recommend not touching shit unless you have no choice."

"Great plan, Jess," Louis said before muttering a few words in the direction of the massive door, standing at least fifteen feet high. It slowly creaked open. I wasn't sure what to expect on the other side, but when the sorcerer finally stepped through, and the rest of us followed, I was completely stunned.

One would think that stepping into a castle, the inside would in some way match the outside – large open foyer, huge curved marble staircases, maybe some long expanses of stone flooring, shiny marble even? Nope. Apparently in this isle of Faerie, what you got inside castles was a massive stretch of meadow, some scattered trees in the distance, and the softest looking grass and flowers flowing out across the distance. The space looked endless; the sky was dark blue, navy, and infused with light.

I couldn't stop myself from stepping further into the meadow, sighing as my bare feet sank into the warm, dry, spongy softness. Wait ... my shoes? I turned back and realized they had been flung haphazardly near the entrance. I must have kicked them off the moment I walked inside, needing to be in contact with the land.

I wanted to run and fly across the meadows. In fact, my dragon had stopped her calm pacing and was now straining against me. All of a sudden I had the feeling that this was her world and she wanted to be free. As if all control had left me, in a roar of fire and magic I felt the shift washing across my body. Braxton's eyes captured mine just moments before my body morphed into my dragon.

My mind went into beast mode, the colors of this place even more dazzling with the extra spectrum of dragon sight. She was pushing my consciousness down, tapping into the base instincts of her kind. We were immediately in the sky, flying, roaring, sending plumes of flames around the world and into the blueness. Everything here felt right for the dragon's existence – the temperature, the air currents, the scents, the colors. It was as if this was a dragon's dream world.

Home.

I sensed Braxton long before he joined us. The wind carried the scent of him to us. I forced some of the dragon down, which was so much harder than it should have been. I feared for a moment that she would never let me take control again. She did not want to leave this world.

Brax...

I hoped he would hear me. I'd dreamed about communicating with him as a dragon.

Jess, babe, now is not the time for a flying lesson.

As his warm tones washed across my mind, I gained more control over my dragon, as if she, too, was unable to stop herself from granting his request.

Apparently what I want is not that important right now. My dragon needed some her *time.*

He chuckled. *I understand. Mine is the same, but that tells me that we're in the right place. This is where we will find the key to defeating Larkspur.*

He was right, and we had to hurry up about it. Who knew what the hell was happening in the human world while we were here. Actually, Louis might know, he'd just been there dropping Jonathon off. I'd ask him, right after he explained about this damn dragon mated thing.

I flew beside Braxton for some time, our dragons companionably gliding through the air. The scenery below did not change much. There were some lakes, a few mountains, trees, and other variances on nature – the most peaceful oasis I could ever imagine.

Time to get back to the others.

Braxton's voice echoed across our bond again, and we banked to the right, turning our large bodies back in the direction we'd just flown. My dragon was calm now, satisfied. Her heart, body, and soul seemed more at peace, and she was content to allow control to return to me.

I tried not to dwell on how easily she'd wrested it from me; it was a relief to have our status-quo returned. We flew rapidly now, our keen sight locking in on the rest of our group. A few pangs rocked my body as we started to descend. I couldn't quite tell if they were from me or my dragon. Still, as I landed, the change back to human was easy, effortless.

Braxton and I were both in our usual after-shift naked-state, but Louis quickly fixed that for us. The sorcerers hand lingered on my shoulder for a few extra moments, as if he knew I was still trying to pull my frazzled psyche together. It was disorienting trying to deal with the dragon's mind as well as my own. I reached out and gripped Louis' shirt.

"I think it's time for you to tell us everything you know about this place."

We ended up beside one of the large lakes, a small stream trickling down a series of staggered rocks. I don't know which one of us decided to jump in first, but before we knew it, all of us had stripped down to our underwear and were swimming around in a sort of reckless abandon. Don't get me wrong, we hadn't forgotten where we were, or what we were doing here, but for some reason the urgency was lost in our need to frolic.

I might not enjoy dark, scary waters, but in a small lake like this, I was in my element, diving and rolling with the cool current, so soothing and refreshing.

"So, Louis, spill." Tyson was flat on his back, floating around, using his magic to power himself like he was a little boat.

Louis sat on the edge of the lake, his pants rolled up and legs in the water, the only one who wasn't swimming. "I'll tell you everything I know, but you must keep in mind that original fey, like the shining ones and shadow spawn, are very secretive. I have inferred a lot from my fact gathering missions over the years, but there are many blanks."

We just waved our hands at him. Even if eighty percent of his facts were made up, he'd still know a hundred percent more than most of us.

He splashed out with his feet as he spoke. "The shining ones are the original gods of Faerie, pretty much. They're blessed to be able to contain and use the Gold. There is only one other race who have the same sort of ties to this pure energy, and that's the dragons. The two are cousins of a sort."

No way! I stopped my frolicking and focused on him with an intensity that would make most supes feel very uncomfortable. Louis didn't even seem to notice.

"The reason there are dragon shifters, that dragons and supes have any relationship at all, is because of their bond with the shining ones. There used to be thousands of dragons, maybe hundreds of thousands. They roamed the lands and were the top predator of both Faerie and Earth. It got so bad that at one point the supes were ready to go to war with the wild dragons, but then the shining ones stepped in. They tamed some of the more animalistic nature of your wild brethren.

"The first dragon shifter was recorded over five thousand years ago, and the story goes that a wild dragonling was born to a weak body, something which happened on occasion, and always resulted in the early death of the young. The problem being that for dragons, even if the body is damaged, the soul is as strong as ever. In a desperate attempt to save him, one of the shining ones managed to set the soul free but kept it contained in the mortal realm. The retaining of an essence had never been done before, and it gave the fey an idea about how they could save these dragon souls. The dragonling was given the choice to bond with a member of Faerie or to move on to the great sky."

I was literally not breathing right now. If Braxton hadn't swum up behind me and cupped his hands under my butt, hauling me into his body so he could hold me up, I'd have drowned. I was all over the feel-o-meter with this story. It was achingly painful and yet beautiful at the same time. I had to know more.

"He chose to be bonded," I breathed, my eyes fluttering closed as my head tilted back to rest against Braxton's hard chest.

Louis made a sound of acknowledgement. "Yes, the dragon young chose to be bonded, but his stipulation was that he would choose the supernatural soul strong enough to house his spirit, one who was worthy. The transformation to dragon shifter would start at conception. He was released, and exactly six months later a child was born, the first dragon shifter, the first supernatural to be dragon mated."

All of us had moved closer, standing in the shallower water, forming a circle around the storytelling mage.

Braxton was running his hands up and down my bare arms, warming me with his fire. "This is why becoming a dragon shifter is not genetic," I said.

"It's an anomaly. The soul of a dragon chooses a shifter strong enough to be part of them."

Louis nodded. "To have your soul be dragon mated is the greatest gift. There are none stronger or more intelligent than the dragons."

"If this is true, then how do I have a dragon and a wolf soul?" My voice was high, and if I'd been on land I'd be pacing. "How the hell am I possible?"

Chapter 11

My entire body was so tense I felt like I could fracture apart with the smallest of taps. Louis shook his head at me.

"I just don't know, Jess. It's almost as if your beast dragon mated to you after you were already developed enough in utero to have claimed your wolf soul. The dragon king did something unnatural to make this happen. Somehow he manipulated a dragon soul. It's possible that's why you needed to come here, because the only ones who could truly tell us are the shining ones."

This was why my dragon and I weren't as connected as Braxton and his dragon. We'd all been dragon mated the same, but I already had the soul of a wolf inside, so my dragon bond was less complete. I went from tense to breakdown in seconds, my emotions spilling over, sorrow burrowing deep into my heart. I closed my eyes so I could focus internally, so I could see my beautiful dragon.

What did they do to you?

She fluttered her wings at me, those large eyes blinking rapidly. Even if she did remember what had happened to her before we were mated, there was no way for her to tell me.

"I'm not worthy," I murmured out loud. "She didn't choose to be dragon mated, she was forced. It's not right. It's not right!" My voice was loud, and without thought I was scrambling out of the water.

Everything inside of me screamed at the wrongness of this. A part of me wanted to claw at my own skin, to release the majestic creature who felt like she was meant to be mine but at the same time wasn't.

Before I could complete my insane breakdown, something changed in the world. An energy infused across the air and the sky darkened. My breathing was ragged as I fought to control the anger and pain lashing at my insides.

I had dealt with fucked up things in my life: my mother disappearing, never knowing my twin, my father's absence and depression, the dragon mark and the subsequent running for my life, but this was the first time I'd ever felt this out of control. I knew that compared to most, my life was pretty great – I'd always had my pack. Still, I was handling this far worse than I expected. My soul actually cried for my dragon.

Again I tried to shelve my emotional leakage. Whatever entity had disturbed this land was getting closer. Reeling in my emotions felt like an impossible task, and it wasn't until arms engulfed me from all sides that I managed a slice of clarity. I was surrounded by limbs, energy, warmth, support. My pack. For many moments we did not speak, we just stayed as a single unit and watched the sky as it continued to darken, waiting for the new interference to show itself.

As the boys wrapped themselves and their energy around me, some of the fissures in my heart and soul – which were so much deeper now – started to disappear. The quads' love and support was a magical putty, easing some of the ache inside.

"I don't know what I would do without you all." My voice startled me. It was far huskier than usual.

Arms tightened even further, and a few more of the cracks were healed. The largest cracks could never be fixed – the one which mourned for the soul of my dragon, and for all those marked who had lost so much of themselves.

"You're worthy, Jess." Braxton was close to my right ear, his words a balm to my wounds. "No matter what the king did, your soul was always strong enough for a dragon. Think about it, you're strong enough for two souls to be mated with yours."

"Exactly, Jess," Jacob said with a touch of laughter. "Are you starting to agree with me when I say you're the dragon whisperer? Double dragon mated: Braxton and your own dragon. Nothing unworthy there, babe."

I don't know why but I laughed. It wasn't funny and I was feeling like ass right now, but Jacob just sounded so proud of himself as he tried to cheer me up. It was the perfect thing he could have said, knocking me straight out of my melancholy, reminding me of all the ways I was blessed.

My dragon might not have been destined for me initially, but she had chosen me and I legit loved the heck out of her. Together with my wolf, we were a soul trifecta and we were totally going to kick Larky straight in the balls and then rip his freaking head off.

My wolf and dragon roared in agreeance. As I straightened and pushed my hair back from my face, the quads unwrapped themselves from me. Everyone is entitled to a moment of hitting rock bottom, it's how we build ourselves back up to be twice as strong, but my moment was over now. Braxton ran a hand across my hair, tangling his fingers through it, as he loved to do.

All of our attentions were drawn back to the darkening sky. Dragon-shaped shadows were zagging across it and the six of us settled into a semi-circle, waiting to see what was about to happen, preparing ourselves. Louis stepped to the front, his power longer-reaching than the rest of ours. Tyson was the next best.

The shadows disappeared, only to reappear moments later. Before I could react my head exploded and darkness engulfed me. For the first time in my life, Jessa was lost to the dragon. The shining ones were here to play.

I awoke in a field very much like the one I'd just left, my head squashed against something quite hard and rough, and by the time I opened my eyes and scrambled to my feet, it was too late to haul butt from the dragon – a dragon who was not Braxton or Larky. Nope, this dragon was so unbelievably stunning it made the rest of us look like geckos – you know, those weird little translucent lizards – ugly bastards, no matter how useful they were at keeping the spider population down.

This dragon was a pure, shimmery gold, like the richest vein of gold you could ever hope to mine from the ground, so sparkling that it irritated my eyes if I stared too directly.

Large, red, jewel-like eyes gazed at me. Unblinking. I sensed no aggression from the beast, even though the wild magic it emitted suggested it was a wild dragon, not a shifter. While it felt like a bad idea to remove my attention from this golden giant, I had to send out my senses to see if my pack was close by.

I got nothing from our immediate surroundings, no other energy at all.

Welcome to my realm, youngling.

The musical voice echoed across my mind and crashed like cymbals into my brain. I shook my head, trying to dispel the lingering fogginess that had sprung up by simply being in the presence of something so magical.

Who are you?

Somehow I knew how to project the words I wanted and keep the rest private.

I am Chrysandra. I am both shining one and queen of the wild dragons.

Holy crap on toast. And I had thought I was a special cupcake. How could she be both?

Have the shining ones always been dragons? I had pictured them looking like pointed-ear elf-princesses.

No, many millennia ago our two races were strong enough to exist separately. Now we are one and the same. After the battle with shadow spawn, those who were left chose to be dragon mated to our most magical of brethren. This is how we survived.

Un-freaking-believable. The shining ones did the opposite of the dragon shifters. The dragons didn't mate to them, they went into the beast.

What do you want with me? What happened when I blacked out?

Images appeared in my head then, flashes of my dragon flying in a large group of beasts, all of them impressive and ancient looking, although none still came close to the spectacular visage of the dragon before me now.

You and the soul of your dragon are innocent victims in something which should never have happened. A thousand years ago a shifter came to our land. He asked for a favor, offering his own boon in return. We refused him, for what he requested was so abhorrent to our kind that there would be nothing he would ever be able to give which could justify it.

Fucking Larky. Bet they wished they killed that arrogant dick right then and there. I certainly wished they had.

He was charismatic and very persistent, though, and somehow managed to convince two of the younger shining dragons to join forces with him. Together they approached the shadow spawn. Our enemy took his offering and granted his request. Even with limited power, they still managed to create a curse, a line of magic which was sent out into the universe. The shifter wanted to bind souls to his own. In the case of his death, he would be able to be reborn with the blood of those who bore his mark.

So it had been the shadow spawn who created the marked.

Why is my mark different than the others? Why did my blood free him from his prison?

Chrysandra didn't answer immediately, and I felt like she was searching my mind, ferreting around in there, probably trying to figure out why I was so special. Finally, her deep tones sounded again.

You're descended from the shining ones, you and your twin both. There was once many supernaturals who were descended from us, but now they are few. You and Mischa are the only two to be both dragon marked and contain the blood of the shining ones. Teamed with the blood of Larkspur's daughters, you held enough power to trigger his curse.

I never even bothered to wonder how she knew Mischa's name. She was a god, they just knew shit.

So, I'm actually descended from ... the shining ones. I trusted the word of this golden beast, but it was still a crazy thing to wrap my head around. Guess I knew now why the labyrinth had let me in and Loch Ness had been like a massive, scaled kitty-serpent. I was family and stuff.

Yes, your family is one of the stronger lines left in the supernatural races, and because you were the first born of your twin set, you're stronger than Mischa. This is why you were the dragon mated.

Yes, how the hell ... uh, how did that happen? I'm a dual shifter. I also have a wolf soul bonded to mine.

Those jewel eyes blinked then, closing in one slow sweep, and stayed closed for many moments. I could hear nothing, but the sorrow that seeped through and into her magic was potent.

That was part of the curse and the reason we would never have helped him. I flinched, her eyes were still closed and I had not expected her to start talking. *He wanted us to forcibly mate a dragon soul with a supernatural, one descended from the shining ones, and in doing so, we would create a mate strong enough to bear his children, a queen to help him lead the five races. This was against everything we stood for, everything we had ever promised to our majestic beast friends.*

My heart was beating so hard it was almost loud enough to drown out the Queen's voice in my head. This was information we needed, that would help us, but I wasn't sure I could handle the full truth.

When we turned him down, he went to the shadow spawn, and while they were able to release the curse, they cannot touch the souls of dragons.

Which is why he ended up turning two of our members. Their betrayal was deep and all encompassing.

Chrysandra's eyes were open again now.

They stole four of our young, newly born dragons. They killed their physical bodies and contained their souls in balls of magic. These four became trapped in the curse of the shadow spawn, cursed to be dragon mated when that was never their fate. The first three were lost to the great sky in an attempt to forcibly mate them to some of Larkspur's men, experiments so they would not make any mistakes with his chosen mate.

They were going to wait on the fourth, hoping to discover the secret to a successful dragon mating, but we thwarted those plans. The moment he killed those dragonlings, he made enemies of the shining ones and the dragons. It was only his ties with the shadow spawn that stopped us from killing him immediately. With his power so linked to theirs, the energy of his death may have given the shadow a window to escape their prison. We would have been weakened, and they would have overthrown us.

Instead we decided to throw as many obstacles in his path as we could, and eventually he was spooked enough to release the remaining dragon soul into the universe. She was still stuck within the marked curse, but instead of being forced to a specific supernatural, she was free to find the mate he needed.

The shining one paused and the air felt heavy. The next time her voice was in my head, it was shaky.

One of the stolen young was my child. Until this day I never knew if she was one of those who were lost or if she was the remaining soul released into the universe. The moment you stepped into my realm, I sensed her soul within you. She survives. The true heir to the dragon mantle, the last queen of our kind.

Holy shit. My heart broke for her. No mother should have to face the loss of a child.

It's been like a thousand years since they stole the dragons, right? It had to be before the king was killed. *So my dragon was just existing out in the universe, waiting to find the right soul to mate with? Larkspur wasn't around to force her? So does that mean it was a natural dragon mating, like Braxton and other shifters?*

I sensed her hesitation before she spoke again.

Larkspur did not force her to choose you, but as I said, the curse was strong and she was a victim as well. Larkspur commanded her to seek the strongest line of shifters, descended from the shining ones. She waited for you through the many centuries. You were the first to call to her, and even though your soul already had a wolf claim, she found a way to make the bond work. Through no fault of either of you, it was this joining which freed the shifter, for he could never have been awoken without the final piece of his curse.

Yep, I knew that all too well. I had been the piece of the puzzle, my blood and dragon mated soul the key to opening his tomb.

Even though she chose you, and you were bonded in the same way as all other dragon shifters, her soul was never supposed to be free to be dragon mated. She should be the queen of her people. She is everything we had hoped and dreamed of to lead our royal line. I have not had any young since. Josephina is the last of my line.

Josephina. The name slammed into me like a bullet to the gut. I played with her name in my head, and my dragon, who had been listening to her mother speak, sent warm energy toward me, trying to reassure me, trying to make me feel better about being the prison binding her soul. Being dragon mated was the greatest gift I could ever hope to have, but this was not the way it should have been.

Josephina wrapped herself closer around me, sending more of that ancient energy in my direction. I wailed my sorrow at her. *I'm sorry. So, so sorry.* And even though we couldn't communicate the same way I was talking with her mother, I could tell that she was trying to comfort me, reassure me that this was not my fault, that she had chosen me for a reason, that even though, by the time she found me, I already had a wolf soul, there had been no one else strong enough for her.

I managed to pull myself together, steadying my breath, focusing again. I sent a question to Chrysandra: *How were the dragon marked chosen?*

Larkspur wanted the strongest minds. Body strength was not as important. He wanted twins and multiples because of the mental link you already possess, a link he could utilize when he tried to control you.

Made sense. Larky was a smug, intelligent asshole. And I was so going to kill him. He murdered baby dragons, for freak's sake.

Chrysandra shifted closer to me, her head snaking down to hover inches from my own. Her eyes stared into my soul again and I wondered if she was trying to see Josephina, her daughter.

I have to go now. There's much we do to keep this world as is, to stop those from waking who should not.

Wait, I blurted. *Just really quickly, why did Larkspur not use magic when he fought against Braxton? And what did he promise you and the shadow spawn? What could he offer that would be worth the shadow ones helping him with a curse? That must have cost them precious energy.*

Our gazes remained locked.

If he managed to dragon mate a soul to a shifter descended from the shining ones, she would be strong enough to produce his young.

I remember.

Her children would be dragon shifters, the first ever naturally born, no need for a dragon mated soul. These young would be stronger than any dragon-mated shifter, a true hybrid of the kind, and would hold power over the five supernatural races. Larkspur plans to build an army of his children to rule over the supernatural races. Even the gods would not be safe.

Fuck! I had kind of skimmed over that before, but I should have paid closer attention to the fact that Larky planned to turn me into a dragon baby maker. A fact which fit with our earlier revelations of my fertility, and his want for an heir.

He promised the eldest of his offspring, a child of immense power. We would never consider it for a moment, but it's a weapon the shadow ones will use against us.

A warning entered her voice.

This is a bargain which still stands. You must ensure this never comes to fruition. Please remember, supernaturals who are dragon mated don't have the same fertile periods as regular shifters. You can have a child at any time, unless you seek spelling from a magic user.

That was weird. Besides my pains very recently, I'd always had normal shifter fertile times ... maybe it was because my mark and dragon had been suppressed, her magic locked down. Either way, I didn't have to worry about having that asshat's child, I think I'd remember if Larky had been close enough to get his di–

Wait...

My heart stuttered in my chest.

Braxton.

We had slept together after my mark was released, and without using protection. I had been ages away from my fertile time, so there had been nothing to worry about. Except ... apparently there was. I could be carrying Braxton's baby, a child that might be a dragon shifter, and was promised to the shadow ones...

The agony must have been clear in my ashen features. Chrysandra offered me some reassurances. *The promise was only for Larkspur's first born, so a child conceived with another would be free from any debt to them.*

The relief was short-lived.

But ... if your child with another is a dragon shifter, and Larkspur steals this young and offers it to them, the shadow spawn will not care that this is not the complete fulfilment of the promise. They want the weapon, and will accept the first natural born dragon shifter. Do not let Larkspur steal your child ... my daughter's child.

I was in the midst of trying to comprehend the gut-wrenching information when she answered one of my first questions. The one about why Larky had not used his sorcery against Braxton. I focused through my shock, it was important to know every single weakness he had.

All of the magic on Earth, all of the magic gifted to the supernatural races, originates from Faerie. Larkspur is not a sorcerer, he is a pure-born shifter, one who must have some powerful friends to lend him magic.

That was one of the more useful pieces of information she had given me. He was not a sorcerer – despite the fact that he'd fooled all the supes in his time to think so – which must mean that any magic he'd used had originated from somewhere else. If we could figure out how to make sure he didn't have access to any magic sources during our next battle … well, that would be a distinct advantage for us.

The golden dragon moved even closer, towering above me. I did not run, but her presence was very overwhelming. *I understand why my child chose you. You're strong, intelligent, loyal, loving, and selfless.*

And sometimes I was an asshole. I guess I was just lucky my dragon liked me for me, even the bad.

Care for each other. The dragon mated bond, and your bond with your true mate, is your key to beating the shifter. We will meet again, Jessa of the shining line. I leave you with two gifts. You will know what to do when the time comes.

As I tried to find the words to express my gratitude and joy at meeting Chrysandra, queen of the dragons and Josephina's mother, a blast of energy rocked out in a circle, starting from the golden dragon and ricocheting outwards like some sort of atomic bomb so fast there was no way for me to avoid the impact. I closed my eyes and braced myself the best I could.

As it crashed against me, the world tilted on its axis and everything went dark again.

By the time I managed to regain control of myself, still naked as the day I was born, the golden dragon was gone. I stared around ... I was somewhere else again.

A flash of something in the distant sky caught my attention, and as I saw the shine of scales I crouched by instinct. It took me a second to recognize the black and blue beast. Braxton. He had come for me, just as I knew he always would.

I bounced with urgency, the conversation I'd had with Chrysandra burning in my mind. I had to let my pack know. Both of my hands dropped to press against my flat stomach; the golden dragon had not confirmed my pregnancy but there was definitely a possibility.

It was too early for any obvious signs of a pregnancy, but I did have the weird back pain and the weird anti-touching thing going on … which could be nothing also.

For now, I was going with a maybe I was pregnant, because my poor brain just wasn't ready to deal with an absolute yes. I wasn't even sure I wanted rugrats. I kind of liked being selfish, and having young would have put an end to that immediately.

Still, if I was preggo I would love my child with a fierceness that would probably scare the shit out of everyone, including the kid. I had no idea what Braxton would say once I told him all of this, but one thing I did not doubt was that he'd love and protect his young with the same ferocity that he loved and protected me. Fuck, he was going to be extra batshit crazy over my safety now. All of the Compasses would. *Fun times, baby Compass, fun times.*

I forced myself to focus on Braxton, until a shimmer of light sprung up close by. The burst of magic took me by surprise but didn't scare me. I was pretty sure this was going to be one of the gifts from the queen. I glanced to the sky again. Braxton was still some distance away, so I had enough time to explore.

As I stepped closer to the shimmering, I could feel the pull of energy. The magical essence of that glowing space was strong, even in a land built on the Gold. Closing in on it, I could finally see through the glow to find a dais in the center. The pedestal was intricately carved with circular patterns, starting thick at the base and getting thinner as it ascended. On top was a circular plate, curved slightly on the sides. I zeroed straight in on the jewel in the center.

A jewel?

I wasn't sure what this was meant for, but it was certainly exceptionally beautiful. I reached for the shimmery bauble, its red tones reminding me of Chrysandra's eyes. The moment my hand closed around it, I heard her voice in my head.

This is the blood of our ancestors forged into a stone of Faerie. It's our offering in the battle, our repayment for all of the dragonlings and supernatural lives lost. Embed this pendant into the heart of the shifter, break the stone, and the shining ones' blood will shatter the bonds between him and his army. It will destroy the curse.

More than one voice joined hers, and I knew the other shining dragon ones were with her again. The tinkling chorus of voices sounded a lot like the ones which had spoken to me in those first few moments after I'd slept with Braxton, quite possibly the very moment I conceived our child.

I still worried about what tough decision they were talking of, the one which could cost the supe races everything? Dammit. I was so not cool with this shit in my life, but at least I had a solid weapon to use against Larky. I would take great pleasure plunging my hands into his heart, especially now that I knew everything he'd done, everything he'd planned. *Impregnate me and then give away my child.* I was not only going to shove my fist into his heart, I was going to tear out that shriveled blackness and feed it to the wolves.

The voices were gone now, and I knew they wouldn't be back. I held the pendant gently, worried that I'd accidentally break it. As I brought the jewel closer, I was astonished at the multiple tones of red in its depths. It was more than evident that this was no ordinary pendant. A chain dangled from it, long enough that I could easily slip it over my head and allow the jewel to fall and rest between my breasts. My own energy took a second to adjust to its power.

Josephina shifted closer to the front of my body, toward the pendant. It called to us.

Warmth washed along my spine then and I shivered as Braxton's energy tugged at my soul. I felt his presence everywhere, all the way to my toes. As I turned to meet my mate – who had just landed and was shifting back to human – there was a flash of light from the dais. By the time I looked again there was a large table in its place.

"Hells yeah." I shouted, fist pumping a little. Gift two was freaking awesome.

Before me was a massive table spread with more food than I'd ever seen in my life, piles of deliciousness, a plethora of colors, textures – and the scents ... shit, don't even get me started on those. I wiggled side to side like a confused puppy. I didn't know which choice to make. I was dying to wrap myself around my mate ... but there was food ... so much glorious food. Braxton laughed then, and my attention was instantly a hundred percent on the sexy dragon shifter. I would never have a single doubt about how much I loved Braxton. If he could draw my attention from food when I was starving, there was nothing that could steal me from him.

I growled as my gaze dragged slowly over him. He was naked and freaking delicious.

Actually we were both naked and alone ... whatever could we do with our time? Ignoring the food, I stepped closer. He wore the wildness of this land across his tall, muscular body. Arms hanging at his sides, palms facing toward me as if he was somehow drawing me closer with his energy, I wanted to go slowly, to savor this moment between us. We'd so rarely been alone since our mate bond kicked in. The chain and pendant swung gently against my body. I paused, just briefly, my smirk teasing as I drew out the last moment before we touched.

A grin cut across his rugged features and those dimples knocked the breath out of me. "Get your sexy ass here, Jessa."

He lifted his arms and my legs scrambled forward. I wanted to be home. I needed him more than anything. I launched myself at him, and with both of his hands under my butt, he lifted me with ease. Our bodies were flush against each other, his hard and unyielding, mine a touch softer.

"We're going to have a little chat about all of this disappearing you've been doing lately, babe." He was being light, but I could hear the tendrils of worry. "But first I think I'm gonna need a second here just to hold you."

Braxton did not like feeling out of control. He wasn't used to it and there were no real precedents for him to learn how to deal with it. This whole dragon marked thing kept shooting up obstacles that he couldn't protect me from. It was throwing him off his game and I wouldn't be surprised if he didn't explode into a mass of angry energy soon. Well, another mass. It sounded like he'd been plenty angry when I disappeared into Faerie.

I hugged myself closer to him, taking this single moment of togetherness. Very soon I would have to tell him what I'd learned from the shining dragon queen, and some of it was life-changing stuff, including the fact that we might be pregnant, and that Larky might be planning to steal our child and give it to the evil ugly-ass Faerie demons.

There were no pregnancy tests this early for shifters. Generally we waited until the first full moon after our fertile period, and a witch would call to the gods asking for an answer.

Shit, I couldn't even imagine being pregnant. I was sure to screw the poor kid up. I had no idea how to raise a regular supe, let alone one with the power to control all five races. I'd have Braxton though, and my pack. We'd all just have to do the best we could and hope the kid was not a little asshole. Plus, we couldn't screw them any worse than Larky, who had zero values, or the shadow spawn, who were kinda on the evil side.

Braxton's lips brushed over my neck; the graze of his teeth followed. "You chose me over food." His low, gruff voice distracted me from my worries.

I loved the hint of humor in his tone. It was enough to bring a smile to my face. "I definitely know you love me now."

I pulled back, chuckling. "Bet you were worried there for a second. To be fair, it was a close call, but in the end … you're naked."

Merriment danced between us, and the lighthearted moment reminded me of the old days with Braxton, the perfect days where he'd loved me and I'd been too stupid and scared to even consider the possibilities. His grin turned into laughter; he threw back his head and laughed as if he had not a care in the world. There was something about this world which soothed the beasts in our souls. The same way being in Braxton's arms felt like home, this place did too.

I made a conscious decision then that I would not stress about shit I couldn't change. If I was pregnant we'd deal with it. If the dragon king had his army ready to rock and roll when we got back to earth, we'd deal with it. We'd always stuck together as a pack, and that wasn't going to change now. Together we could do this.

"Where are the others?" I asked. I was dying to tell them everything I'd learned. But mainly I needed to know how much more alone time we had.

Those blue eyes, locked on my face again, darkened to rich, cerulean blue. "They're close. We'll see them any moment."

He sounded disappointed, and I totally got that. Was it too much to ask for a few moments to be together as a proper mated couple? We were constantly being torn apart, and I wanted to hole up in a room with Braxton forever and explore him – literally, emotionally, mentally. I'd never cared before, not with any male – my past relationships were purely fun and sexual – but I wanted it *all* this time. Despite the fact that I knew him as well as any supe in the world, I wanted to relearn everything. And I'd also like some sex, because the few times with Braxton had been amazing. Like mind freaking blown. I figured I was due about eight hundred thousand more of those orgasms.

I placed my hands on either side of his face. "Here's some real talk. We're in desperate need of some bonding and sex, so let's just kill the king quickly, then you, me, and a cabin in the woods or some clichéd shit."

He laughed again, but the heat in his gaze was all I needed to know that we were both on the same page. "I'm going to kill the king, babe, don't you worry about that. Then we'll have our romantic cliché moment." The rolling timbre of his voice had me squirming. He was a deadly weapon against females. "I want to strip you bare and taste every single inch of your body."

My breathing was getting all heavy, and of course right at that moment our pack rocked up. They were moving fast, coming up behind Braxton. With a huff, my mate lowered me to the ground, his lips grazing mine as he let me go. None of the guys would have blinked twice to find us naked and wrapped around each other, but it was time to focus on other things, which was a real buzz kill.

Jacob the jackass was back. "Fuck, I knew we wore the wrong thing to this picnic. You should have specified on the invitation that this was clothes optional."

I stuck my tongue out at him and he shook a finger at me. "You're in big trouble, Jessa babe, flying off like that and leaving the rest of us behind. Do you know how far we trekked to find your cute butt?"

Before I could reply, Louis stepped up and in an instant Braxton and I were clothed again. "You two are lucky I have the ability to weave clothing from material in Faerie. If I were constantly dragging these outfits across the realms, my powers would be too depleted to get us all home."

No wonder my army-style pants and tank were so soft to touch. Faerie material was weaved out of the clouds or some shit.

"Is there a reason you haven't demolished this food yet?" Maximus said, looking between me and the lavish picnic left by the golden dragon. "Is there something wrong with it? It's bad, isn't it? What sort of cruel bastard would lay out a meal like this and then taint it with bad-ness. I'll fucking kill them, seriously. I'll kill them."

The small tendrils of tension which had been riding our group dissipated then as we fell about laughing. The look of actual despair on Maximus' face was pure comedic gold.

A funny which all of us desperately needed. It reminded me again to be grateful for the little things. We were all here, alive, and about to eat a kickass feast. Food was my focus, not the fact that after this it was back to the real world. The weight of the pendant, which was nestled safely under my shirt, was a reminder that a lot more darkness was coming for us. I was already praying that we all survived.

Chapter 12

I didn't have a single doubt that the food was safe for us, and it took zero effort for me to convince everyone of this. I trusted the golden dragon. In a way, she was mother to me as well as my dragon.

The six of us wasted no time stuffing our faces. Food in Faerie was not like any other. It was bright and rich and filled with flavor. The table was well stocked with fruits, seeds, nuts and vegetables, foods directly from nature. I particularly loved the mixed berries and salad type concoctions, which were wrapped up in greenery and filled with some sort of creamy cheese.

In deference to the carnivores of the group, a few meats were provided as well – small whole birds which had been marinated in something both spicy and sweet, and a large roasted boar-looking animal. It was different than the pigs from earth, taller, with long, slender legs, but the same general flavor applied.

No one spoke for the first ten minutes. We just sat and ate, absorbing the tranquility of this world.

Honestly, if I ever wanted to escape life, this is where I would come.

Louis broke the silence, his eyes focusing off into the distance. "This is a kind of peace I haven't experienced in a long while." I wasn't the best with emotions, but it felt as if some of the heavy sorrow he carried around with him had lessened. "It's so rare to find peace in our world. Supernaturals are filled with passion and violence and love. But peace … that's much harder to achieve."

He was right. Supernaturals had an overabundance of emotion, but we were not a peaceful lot. I reached out and grasped his hand. "You'll find love and peace again, Louis. You deserve happiness."

Suddenly those eyes were locked on me, and as always his power wrapped around my mind. "I'm not sure I want to be happy again when my mate is gone. I don't think I deserve it. I couldn't protect her. I wasn't enough."

I snorted then. Yeah, okay, not a very sympathetic response from me, but it was time for me to up the real talk again.

"Louis, you're a powerful male, we all know that. Something tells me the female you loved was also crazy strong. Which leads me to believe I might know some things about her. What you need to understand about us females is that we don't need you to do anything but love us, love us as much as you possibly can, support us through the trials of life and even treasure the parts of us which are not all that lovable. Protecting us ... well, that's nice, but it's something that goes both ways. Mates protect each other; it's not the dude's job to bodyguard us. We're adults and are capable of kicking ass all on our own. In fact, I'm pretty sure your mate would kick *your* ass if she heard the way you were talking. I'd kick Braxton's." I grinned at the dragon, before giving him a wink. "I definitely don't want him to be with anyone else. The thought rips at me, like broken glass across my skin. But if I was gone from this plane and he was still to live out hundreds of years, I would hope he found someone else to love, to share his life with. I want that for him."

My mate growled long and loud. He was not happy about me even mentioning being gone from his life. "Never going to happen, Jess. If you die, I'm hunting death the fuck down and I'm getting you back."

I reached out and patted him on the shoulder. "That's my man, always saying the sweetest things."

It really was one of the sweetest things he could say. He would never stop fighting for me, through this life and the next. But Louis' mate had also not been his true mate, so there was still a soul out there to complete his. The fates still owed him.

The sorcerer was frozen in place, his eyes like purple chips of ice. He finally moved, but it was only to pull his hand from mine. I was worried for a second that he was truly angry with me, but then with a sigh, and a brief smile across his aristocratic features, he said, "Regina would totally kick my ass if she saw me moping around. Even though my pain has somewhat eased in the last few decades, I'm still struggling to fully let go of her."

Regina. That was the first time he'd said her name.

As he faced his plate of food again, there was still pain on those perfect features, but also a sense of something more. He wasn't healed by any stretch, but I could see that over the last few months he was starting to let go of his guilt, guilt which was not his to own. So much of Louis' pain stemmed from his own personal blame game. Supe males were crazy with protecting their females.

Tyson leaned in closer, the light shimmering off auburn hair, honeysuckle eyes. "So, Jess, I think it's time to tell us what happened when you disappeared on us ... again. I mentioned *again*, right?"

Smartass. At least he took the focus off Louis. The sorcerer was still in the midst of some sort of mind-fuckery and pain. My story was definitely going to get his mind off Regina; it was a hell of a tale.

I leaned over. "I've got an ass ton of information to tell you, but first I want to know what happened when the dragons appeared. The Jessa part of me blacked out and the dragon was in control of the brain steering wheel."

I'd seen a brief glimpse through the vision of the queen dragon, but I wanted to know more.

Tyson jumped right in. "There were seven dragons. Six flew in a V-shape, protective style around the huge golden dragon in the center. When they were about a hundred yards from us you started to shake. Your eyes were locked on them and there was no way to break your gaze."

Braxton interrupted: "I felt the pull toward them also, but I didn't lose control of my dragon. He wanted to fly, but I kept him under control."

"Yeah, Brax did the weird shaking thing too, but he didn't shift. You did," Jacob said. "There was a burst of light and energy. My fire power was going crazy inside of me, responding to the heat rocketing from you. I've never had that happen with a shifter before, but it was something that the wild dragons from the sanctuary did to me. They have an elemental fire inside of them which calls to my own."

Braxton's voice was lower than the others. "You flew away. You flew so fast that even with me shifting instantly and following, I couldn't reach you before you disappeared. The golden dragon had you tucked in under her wing, and then you were gone. There was no way they could have flown that fast for me to not see you in the distance, so I think there was some sort of magic or step through involved. I followed the path, and eventually started to feel your energy again."

Five sets of eyes were on me. They'd explained their small part in the tale and it was now time for my much larger, batshit crazy part.

I took a gulp of the Faerie nectar, which was a lot like wine but without the kick, and then I opened my mouth and let it all fall out. I told them about waking in the other place and how the golden dragon was wrapped around me. I tried to keep the information sequential, but so much of it was still jumbled. Luckily my pack was a smart bunch of supes.

No one interrupted me. There were mirroring expressions of shock across all faces. I swear none of them were even breathing.

To finish up, I took another drink of the nectar, totally wishing there was some alcohol in it this time, and spilled all the details of the fertility of my body, and the things Larky planned to do with our offspring. This was the point Braxton lost it ... like, snapped off the side off the thick table, picked up the rest of the structure and punted it about twenty yards into the distance.

We were all on our feet now; his entire body shook as he fought for control. The blue flames licked across his skin again, and I could see the shift of scales playing along the tawny darkness of his arms. Before he could do anything else, like snatch me up and hide me away for the rest of our natural lives, I pulled the necklace free from my shirt, and held it aloft.

"This is the weapon we have against the king. This contains the blood of my ancestors, blood of the shining ones. We will defeat him, Brax." I didn't want to take my eyes from my furious mate, but I needed to tell Louis one thing also. "He's not a sorcerer, Louis, he is borrowing that power from somewhere. Do you have any idea what might be powering his magic?"

Louis' expression morphed from stoic into narrowed eyes and furrowed brow. He looked almost as pissed as Braxton. It took him a few moments, but he finally answered me.

"It has to be the mystics. When Larkspur was alive the first time, his council were simply powerful fey who joined his cause. But after his death, whatever curse he enacted from the shadow spawn actually gave him ties to the next generation of mystics. The marks used to be magically tattooed on the mystics, but for Quale and the rest, they were born with them. I wondered what their role in this was. If they're the ones who prepare the spells for Larkspur, then he's weaker without them."

I sucked in deeply. "We need to take them out." I hurried on, not liking the bleak expression on Louis' face – one of them was his brother. "I don't mean kill them, I mean lock them down or something. We can't let the king bring them into this war, we need him as weak as possible."

I couldn't stop myself from moving to Braxton then. He had calmed slightly; the flames and scales were gone now. I understood why he was so upset, there had been nothing nice or pleasant in my Faerie tale. It was filled with heartache, pain and an unknown future for us all. Still, lots of our questions were finally answered and we had more than one weakness of the king's to exploit.

Braxton's arms closed around me and they were so gentle that I had to pull back and see his face again. It was clear that he was still beyond words, so instead we just used our bond to express all the emotions we were currently feeling.

Jacob interrupted with a snort. "I can't … for shit's sake … goddamn unbelievable. Still, I guess that explains the dragon whisperer thing you had going on with those wild ones in the sanctuary. You have their next queen dragon mated to your soul, and she will call to her people." His hand was rubbing across his chin. He was the least hairy of the brothers; the fey could not shave for a month and still barely even have stubble. Braxton, on the other hand, could have a magic user remove his facial hair every day and still have a shadow by the afternoon. Not that I minded. Not. At. All.

Braxton's hands were running over my back, again soothing that ache which never quite disappeared. I was going to call it the "I got unknowingly knocked up" ache.

I felt his chest heave and I waited for his words. "So the queen of the dragons told you that Larkspur plans to produce dragon young with you, then use them to control the supe races, like he attempted last time…" The pace of his words increased, anger brewing again. "And that he promised your firstborn child to the shadow spawn so that they could overthrow the shining ones. I don't … what the actual … how am I supposed to respond to this, Jess?"

I shrugged against him. "We respond by making sure that never happens. I would never allow my child to fall into the hands of those evil assholes, I will take my last breath making sure that doesn't happen. Plus, Larky has never gotten his tiny dick near me, so there's no way I'm pregnant with his child." I pulled back to see Braxton's face. "Let's be thankful that the fates and shining ones hate him. They made sure I had a dragon shifter mate already, the only other one who could produce a dragon baby with me and thwart his plans."

Braxton's eyes were practically black now, black with flickers of blue flames deep inside. A plethora of emotions crossed his face – joy, fear, anger, excitement. The entire feels scale was hitting him. "I'm torn between hating that you have a nickname for him and loving that it's a nasty little derogative one."

He was trying to compartmentalize his emotions, focusing on the small insignificant ones so that the rest didn't crush him. But there were some we couldn't ignore.

He rested tumultuous eyes on me. "If you're pregnant with my child, I will fight beyond death for you both. I will never stop. I will never fall. I will never let another male take what is mine to protect."

And we were back to the caveman supe protecting their mate thing. I could sense Louis was giving me that look of his, the one that was all "See, I told you so, it's our job to protect our mates." Stubborn males.

It was definitely not the ideal time to have me pregnant and vulnerable, especially if I was carrying some sort of magical warrior child. I could find myself hunted by more than just the dragon king. But still, we might have created a child together and it was something to be joyful about. Braxton was still just holding me, his features and grip calm.

"Despite your freak out over Larky, you're acting very chill about our possible pregnancy," I said, my eyes narrowing. "Why are you not more surprised?" Sure, I'd explained to them what the queen had said about me being fertile from the moment my mark's powers were unlocked. That this was part of the curse of the dragon marked, the part which Larky put into play to make sure he'd get his dragon babies. *Fucker*. But still, I expected that the news of our possible baby would have taken Braxton by surprise, instead he seemed content with the knowledge. Like he'd known all along.

"Your scent has changed a little," he finally said. "I thought pregnancy was impossible because of your fertile time, so I assumed it was to do with being stuck in Faerie, the absorption of some of the magic here, but with this new information, your backache, and you not wanting to be touched ... it makes sense."

So basically he had known the second I reached that part in my story. My mate was all about being an overachiever on the intelligence train. Which was both annoying and hot as hell.

Braxton turned to Louis. The sorcerer was back to being blank-faced. "Is she far enough along yet for you to try the pregnancy spell? We need to both confirm and to make sure everything is okay."

The other quads were all eyeballing the magic user, each of them outwardly expressing their extra surge of over-protectiveness toward me. This child was not only going to have a dragon shifter for a father, but three uncles of scary-ass nature. Plus, Jonathon. Holy freakin' hell, this kid was going to be one spoiled and protected pup.

Louis stepped closer to me, his eyes scanning across my body. My stomach was flat, no signs of a child there at all. Most supe races have different gestation periods. Shifters were about six months, magic users nine. Vampires were very short, only two to three months; and fey were the unlucky bastards at fifteen months' gestation for their young. The demi-fey all varied, and some of them didn't even carry their young in their bodies. Some had pods, or capsules or eggs.

Louis lifted both hands as if sensing the air around me, before taking a step back. "If she is pregnant her body is hiding it well. No magical essence of another is clear. It's hard to tell how far along she is. In Jess's time it's been no more than a week since you were together, but being in Faerie can mess with timelines, so it's hard to know what her body is doing development wise. I need some ingredients from home to do the gestation and pregnancy spell, so for now we can be cautiously optimistic that we will have a child in our lives in six months."

"Don't you need the full moon?" I asked.

Louis shook his head. "Nah, I think I'll manage without it."

"Showoff," Tyson muttered.

The sorcerer shot him a smile. He enjoyed taunting the brothers, but there was actually something genuine in that glance. "Don't despair, young wizard. I sense your powers are awakening. It started when you joined with your brothers in the sanctuary. I don't think you'll have to wait long until you unlock your sorcery energy."

Tyson narrowed his eyes. "Are you fucking with me? Because that would mean I'm going to beat your record."

Louis gave a single nod. "Yes, if you make sorcerer in the next few years, you would be the youngest mage in our history. Of course, you haven't actually made it there yet. I just sense the power emerging."

Tyson grinned. "Oh, I'll make it, don't you worry. I'm going to be wizarding the shit out of things, getting those powers going."

I shook my head, laughter unfolding from me. Braxton distracted me by cupping his hands on either side of my face. As my chuckles died off, I was captured by the emotion in those stunning blue orbs. His words were equally as emotional.

"Despite the fact that this pregnancy was not planned, I need you to know that if you're carrying my young, there's no better gift you could ever give me. The joy thrums through me and my dragon. You're our true mate, our other half. There'll never be another for me." His lips touched mine, and I could actually feel that joy he spoke of. He pulled away too soon, his hand lowering to fall against my stomach. The other hand threaded through the hair at the nape of my neck. "I'll die before I let anyone touch our child. I have no doubt you'll do the same. Your fierceness is going to go into overdrive now."

I heard laughter from behind him. "Holy shit, Jessa is going to be a freaking nightmare. Food cravings, weird hormonal outbursts…"

"Sounds normal to me," Tyson said with a snort of laughter.

Great, not only did I have to deal with Jacob the jackass, but Tyson was joining in too. Still, they both made good points. I would probably be a nightmare. The quads must have decided that they'd held back long enough. The three of them wasted no more time pounding over and stealing me right out of Braxton's arms. I was passed around for hugs and cheek-kisses, before ending up in Maximus's arms. He gave me the gentlest of hugs I'd ever felt from him.

"I'm not breakable," I said to him. "If I'm pregnant – and remember we haven't confirmed this yet – then I'm only just pregnant. At least wait until I'm six months and the size of a house before you start treating me gently."

In my younger years I'd always feared that if I let these guys start handling me like a "girl," their chauvinistic brains would kick in and I'd always be separated from them, left to the side. It was something I had eventually stopped worrying about, realizing that even if I was female and a little different, I was one of them. We were pack and that would never change.

Of course, I somehow still knew that no matter what I said, I'd be handled like fine china by the big brutes.

"So it's time for us to head back now, right?" I found myself turning to Louis, who was best at adulting in this group. "Where do we go? What's the plan?"

"I think the best thing is to head to Stratford. It's where your families are, and the Four. Even though you have the necklace and a plan, we need power on our side before we go up against Larkspur."

"Who will go to the sanctuary and disable the mystics?"

His eyes shuttered. "I'll do it. Quale trusts me, and I think I can get him to help. With him on board, it will be simple to take them unawares. I won't hurt them, I'll just disable them until after we take out the king."

The sanctuary reminded me of something. "Does anyone know if the marked who were not in Drago or the sanctuary survived after the release of the king?"

Braxton answered. "When you got taken, our parents were on their way to the sanctuary with Nash, trying to get him to safety. Their plane was delayed, so they didn't make the flight. Nash ended up being okay." Thank the gods for that. "I'm guessing that was just a rumor started by his daughters, something to make sure that eventually the dragon mated female would get close enough for them to use her blood and open the tomb."

That's what I hated about rumors. They were like friggin' Chinese whispers. The information by the end was ninety percent bullshit.

"That's also why they waited so many years until they freed all those in the prisons," Louis added. "Basically they started to get serious about their father's plan from the moment Jessa and Mischa were born. Before that they spent their years running from the Four."

"How did they know we were the ones they needed?" So many annoying unanswered questions.

He shrugged. "I don't know. I believe Larkspur left some sort of way for the curse to communicate with his helpers. And don't forget that the twins mother would have had information to impart in their younger years. Of course, we'll never know for sure since they're all dead."

I kicked out at some of the dirt and grass, clipping some debris from the destroyed table as I stomped. "We need to make sure that no more of Larky's plans come to fruition, which means we'd better get back and gather our army."

I didn't really want to. Staying here in this tranquil, home-like world was much more appealing, but there was no way I'd ever abandon my family. I was missing them a lot, especially Mischa. Even with her stupidity, she had wormed her way into my heart.

Wait a damn minute.

"Did you say the Four were in Stratford?" I must have blocked that part out for a moment or some shit. But seriously, what were those assholes doing in my town? I knew that the Compass quads had said they ran into them, and that some sort of asinine plan was hatched to fight together. But why in the good name of fuck were those douchebags hanging around in Stratford?

Louis looked cautious as he reiterated the quads winning argument: "They're going to help us fight the king. Their energy can hold the marked at bay, and teamed with the Compass' power, which we're hoping can hold the king at bay, there might be a shot at truly defeating him."

The sorcerer was right to be cautious, even with the previous heads up from my boys, I wasn't happy about this at all. "Sounds like we're asking for trouble just letting them hang around our town. With our families. What if this is just a ploy to get to me? Or the other marked?"

Jacob shrugged. "Then we kill them. Easy."

I snorted. "Great plan, tough guy." *Fuck.* There was really no other option here. "Okay, for now I'm willing to let this one play out, but if they do anything suspicious … one chance is all they get with me."

I hadn't forgotten their creepy fuckery when they tried to take me from Stratford. I still owed them some sort of ass kicking for that, but since they had been able to use their powers against me, I wasn't sure that opportunity would easily present itself. My dragon lifted her head then and let out a snort of smoke and heat. She remembered too, and our connection was much stronger now. She felt that this time we could take them.

I gave her a mental pat. *We'll see what happens,* I promised.

"So how do we get out of here?" Tyson was pulling energy. I could see the gold threading his eyes, similar in color actually to the golden dragon queen. I was reminded of her words, that all magic was from Faerie. All supes were connected to this land and the golden energy threading through it. This was information we all learned in basic Intro to Magic classes. But seeing it first hand, well, everything felt more real.

"I don't think I can get us out of this part of Faerie," Louis said. "This world is locked down. The shining ones control the ability to step through and they aren't sharing."

Great, so that meant we were going to have to trek back the way we'd come, which was a massive waste of time. Then we'd have to figure out how to get back up to the land above.

With no time to waste we started to move toward the gateway of this land. My dragon knew the way, like she'd spent her entire life here and not just a few precious moments.

A flash of gold caught our attention. We all stopped and stared as a shimmery wall appeared to our left. It was circular, large enough for all of us to step through in one go. In my mind a flash of golden scales brushed against my dragon, and I knew this was a parting gift from the queen. She was giving us a direct step through back home.

"What the hell is that?" Maximus said.

Louis strode right up to it, his hands held out to feel the energy. "Appears to be a step through, on a massive scale, but I can't know if it will take us anywhere safe. Faerie is unpredictable.

To save time arguing about its safety, I just took off, ducking between them, my size an advantage for once. I was fast, arriving at the shimmer before most of them even took their first steps after me.

"Trust me," I yelled, "it's safe!"

The quads curses and shouts were cut off as I stepped into the shine. I never liked the sensations of being in a step through. My body always rebelled at the cloying nature of it, the way it sort of sucked me through to the other side, but I was ready to see my beloved Stratford again; it felt like years since I'd been there. I also had that terrible feeling that while we'd been doing our thing in Faerie, the king had been up to some bad shit, and that we were going to walk back into chaos. Pure chaos.

I stepped out to the other side and found myself in Stratford's city center, next to the water fountain. The icy wind shocked me at first; it had been so temperate in Faerie, but here we looked to be in the tail end of the cold months, no snow left, just that frigid wind which could cut right through to bone. My shifter metabolism kicked in, sending heat through my veins. Thank you, genetics. Hugging my arms closer, I looked around the square.

The town was eerily quiet. There was no one around, which was odd. With over six thousand inhabitants, there was always someone here. It was a central gathering point, and the town hall was used often for various events.

I kept myself in the vicinity of where the others would soon emerge. I was extra cautious, worried I was about to be ambushed by the freaking king again or something. Not only would the quads be pissed at me, but I'd be pissed at myself if he managed to get the drop on me twice. Thoughts of my "maybe baby" flittered across my mind too, and I knew I had to be careful for more than myself now, had to be smarter than ever. All I had to do was protect everyone, defeat the king, and not hurt my possible offspring in the process. Yeah, no worries.

The silent eeriness remained unbroken around me. What was going on in Stratford?

A whoosh of energy trickled across my back, followed by the deep voice of my mate. "Just because you might be pregnant, Jessa, doesn't mean I can't take you over my knee and spank your ass."

His presence and energy filtered around me, and it finally felt as if there were more here than ghosts. I wasn't surprised at all that Braxton was the first through the step through. He would have been right on my butt, as usual.

I smirked as I tipped my head back to see him. "A spanking is starting to sound pretty good to me right now. We're in some serious need of alone time."

His thumb grazed my lips, slowly tracing across my skin and down to my throat. "We'll have our time, and it'll be soon. We just have an asshole to rid ourselves of first."

Asshole was right, and judging by the empty Stratford streets, and the cramping worry in my gut, I was just hoping we weren't already too late to save the supernatural world.

Chapter 13

I forced down my fears and focused on the creepy Stratford we'd arrived in. "Can you sense anything about what happened here? Do you think Larky took them all?"

As I had done, he took a few moments to observe the area. His eyes morphed into that striking blue, with the glowing flames in the center, that came out when he used his dragon senses.

Tyson, Jacob and Maximus exited the step through and joined us. Our pack was silent and watchful, each of us trying to figure out what the freak was happening here. Louis was the last to reach our side. Even though the step through was courtesy of the golden dragon queen, he'd probably remained behind out of habit. He generally liked to make sure everyone made it through safely. It was one of those things which showed how truly courteous and kind Louis was. Most people saw his power and nothing else, but while power was something I appreciated, it was the true goodness in his heart I cherished the most. My self-appointed big brother.

"I don't know what happened here," Braxton eventually said, his keen gaze still focusing on our surroundings. "There's no lingering magic. No misfires of spells. There's no blood residue. No weapons of steel or iron in the vicinity. I sense no disturbance on the security around the borders. The only odd scent is an extra strong burn of diesel in the air."

Louis held both hands out and started to murmur. There wasn't as much general magic in the air here compared to Faerie, so when he cast his spell it was strong enough to leave a woodsy taste on my tongue and tingles on my skin.

I knew from school that magic users pulled energy from the gods. Of course I couldn't remember all the different deities, except for the shining ones. They were the most important, which made perfect sense, as our magic originated from Faerie.

A scuffle of footsteps behind us was the first indication we weren't alone. The five of us were already on high alert; we spun and fell into a fighting stance. And I didn't relax my pose when I saw who was standing there. If anything, my beasts inside were closer, hands semi-shifted into claws.

It was the Craiz brothers. The Four. Spread out, standing in a line about twenty feet from us. They weren't moving, and their expressions were benign, nothing threatening in their demeanor at all, but I was still wary. They were the assholes who had locked away babies and innocent victims of Larky. Some of those supernaturals were in chains for hundreds of years. There would be no forgiveness for these males, no matter how justified they were in their actions. They would have killed every single marked if we hadn't been unkillable at the time. They'd basically admitted that they'd tried every way possible over the years. I couldn't even comprehend the level of torture some of the marked must have gone through at their hands.

When Louis and the quads had mentioned that they would work with the Four, I thought I was okay with it – not happy or anything, but it was a means to the end of Larky, and I would do anything to end him. Now, though, as I stood before them, with growls rumbling my chest and my dragon straining against me, I wasn't sure I could do it. I couldn't fight with them when I really wanted to kill them.

"Jessa, babe, a little care with the muscles please."

I glanced down and realized my clawed hands were ripping Tyson's biceps to shreds.

"Sorry." I relaxed my grip but the growls wouldn't cease. My animals were just too riled up to settle, and therefore I couldn't settle either.

I eyeballed the Four. "I don't think I can work with them. I really want to kill them. Can't we just kill them?"

I heard Braxton chuckle, and turned to see him flashing me that smile, the one with the double dimples. "As soon as we deal with this crisis, you have my permission to destroy the Four. I'll be right there to help you hide their bodies. But for now we need them, and so do the rest of the supernatural world."

I knew the Four could hear us. They were not that far away. None of them showed any concern, and I realized how much they reminded me of soldiers, the ones who go out there and do horrible shit so that the rest of the world doesn't have to. I knew that in war you had to make tough decisions – sometimes it might seem cruel, but the greater good was important. Still, I believed every supe, human, and other, needed to have a set of morals they stuck with. You must draw a line in the sand and never step over it. Otherwise, how will you ever know when to stop?

Some things were too much, even in war. Children was where I drew that line, and it made me more than a little angry that the Four had not felt the same way.

The one on the far right spoke first. "We promise we're only here to defeat the king and make sure he doesn't gain control of Jessa or any more of the supernatural communities. We mean the marked no harm unless they're part of his army and need to be subdued. We have the power to hold them, to counteract their dragon ghosting abilities. You need us."

Truth. Dammit, I really had no choice. They were right. We did need them.

Somehow I managed to get my animals to settle, and my hands returned to their nice human shape. I turned my back on the Four. I did not fear them any longer. I could access my dragon on command now, and I doubted their power could halt her change.

I focused on Louis. "Did you figure out what happened here?"

His expression was stone cold. "Don't worry about the Four, Jess. If they step out of line, I will not hesitate to end them."

Truth.

He continued: "Stratford wasn't like this when I left your father here, but clearly in the additional time on Faerie, a lot has happened. I'm pretty sure most of Stratford has been evacuated. They left in their vehicles, which is why Braxton could smell the diesel. There's still some energy inside the town hall. I think a few members remained behind."

All of us swung around to face the large building behind us. I knew it was heavily spelled to protect its contents, including the *Book of Guidance*, which would explain why none of us – except the powerful sorcerer – had picked up on the life inside. I didn't hesitate, I needed to know if my family was in there. I needed to see my parents and Mischa. Fear for them was a hot thrumming in my veins, and until I saw with my own eyes that they were safe, I would not be able to calm.

The moment I thought of Mischa, it was like our bond kicked into gear, pushing through all the other bonds inside of me – dragon, wolf, and partial mate bond – urging me to find my twin. I had to see her. I moved swiftly, the others a step behind. Even in my haste, I kept one eye on the Four. They fell into the back of our group, keeping a decent distance between them and us. It was smart of them to not get close. I wasn't sure I could control my actions.

I slammed against the main entrance but it was locked down in that unbreakable magic way, like when there was a trial going on. I knew there was no way to budge it with so much magic slicked across it, but the quads were still going to have a go.

Braxton came first, barging against the door with his shoulder. The building shook but the doorway held strong. I was lifted and deposited to the side by Maximus, and then he joined his brother. The two of them were the biggest and strongest of the quads and had the best shot.

They both smashed against the door, and this time I felt the rumble under my feet, but still there was no opening. The four Compasses were just stepping up when Louis spoke.

"Before you guys get any more Rambo on us, maybe give me a shot to see if I can circumvent the magical barrier. I set most of them up in this town, so I might actually know what I'm doing."

"Why the fuck didn't you do that straight away?" Maximus growled.

Louis just grinned. "It was good to see my magic hold up against the famed Compass quads."

I couldn't tell if the boys were pissed at his tactics or kind of pleased that he thought they were that strong. Looked like a bit of both to me. They said nothing more though, and stepped back to allow the sorcerer access to the doorway. His shit-kicker boots were loud as he strode over. He touched his hand to the building, muttered a few phrases, and stepped back as the doors swung open.

"Still a friggin' showoff," Tyson muttered.

I hid my grin. He had such a competitive streak and was going to stop at nothing to reach sorcerer before the age Louis had. He wanted to have something to lord over the legendary magic user.

I was in the middle of my pack as we scrambled to get inside, all of us wanting to be first.

"Jess!" I heard the shout before I saw who was in the room, but I would know my father's voice anywhere.

I pushed through the boys and dashed along the aisles. The long pews and chairs were still set out in the same pattern used for our town meetings, and at least two or three of these rows were filled. There were quite a few members of Stratford here. I ran until I crashed into Jonathon, his strong arms and energy wrapping around me. All shifters felt better when they were close to their alpha and I had been spending so much time away from mine.

"You've been gone for so long," he said, voice low over my shoulder. "We were worried you wouldn't make it back in time."

I pulled back to see him. "For me it was only another day or so in Faerie."

"It's been three weeks here. Larkspur has gathered his army from the sanctuary. They've been moving on the supernatural prison communities through Europe. After he smashes through their securities, his army takes out the inhabitants and Larkspur kills their council. Then he captures their *Book of Guidance*, which allows him to control the town, its magic, and any members who were not cut down in the battle. He makes all survivors swear fealty to him in the ancient language, the same as when council leaders are elected. If they don't, he cuts their heads off."

"Holy shit," I said breathlessly. "How many towns has he hit? He must have a massive army now. Is that why there's no one here? You sent them out into the human world, didn't you?"

Jonathon nodded. "Yes, we received word that he was moving on Stratford next. He has taken at least five of the European cities that we know of, gathering numbers. He must have many thousands now, and there have been a lot of deaths. It's damn chaos."

I had expected chaos, and yet … I rubbed at my face, trying to control my emotions and thoughts. It was so odd. In the small time I'd spend with Larky he had been polite and cultured, even caring at times, not at all like a murderous crazy tyrant. If it hadn't been for Rose's stroll through memory lane, I'd forget how much he had been feared, how much carnage he had wrought the last time he had tried to take over the five races. I had no doubt that he was making sure he was at full power before confronting me and the Compasses. He knew the five of us would be together, and he wanted my magical dragon baby. Another means to achieve his endgame of ruling all five supe races.

"If he controls all copies of the *Book of Guidance*, and all the towns and their people, that means he will receive energy from them also, right? He's going to be so much stronger than the last time we saw him."

I knew the quads and whoever else was in the room was listening, but I was so focused on Jonathon I didn't even have a clue who else was here. Except for Mischa. I could feel her quite strongly, though it was strangely muted, like she was in the room next door with walls between us or something.

Jonathon's answer was quick, his features tightening. "Yes, all council leaders and alphas receive portions of power from their people. Larkspur will now be reaping the energy from all those he has forced into his servitude. Not as strongly as the ones who voluntarily pledge their allegiance, but enough to make him formidable."

We couldn't rely on Braxton to beat on him this time. Larky would be back to his full power, all his followers behind him. I turned and found Louis in the crowd. The sorcerer was chatting to some of the magic users. I could hear them discussing strategy and backup plans.

"Louis!" I shouted, uncaring that I was interrupting. "Remember that thing you needed to do?"

Lots of faces were staring at me, and I gave zero fucks. He nodded, then turned and walked straight out the front door. He would take care of the mystics, I had no doubt. We had to make sure that part of Larky's power was locked down before he got here.

When I turned back to Jonathon, Lienda was right behind him. I barely flinched when she swept me into her arms. I hadn't known my mother for most of my life, but she had proven time and again that she was worthy of being a member of my pack. She had sacrificed and fought for her children, and now, possibly carrying a young of my own, I understood why she had to do what she did.

I wondered how my parents would react once they knew everything we had learned from the golden dragon. I shifted to find Braxton's gaze on me, and as if he knew what I'd been thinking his eyes dropped to my stomach, before lifting to my face again. He gave me a gentle smile, something I'm sure he was trying to work on – the gentle thing. It wasn't really in his nature, and yet didn't seem that odd either. I was kind of liking this side of him, because it was all for me.

Lienda finally let me go, even though she kept running a hand over my hair, seemingly trying to convince herself that I was actually home and okay.

"Where's Mischa?" I asked, scanning the room.

Amongst the many Stratford inhabitants I could see the council leaders: Torag, from the Eastland trolls; Julianna Medow, the six foot, stunning redheaded vampire; and Galiani of the Greenlands, the fey representative. Kristoff was still missing, which was lucky for him, because he was a dead man walking when I finally dealt with Larky and had time to hunt down his slimy sorcerer ass.

The quads' parents were there; the boys were with them. I couldn't halt the pure joy I felt at seeing Jo and Jack Compass. They were like a second family to me.

No one answered me, so I asked again, with more force this time. "Where's Mischa?"

Jonathon sucked in a deep breath. "I'll show you. We've had to lock her and Nash away for the moment."

Shit. I followed my father as he strolled along the row and past the front dais, where the council members ran the town meetings. He took me to the side of the huge room, stopping in front of a set of double doors. I'd never been in this room but had seen council members and elders emerge from there. Always figured it was some sort of "leaders' lunchroom." Inside, they sat around bitching about us, drinking coffee and eating cookies.

I really hoped there were some cookies inside. Chocolate chip – double chocolate would be even better. Fuck, I'd even eat oatmeal and raisin right now.

Jonathon pulled a large key from his pocket; it slid easily into the huge, magically-etched lock holding the entrance closed. The click was silent, as were the doors as they slid across. I was sort of holding my breath, having no idea what to expect on the other side.

Braxton moved toward me, the warmth at the base of my neck firing to life. I had to stop the stupid smile from spreading over my face. Just having him close made almost every situation better. Yep, I was a sap, but might as well own it. Plus, it was Braxton. There was not a single thing about him which was not worth a decent fangirl. Not one thing.

I don't know why but I expected the room beyond to look like a dingy dungeon. When I stepped inside, I found it was light and airy and about twenty feet wide, a big room, outfitted with a round meeting table, a few couches, a kitchenette, and a wall filled with books – spell books by the look of their spines.

Two figures sat on the furthest couch, watching a television which was mounted to the wall.

"Nash..." Braxton brushed a hand along my back as he strode past me and across the room to the little boy, before hauling him up off the seat and into his arms for a hug.

I took a moment to note how much better the six-year-old supe was looking. Healthy, well fed, shiny brown hair and nice olive skin tones, instead of the sickly white he'd been when we found him. He was living with Jo and Jack now, but I knew the plan was to find his family as soon as all of this dragon marked stuff was over. Until then, the Compasses were sharing their overabundance of love with the young supe.

I was distracted then by a pair of green eyes and a face very much like my own.

"Jess?" Mischa's voice was hesitant. She'd said my name like a question, as if she couldn't believe I was here.

"Hey, sis," I said. My smile was slight but natural. I wasn't mad at her any longer. Okay, I for reals thought she was an idiot, but that didn't mean she was a bad person.

She rose from the couch, and I had to say, she looked like shit, wearing sweatpants and a baggy shirt which hid most of her body – a body which looked extremely thin, the bags under her eyes so dark and pronounced they might as well be suitcases.

"Why are they locked in here?" I asked Jonathon, but Mischa was the one to answer.

"Because when the dragon king calls for the marked, we have no choice but to follow. He's stopped projecting at the moment. He must be traveling. But when the call comes we have no power against him."

Shit! I'd felt nothing from him in Faerie. Now that I was back in Stratford, I was genuinely curious as to whether it would affect me the same way as the others. My dragon was pretty great at resisting magical stuff. By forcing Josephina to choose a soul to be mated to, Larky had made me – his alleged mate – so much stronger than he probably imagined.

I had another thought then. "Why is Cardia not locked up too, she's dragon marked, right?" This time Jonathon answered.

"For some reason his call is not affecting her. We have surmised that it's because of her bond with Max, and his calling to the dragon king."

Okay, still strange. I felt like there was more to this story, but it could be her bond with Maximus. The Compass quads were very powerful in that way.

Mischa paused before me, and there was no way to miss that we were twins. She opened her mouth but slammed it shut just as quickly. I hated when she got all weird like this. I blamed the human influence from her years raised amongst them. Just spit it out, seriously, this waffling was more annoying than anything she could say.

"I've got to get back out into the hall, so I'll leave you two alone for a bit," Jonathon said, giving me a kiss on the cheek, and then Mischa. "Nash will be leaving with Jo and Jack just as soon as he's finished visiting Braxton. The little one wouldn't leave until his friend was back, but it's too dangerous for him to be here." His eyes flicked across to his other daughter. "Mischa also, but she refuses to leave."

Mischa crossed her arms and got a stubborn look on her haggard face. "I won't let him drive me from my home again. I spent too many years hiding in the human world because of that di ... piece of crap. I stay here now. With my family."

Hells yeah! I loved her fire. It was the supe in her; no amount of time in the human world could squash it completely. Although her fear of cursing was both funny as hell and weird to the nth degree.

Jonathon shook his head, but he wasn't really upset. I could tell that he liked her fire as well. With another kiss on the cheek for both of us, he left. Mischa took my hand, and the moment we touched the bond between us flared to life.

I've missed you, I said to her mentally.

She jumped. *I forgot we could do the mental talk thing now. Do you think we can shut it down for a bit? My mind is messy enough with just me in here.*

Sure, I'm getting better at controlling it now. My dragon is teaching me. I erected the mental blocks I had been working on, and immediately the sensation of being linked lessened. Our bond was still there, but we were no longer in each other's heads.

Mischa smiled. "Thank you. And I've really missed you too." Her voice shook then. "Jess, I'm so sorry. I've been freaking out worrying about you, not to mention kicking myself for being the world's biggest idiot."

The girl was not kidding about her mind being a mess. She was a hot mess like nobody's business right now.

I led her across to a small double couch, farthest from where Braxton was quietly talking to Nash. I took a second to watch the pair of them together, loving how happy both the boy and Braxton looked. Nash loved the dragon shifter that had befriended him when they were both locked in Vanguard, and I could see my mate felt the same. He was going to be a wonderful father, as long as we could stop our world from crashing down around us. At least Nash and the Compass parents would be away when Larky hit.

Focusing on Mischa again, we sat down facing each other. I gave her a moment to pull her shit together. Tears had formed in the corners of those stunning turquoise eyes and she was blinking rapidly to stop them falling. Finally, I tried for some reassurance.

"Misch, it's okay, I'm not mad at you."

She shook her head hard, black hair flying around her face. "I'm mad at myself and you should be mad at me too."

I laughed. "Truthfully, shit happens. If it wasn't you helping the bitch twins, it would have been someone else. Blame game is not my deal, and since you've clearly been beating yourself up about it the entire time I was gone, there's really no need for me to lump in too." I reached out and hugged her. Hard. I was fast realizing that you only got one family, and that they could be taken from you in an instant.

"I've been worried about you," I said to her. "It really sucked balls being stuck in Faerie and not being able to talk to you."

She nodded, losing the battle with her tears. They silently streamed down her face. "Dad has filled me in on what he knows, but I want to hear from you. Tell me everything that happened after I lost consciousness in the prison."

Shit. Really ... everything? It wasn't exactly a short story. Still, I would want to know everything too, so I couldn't blame her curiosity. I started at the beginning, the castle in the land of illusions, Rose, all the rest of the assholeness which was Larky. My story wrapped up with everything we'd learned from the golden dragon, and I could see the absolute astonishment in my sister's face.

"So, you might be pregnant with a magical dragon baby." For some reason her voice broke there, but she managed to keep going without more tears. "And your baby could be strong enough to control all the races. And Larkspur is on his way here to both find you and destroy Stratford…"

She jumped to her feet, running both hands haphazardly through her hair. "I'm struggling to process this information. How are we supposed to fight the king when he's so powerful now? You're so lucky you haven't felt his call yet. It's … horrible. His voice and power fills my mind and overflows until I can't even remember who I am. I know deep down that I need to fight against him, but there's nothing left of me to do it." She hung her head. I was starting to understand why she was a walking skeleton.

I watched as she started to pace. "Having his presence in your head must be just delightful," I said, letting my sarcasm run free. "I'm guessing you aren't getting a lot of sleep."

She shook her head. "Nope, sleep is the easiest place for him to reach us. Our minds are open and vulnerable to his manipulations." She swallowed roughly, and dropped back down beside me. "I'm going to ask you something now, but I don't want to cop any crap for it. Can you do that?"

I was instantly curious. "Can't promise anything, but I'll do my best."

"Is Max back? And is Cardia out there with him?"

My curiosity fled. "Seriously? Babe! Seriously? You've got to get over it. He's mated. There's never going to be a chance for you."

She leaned in closer to me, her voice barely a whisper. "Jess, I'm not a complete fucktard. I know he's not in my reach any longer, but I have to tell you something, and it affects Max. I need to know you won't tell him yet, at least not until I figure out how to break this news myself."

My sister had cursed. This was bad.

Something hot and potent licked across my body – fear. I hated promising to keep secrets from my boys. That had caused me nothing but trouble recently. Still, it was clear that Mischa was desperate to offload and I could tell by the stubborn tilt of her jaw that if I didn't promise to remain mute on it she wouldn't tell me.

"I'll keep quiet for now, but you better sort yourself out and tell him soon. Secrets are the death of relationships, and I for one hate them."

Mischa nodded. "Trust me, he's going to find out."

Holy flaming ogre balls, this was going to be something insane, I just knew it. My mind started spinning with all the possibilities. Mischa took a few deep breaths and leaned in close to murmur.

"So ... backstory first: I've never had a period in the human world. Mom was always telling me I was a late bloomer, but I knew there was something weird about me. Still, she would never let me go to a doctor, and since I wasn't sexually active, there was no reason to worry about periods, or babies, or birth control."

Okay, this was a weird and slightly disturbing backstory. She'd better get to the point fast. Her voice was so low there was absolutely no way for Braxton to hear. Still, I glanced over and was relieved to see the dragon shifter down on the floor playing some sort of army game with Nash and his little figurines. Dude even made playtime look badass.

"So then when my shifter side was unlocked, and Max and I were hanging out heaps, I never even gave birth control a thought. I really liked him, Jess, and we got along so well. He was the first real friend

I had beside you. He seemed to like me also, even though I think for a time he was just confused about his feelings for you and me."

Maximus had all but admitted that to me, but there had been a real thing between him and Mischa, even if it started because she looked a lot like me.

"You remember in the trial how Max wouldn't give his alibi?"

I nodded. I had thought at the time it was about a girl.

"Well, he was with me, just kinda hanging out, but I made him promise not to tell anyone. I was insecure and trying to learn my way, still embarrassed from that first time when you told me that everyone could scent my attraction. Mostly I didn't want to be defined by what I was doing with Max, so he kept it private for me."

Asshole. Always on my case for keeping secrets, but looked like he had a pretty big one of his own.

"So you two did have sex," I said. "All the times you told me you were a virgin, you just lied right to me?"

She crumbled forward. "No, I was a virgin for a lot of that time. We slept together once, just before the Four came to Stratford, when you and Braxton were in the prison. It was a sort of spur-of-the-moment comfort thing. I don't remember how it happened. One minute we were talking and worrying and the next…" She trailed off, flashes of memory in her gaze.

She focused again: "I was really happy it happened, but he withdrew then. He said we had to focus on you and Brax, on getting you out of Vanguard. He distanced himself from me and never looked back again, and then the next thing I knew he was mated to Cardia."

I blinked a few times. "You were still saying you were a virgin in the sanctuary though."

She nodded, her movement shaky. "I thought if you knew what had happened you would lose your shit at Max or me. I worked double-time to pretend I was still the same virgin that had first come into your lives rather than a slutty chick who gave it up to a guy who didn't really give a crap about her."

I tried very hard not to sigh. "That's some sort of human shit there again, isn't it? Why would you think any of us would have cared that you two slept together? And the word *slutty* is not even in a shifter's vocabulary. You'd have to sleep with twelve men in one night, minimum. Did he hurt you?"

My voice rose a little, and I saw Braxton glance our way, but when I gave him a ghost of a smile he turned back to Nash.

She shook her head violently. "No! Of course he didn't. It was probably one of the best nights of my life, and that was with the fact that I was stressed and worried about you being in the prison. By the time we were escaping to the sanctuary, things got really weird between Max and me, and then he met his mate. It was so fast there was never enough time to even process my true emotions on it all." She hung her head, dark hair falling to curtain her face. "I was an idiot, Jess. You warned me that we couldn't be true mates, and I knew it was one of those things which happened because of the circumstances, but still ... I couldn't let him go."

She rubbed a hand across her face, and I sensed something much bigger than her giving it up to one of the Compasses was coming. Something to do with the fact that she was talking about birth control earlier. She honestly couldn't be...

"Just after you disappeared into Faerie, and Max met Cardia, I started to get sick. Pains in the stomach and lower back. Eventually I went to one of the healers in the medical ward, and they figured out what was wrong with me. When they told me I kind of lost my mind ... hence why I acted like such a dumbass ... dummy." Her hand dropped to her stomach, and even though I knew it was coming I still gasped loud enough that Braxton was basically at my side in a second, Nash tucked in under his arm.

"What's wrong, Jess?" He was speaking but I wasn't comprehending. My eyes were locked on my sister, my brain a fuzz of confusion.

She was actually pregnant. With Maximus's baby. It was all starting to make sense now. Her desperation in the sanctuary. The reason she did everything in her power to try and bring him back to her. She had known the entire time and he'd been holed up with his new mate. Mischa must have felt like her entire world was crashing down … and no one had been there to help her.

"Mischa?" Braxton's voice was harder but not mean. He wasn't angry with her any longer either, even though I knew he had been pretty brutal with her when I'd first disappeared. "Someone better speak."

I finally raised a shaking hand and laid it against his chest, letting the familiar beat of his heart soothe me. "I'm okay, Brax. Misch just surprised me with some information."

Concern lined his face and eyes, and I could tell he was going to push me for more details. "I'll tell you later. Go back to your game with Nash." I gently ruffled the little boy's hair. "He needs some playtime and so do you."

Braxton very reluctantly left us, and I recognized the look he bestowed on me. I would be telling him later what happened, there was no doubt.

For now, I needed to sit down.

Chapter 14

Mischa and I sat side by side, our emotions all over the shop. I knew this information wasn't anything which should have knocked me like this. Supes got pregnant; it happened by choice and accidentally, even with our very clearly defined fertile periods. Unplanned young didn't occur as frequently as with humans, which was no wonder with the way they seemed to have a fertile period every month.

Mischa was barely holding it together. "What are you thinking?" Her voice was low and crackly.

"I'm the first person you've told?"

She nodded, wringing her hands together. "Yes, I was in denial for ages, thinking the healer made a mistake. I mean ... I've never had a period. Maximus didn't seem to think I needed any protection. I was just stupid."

I shook my head. "Shifters have four fertile periods a year, and we're always aware when they are. Maximus would have assumed you would know if it was your time. Like the rest of us, he probably forgot that you know next to nothing about our world."

She nodded. "Yeah, I went back to the healer and demanded to know how it had happened. He thought that because my marks were bound by magic for so many years, before slowly starting to release, there was no way to predict my fertile period. Basically I wasn't following any normal pattern for a shifter. My body was all out of whack, and with the surge of hormones it was like I created my own fertility."

I shook my head. "We went true twin style there, doing everything together. Both of our fertile times were screwed up as a side-effect of the dragon mark." Fucking Larkspur. I reached out and hugged Mischa, squeezing her frail body. "We need to get some food and sleep into you. You have to be healthy so my little niece or nephew thrives."

She shook against me, but I sensed the tension which had been plaguing her for so long starting to ease. Sharing her secret had taken some of the burden which must have been weighing her down.

I had a thought. "You're lucky those bitch twins didn't hurt the baby when they attacked you in Krakov." A sense of horror stole over me. The memories of her injuries were so much worse with the knowledge of her pregnancy. So much of her blood had coated the ground.

She wiped her face on her sleeve, and gave me a tired smile. "Yeah, I think the fact that the mark was keeping us safe helped. Then Grace healed me so quickly that I was okay, and I feel the baby moving now, so I assume it's okay too."

We needed to get another healer in to check on her. I wasn't too worried, shifters were tough and so were their babies. I mean, I had no personal experience of course, but there had been a lot of pregnant shifters move through our packs over the years, and as far I knew there wasn't much that could go wrong in healthy shifter pregnancies. Still, she was probably a few months along now and should be checked out.

We at least needed to find out the gestation period for this shifter-vamp hybrid fetus. Calculating this was left up to the magic users, because it changed every time in hybrid births. Just depended which genetics was stronger. I would think that if she could feel the baby moving, then she was a decent way along.

A quick glance to check that Braxton wasn't watching, and then I reached out and smoothed down the huge shirt she had on. Sure enough, there was definitely a baby bump there.

"Cardia's going to lose her shit," I said, a burst of laughter leaving me. "Seriously, we're going to have to make sure she's occupied while you tell

Max. Then he can have the joy of breaking it to her."

A smile wavered on her lips. "It's not really funny, Jess."

I snorted. "Sometimes you have to laugh. Honestly, you and I might both be knocked up because fate was fucking with us. We should have known when our fertile periods were, and yet they made sure we didn't. These babies are meant to be born. That's just how fate works."

Mischa let out a deep, ragged breath. "In the human world I'd just be a moron who let some dude have sex without protection. Max and I did talk about it, but when he told me that supes didn't have to worry about diseases and such, and that if I wasn't fertile there was no way to fall pregnant, I thought it was okay. Like I said, I'd never been fertile before and I figured I was just some sort of supernatural dud in the baby-making department."

Sounded like she'd been waiting to bleed like humans. We weren't the same as them and therefore did not have the same sort of fertility symptoms.

"Girl, you seriously need some basic supe classes. These are the things we learn in our first years of schooling. Or from our moms. Of course I didn't have a mom here, and you clearly had one who was more concerned with keeping this world a secret so that no dragon marked hunters found us –

are we both starting to see how this all happened? Bad timing really."

Mischa leaned in closer. "I know it's asking a lot for you to keep this a secret, but for now I think it's better that everyone focuses on the dragon king. We'll deal with the pregnancy thing after. I mean, it's not like it's going anywhere."

Her hand rested against her tiny bump again, and I could see the protective way she already cradled the life in her body. If this was what she wanted, I could stay quiet for a few more days.

"I promise I won't tell anyone – except for Braxton. I will never keep secrets from him again, and there's no way he won't demand answers. I'm pretty sure I can get him to give you some time to tell his brother. We understand that this is not our secret, but you can't wait forever. Our pack is so close because we try to always be open and honest. Not to mention our parents are really worried about you. It will be better for all once they know the truth."

Mischa gave me a side hug. "Thank you, I appreciate that. I will tell him, and everyone else, as soon as we've dealt with this crisis. I just want Max to be able to focus on this fight. Distracting him and his mate now … well, it could be fatal."

We both knew there would be a massive fallout between Maximus and Cardia – a definite distraction during our fight with Larky. Supes did not share their mates well, and the fact that Mischa would give Maximus his first child would forever grate on his vampire mate.

We were interrupted then by the door swinging open. Jonathon appeared in the entrance. His face was neutral but his eyes darker than usual.

"Louis just arrived back. He said to tell you that it's all taken care of, but that Larkspur will be here early tomorrow morning. He's suggesting we all head out now and get some sleep. We don't know when we'll be able to rest again after this. Lienda and I are going to stay here with Mischa. Jo and Jack are leaving right now." He strode closer to the little dragon marked child.

"Come on, Nash. Time for you to say your goodbyes."

The dragon marked child hugged Braxton hard, before crossing to take Jonathon's hand.

My father turned to me as he was leaving. "Go and get some rest, Jess. Just make sure to listen out for the alarm."

I looked to Mischa, silently asking her if she was going to be okay or if she wanted me to stay with her. I was feeling strangely protective over my fragile twin ... and the tiny baby nestled inside of her.

"Go," she said softly. "Spend this last night with Braxton. It doesn't sound like you've had much alone time."

Try none. I kissed her cheek with a swift peck and jumped to my feet.

"I'll see you in the morning."

She just nodded before lying back on the couch and getting comfortable. I reached across and snagged a throw and dragged the blanket over her. She closed her eyes. Exhaustion was clear across her face.

My father must have deposited Nash with the Compass parents in record time, because he was back in the doorway before Braxton and I even made it outside. As we stepped into the main hall, he took a second to stare at the still form of his daughter before quietly closing the door and magically locking it down again.

I could see the true worry in his dark eyes; the color was more black than blue. "Is she okay, Jess? She won't talk to me or Lienda, and frankly, ever since Krakov, she's been suffering. I don't know how to help her."

I refused to flat out lie to him, and tried to think of a way to reassure him without completely spilling her secret. "She's not exactly fine, but for now she's dealing with everything, Dad." I threw my arms around him and he lifted me up into one of his warm hugs. "As soon as we destroy Larky, we can all start to recover, get back to a normal life."

"Okay, I'll take your word for it," he said as he set me back on my feet. "But if anything changes, and you're worried about her, I expect you to immediately come and tell me what's going on."

I nodded. "Promise."

Braxton was quiet as we made our way back into the main part of the town hall. The members of Stratford were dispersing through the double front doors. Within a few moments the rest of the quads found us in the crowd.

"So are we heading to our place?" Jacob asked. "I'm pretty sure there are some meals in the freezer. It's not ideal, but better than nothing."

My eyes were drawn for a brief second to Maximus. Cardia stood beside him, the pretty and petite vampiress had her black curls artfully pinned atop her head. She gave me a nod but there was no friendly smile to follow. She actually looked kinda pissed, which I couldn't be bothered dealing with right now. I'd never had the best feeling about her in the sanctuary. Something about her attitude screamed *fake*, even when she was trying to be nice. But for Maximus's sake I needed to learn to deal with her. They were a package deal now.

Poor Mischa.

I forced a smile across my face. "Yes, I think one night of normalcy in the Compass castle is exactly what we all need."

I felt homesick and couldn't wait to get back to my pack home. Braxton tucked me in at his side, his lips grazing my temple while his right hand dropped onto my ass. That move was a hundred percent my dragon shifter, confident with a touch of arrogance.

I couldn't help but chuckle. "You love me the right amount of perfect, you know that, right?"

He answered with another kiss, this time on my lips. I could not wait for tonight.

Eventually I was wrenched from his arms. Tyson held me captive before passing me to Jacob like I was some sort of parcel.

"Time to go, lovebirds," the fey said, giving me a cheesy grin. I punched him in his shoulder, and he conceded by lowering me back to my feet and letting me walk from the hall.

As we crossed the foyer, pushing through the masses of supes, I saw a familiar elfin face.

"Grace!" I jogged to her side and wrapped my arms around the healer. "Thank you so much for what you did in Krakov."

She had saved my sister's life, and the baby she didn't even know about. We owed her big-time, and I needed her to know how much I appreciated her help.

"Will you come and hang out with us tonight?" I said as I pulled back. "It'll be fun."

I knew she would immediately look at Tyson. Those two just couldn't seem to get their shit together. If anything, it felt like there was even more distance between them.

"Come on," I said, distracting her from the intense stare between them. "I don't want to be the only girl."

A throat cleared behind me and I turned to find Cardia glaring. "Oh yeah, right. Cardia and I don't want to be the only girls."

Whoops. My bad.

Grace looked so torn. She was still sneaking glances at the handsome wizard. Finally she nodded. "Sure, I'd love to hang out with you all for the night. My family left, so it would just be an empty house for me."

I clapped my hands together. This felt like something fun and exciting. Sure, the world might end tomorrow, but tonight we would all be together and safe. I would cherish every second of this time with my pack. There weren't many people left in the hall now. I was sad to see that Jo and Jack had already taken off with Nash. I'd wanted to say goodbye – though I felt reassured knowing they were safe. I gave Lienda and Jonathon one last wave before leaving them to their Mischa babysitting duties.

My father warned Braxton before we left: "If for some reason the king puts out a call again and Jessa is able to be controlled outside of Faerie, you must get her back here immediately. The only reason I'm letting her leave is that you're a dragon, and should be strong enough to contain her until we can lock her down."

I snorted. "Standing right here, Dad."

I was hoping like hell the king had no control over me here. Surely if he could influence me even a little, he'd have tried to use it when I was in his castle in Faerie.

Louis pulled me to the side just before I was about to leave. "You got my message about the mystics?"

I nodded a few times, a smirk quirking my lips up. "I have a good feeling about taking them from the equation. How were you able to get them away from the king?"

Every facet of his purple eyes was visible, sparkling like precious stones. "Quale helped me. The mystics are connected, similar to the marked. He brought the other eleven across to a secure location. I have a potion which can render a supe into an unnatural sleep. Generally lasts anywhere from four days to two weeks, depending on the magic strength of the individual. If we can end this thing with Larkspur without much delay, he won't be able to call on the mystics."

Braxton, who was standing close by, tuned into our conversation. "Were the mystics with Larkspur? Does he know they're out of commission?"

The sorcerer grinned. "Quale arranged it so they were left behind to ferry the last of his marked across. The king was already on his way, so he may not be aware until he gets here."

The magic user quickly switched topics. "I know you're probably anxious to have me perform the gestation spell, but I'm not sure I can spare the time or power. I have to make sure I can hold the wards as long as possible."

I wasn't going to lie, there was some disappointment there. I really wanted the confirmation of pregnancy, followed by the knowledge that everything was okay. Still ... it was definitely more important to keep everyone safe.

"It's okay, if I'm pregnant, that's not going to change today or tomorrow. Waiting is the right thing."

Braxton draped an arm across my body, pulling me into his side. We were both anxious to know, but it didn't change anything. Either way, we'd deal with it. And right now, everyone was waiting for us. Louis walked us out and locked down the hall again.

Some of the members felt safer staying inside. Others, like us, were heading to their homes for a decent sleep. The sorcerer was going to be up all night keeping an eye on the perimeter and controlling the security systems here. He really did need all of his power. He was our best weapon, as well as an early detection system for the king.

Once we were past the fountain in the center of the town, I dropped back a few steps, and just as Braxton was turning to see what I was doing, I took a running jump and launched myself onto his back. Lucky I had wolf reflexes, because those broad shoulders were really far off the ground. I wrapped my arms around his neck and snuggled myself into his back.

He twisted to see me better, his blue eyes twinkling as a lazy grin spread across his handsome face. "I have no idea why you wanted Grace to come tonight. If you think for one second I'm letting you out of the bedroom, you're crazy."

My entire body tightened, and I found myself slightly breathless just thinking about that. Braxton had a gorgeous bedroom on the top floor, one he'd won through bloody battles with his brothers. I had never slept in his room. We all tended to share the largest room downstairs when we slept as pack. I wasn't sure I'd ever seen him take a female to that room either. On those rare occasions he'd been more inclined to go to their place.

"Are you actually going to let me into the sacred space?" I let my lips graze against his ear and felt the rumbles increasing in his chest.

"Babe, that room has always been yours. I was just waiting for you to figure it out."

I buried my face against his neck. *Perfect, he was just perfection.*

"Are you concerned that our bond is still not fully formed?" I murmured.

He took a moment to answer, continuing to piggyback me toward their place. His voice was a little rough when he finally spoke. "I'm not happy about it, but as long as we're together, the rest we can figure out." The gruff tone got more pronounced. "When you were taken from us, well, that was the worst thing I've ever experienced. Life is more in perspective now. As long as we're both alive and free, everything is okay."

I pressed my lips to his cheek, the slight stubble rasping across my skin. "I can't wait for tonight, but I'm telling you now, food first, then sex. I need my energy."

He laughed loudly. "Very true, Jessa babe. You're going to need a lot of energy tonight. I'd better find you some cake."

I groaned. He knew the way to my heart, that was for sure.

Beside us, the other five strolled along quietly. It was just on dusk now and the town was still all creeped out in silence. It was like an abandoned ghost city, and I couldn't wait to feel the life return to it again. I don't think I ever realized how much I loved my home until I was forced to leave it. I did enjoy the adventure, traveling the world, and planned on doing much more of it in the future, but I'd always hoped that Stratford would be here to return to. It was where I wanted to raise my kids, with family and pack close by.

As the large wooden wraparound porch of the boys' home came into view, I wiggled my way down off Braxton and ran up to the door. Cardia gave me another glare and I wondered what the bitch's problem was now. Did she think she owned Maximus and the house? I was sure she'd been staying here while the boys were in Faerie, but that was no reason to get all territorial.

I'd been here when they built the damn place.

I guess, if I was being fair, I might be a smidge on the upset side if my mate disappeared for weeks to look for another chick. I didn't actually know how much time they'd been apart since Romania, but I was thinking a lot. When they had first mated, and I'd kind of lost my mind worrying that our pack dynamics were over, Maximus had told me he would choose me over Cardia, over his true mate. His loyalty and sincerity had melted my heart, but I'd still always known that was going to cause problems between them.

True mates was a magical bond – you were magically predisposed to love them – but it didn't mean you always got along perfectly, or that they were even the best suited to you. Unfortunately, you didn't get much choice in the matter. The fates decided who your true mate was, and you just had to hope they chose well.

So, I guess Cardia had every right to be upset about his choices. My eyes alighted on Maximus. I'd been avoiding his gaze, worried he'd somehow read the truth about Mischa in my face. Probably just my own guilt talking, but this secret felt so big and I was bursting to tell him.

Examining my emotions, I was glad I wasn't mad at him. Sure, he made some bad decisions with Mischa, but there was nothing innately bad in what he did. Sex happened, especially during highly emotional times. I had no doubt Maximus would step up and be a great father and support to my sister. It just sucked that Cardia and Mischa would be caught in a territory war, one which could divide our pack. We had to make sure that didn't happen.

We had to think about the new pack young on the way.

Opening the front door, I stepped inside and the scent of home surrounded me, that rich, spicy heat that all of the Compasses exuded, all male and all delicious.

I pretty much ran down the long hall and threw myself onto their large, comfortable couch.

"Food me, bitch," I hollered to Jacob when he burst into the room after me.

"On it," he said, cutting left into the rustic-styled kitchen.

As the rest of my pack wandered in, rustling and clanking could be heard from the other room. Braxton gracefully dropped down on one side of me, Tyson on the other. Grace took the seat across from us, leaving enough distance between her and Braxton to label her as an outsider of our pack. I was wondering if Tyson's tense face had anything to do with that distance.

I ran my hand through the wizard's shorter hair. "I'm still a little weirded out seeing your hair all gone."

His eyes crinkled. "Well a lot happened while you were missing, and none of it good. It's in my hair's best interest that you don't get kidnapped again."

I looked over at Grace and was not surprised to see a secret grin tipping up the corner of her lips. I had to give her props for not caving into the charismatic wizard. Even if she had forgiven him for past hurts – and I think she had – it was not as easily forgotten.

Braxton shifted next to me, and I found myself eyeballing him hard. "You ever going to tell me exactly what happened when I was kidnapped?"

He let me have that lazy grin of his. "I think it's better that we don't go too deeply into it. If the councils ever get their shit together and come calling, I'd rather you didn't know the details."

I punched him in the ribs. "Dude, if you go down, I go down. We ride or die, right? In this together forever."

His grin spread, and he looked extremely pleased with that response. "Let's just say I had to hurt a few people to get information about Larkspur, although no one was really up to date seeing he'd been absent for a thousand years."

Jacob's laughter could be heard from the kitchen. "Hurt?" He hollered between laughter. "I think the death count was five, including the bitch twins."

I raised both of my eyebrows at him. "Five?" That was kind of scary and impressive.

"I can only really claim four," he said. "The second twin killed herself before I could finish my interrogation."

Might seem harsh to most, but I didn't care. I would have done the same thing if someone had hurt or stolen one of my Compasses. I probably would have killed more than five just in the first few days of raging around.

Through our bond I could sense Braxton following my bloodthirsty thoughts.

"The boys stopped me from completely losing my mind and soul. The moment you were gone, the world stopped spinning for me. I lost who I was. I became a mindless beast. I killed one of the twins in a blink of an eye, and the other only survived then because I knew I needed information from her. The bond with my brothers is the reason I'm still Braxton."

I leaned up and kissed him hard. "You're the sweetest mate any supe could ask for."

I peppered more kisses across his face.

"Humans would think we were all homicidal sociopaths if they spent any time with us," Grace said.

Saying that, she reminded me of Mischa and how odd my sister was at times. Being raised with humans sounded a lot like being raised with alligators, weird and dangerous. We sat for a while chatting and relaxed. All except Cardia who was a stiff, silent supe. After about forty-minutes Jacob emerged from the kitchen and he was bearing gifts. Beautiful, beautiful gifts. I didn't hesitate, jumping to my feet and dashing into the dining room.

"Hello, old friend," I said as I ran my hands along the stunning table.

If one could have a favorite piece of furniture, this was mine. Not only was it absolutely spectacular, it had been carved by my mate. My hand fell to my stomach. Was I pregnant? Would our child one day sit at this table and enjoy massive family dinners like we had? The thought had me both freaked out and filled with joyful anticipation. I slid into my usual seat. Generally, Braxton would sit on one side and Maximus on the other, but now that he had Cardia, I wondered if my vampire would move so as not to annoy her further.

Jacob was next to venture into the room. He placed two large platters into the center of the table before heading back to the kitchen and returning moments later with two more huge platters. Lucky it was a really large table, because he'd just dropped enough food here to feed a small army. Chicken, pasta, scalloped potatoes, sandwiches, and heaps of other bits and pieces filled the large plates. Impressive. If this was his definition of frozen meals, I'd love to see a home cooked feast.

The others filed into the room, but not Braxton. I briefly wondered where he'd ducked off to, but didn't worry too much, he'd be back for the food. I had no doubt of that. Tyson and Jacob settled in across from me, and my heart kind of fluttered when Maximus took his usual seat beside me, Cardia sliding in on his other side. Grace hovered in the doorway for a bit before she finally crossed and sat next to Jacob. Tyson's face was stony but he didn't say a single word to the witch. Everyone grabbed a plate and started filling it with whatever food they could reach.

For some reason I hesitated. Where was Braxton? My stomach growled, and I was just about to jump up and find him when his massive frame filled the doorway. He grinned as he crossed to me.

"Jess, you didn't have to wait for me."

I *had* been waiting for him. What sort of sappy, love-sick, shifter spell did he have me under?

He slid gracefully in beside me, and without hesitation piled ninety percent of the remaining food onto my plate.

"You eat first. I'll finish what is left."

Sigh. Shifter males ... every female needed to get one. They were the best.

It looked like Cardia felt the same. She narrowed her eyes and growled a little at Maximus. My vampire quad got that look on his face, a cornered predator. On the one hand he knew he was in trouble for something, and on the other he had no freaking idea what it was. Vampires were not like shifters, they didn't have the same relationship with food, and they treated their mates special in different ways. Still, he was being extra dismissive of Cardia, fighting the mate bond for some reason, and his girl knew it.

Knowing Braxton would wait until I was done, I ate as quickly as I could and then transferred the rest of the food across to his plate. We chatted over dinner, light conversations about nothing in particular, followed by moments of silverware clinking and comfortable silence. I wished Mischa was here right now. I had missed her. I hadn't realized how much until we were back together, until our bond was cemented again.

I had so many bonds now. Were one of them the reason I didn't have a complete mating bond with Braxton? What would I have to sacrifice? What choices would I have to make in the following days that might change everything?

Chapter 15

After dinner we all dispersed. Most of us were exhausted. I was way past exhausted, I was wrecked. I'd barely slept in days, and tomorrow was going to be hectic. After hugs and good-nights all round – Grace was all snuggled into my old room; I thought it was a perfect fit for her – I followed Braxton up the stairs to the highest room in the three-story home. He had the entire top floor, which was much smaller than the two floors below, but still a massive expanse of luxury and workmanship.

The bedroom's décor was cozy and masculine. A king-sized bed dominating the space, the bed base and headboard were both hand-carved, dark timber. There were some other large, heavy furniture pieces scattered about, expensive looking but practical also. The wide floorboards were stained timber, set off by a few thick cream-colored rugs. A fire was crackling in the large fireplace near the foot of the bed, and since I loved the piney scent of freshly cut logs, I took a second to breathe it all in.

"Would you like a bath first, Jess?" Braxton stood beside his bed. The room was dim, just the natural wash of firelight.

I nodded, my body already humming at the thought of being naked with him. I crossed the space swiftly, but before I could push past him into the large en suite, he swept me up into his arms.

"Tonight we do things my way," he murmur-growled at me.

I patted his shoulder. *We'll see, mate, we'll see.*

I was distracted from arguing my point as I caught sight of something inside his large, white and navy tiled bathroom. I sucked in deeply, my heartbeat pattering so hard I could feel the surge of hot blood through my veins.

I had to blink more than once, trying not quite successfully to stem the tears sprinkling in the corner of my eyes.

"When did you have time to do this for me?" My voice was breathless, my heart still pounding. My overwhelming love for Braxton had me all lightheaded.

The bath was filled, bubbles fluffy across the surface. At the far edge was a bamboo board, the kind used to hold drinks and books while in the bath. Sitting atop of it was an array of cakes, and two glasses of what looked like wine but smelt like apple cider. Nonalcoholic.

I tilted my head up to him, letting all my emotions out. "Most guys would have filled the room with candles and rose petals or some shit," I said. "But you, my mate, know for sure the way to this shifter's heart." I turned back to the tub, still astonished by the collection of beautiful desserts. I knew now where he'd disappeared to at dinner, but I had no idea how he'd managed to find so many cakes. I felt extra special tonight.

He gently lowered me down, and in seconds had stripped both of our clothes off, leaving my necklace in place. We both knew it had to stay there until I was ready to crush it into Larky's heart.

Again Braxton distracted me from food as I drank in the sight of him. As much as I appreciated his body, I hated to think the new definition to his muscles was because he'd been doing nothing but training and fighting while I was gone. I hated that he'd been in so much pain.

Time to wash that away with some new memories.

I stepped into the warm bath. Braxton followed me, and as we both sank down, water splashed over the side. Settling back, I made myself comfortable. It was a large, deep bath, with powerful jets at either end.

Braxton's strong features were relaxed as he settled in close to me and the tray. There were a multitude of jets pulsing around us. He pulled me back against him and I found myself going all tranquil-like. We sat like that for an hour. He fed me the cake, and I even shared some of it with him. We sipped the cider, and it was warming as it made its way through my body. Between the snacking we talked about Maximus and Mischa, and I was surprised to learn that Braxton had noticed no changes in my sister or her scent. So either he hadn't paid close enough attention, or her hybrid child was masking itself. Thankfully he didn't fight me on keeping it from Maximus, but I could see that he doubted the information would remain secret for very long.

As the water finally started to cool, I realized how boneless I felt. These peaceful moments with my mate had my body and mind in such a happy place. For the first time in a long time things felt right.

The longer I spent pressed against the length of muscled body beneath me, the more difficult it was to ignore the urges clenching my insides. Braxton and I were newly mated, and would usually have been locked away from all civilization for the first few months. Instead, we had barely had a night together, and had a lot of time to make up for.

I spun around so I was straddling him, and his lips were on mine in seconds. I was burning up, all rational thought gone.

His hands found their way under my ass, and I was pressed so firmly against him that I could feel each and every one of those very defined muscles. The kiss deepened, my body rocking of its own accord. I moaned as his lips left mine and he started to kiss down my neck, devouring me, tasting every part of me that he could reach.

He lifted us up then, flipping our positions to press me back against the far bath wall. My head settled comfortably into the indent of the bath as he raised my lower half out of the water.

"I have to taste you," he said.

I pretty much orgasmed right then, like no touching required at all.

Okay, some touching better be–

He lowered his head and my eyes rolled back at the first sweeping brush of his tongue. He growled, low and hypnotic. "So sweet, so perfect."

I had to reach out and grip the side of the tub so I didn't drown. My muscles were pretty much useless. Braxton kicked it up a notch, using his talented tongue and hands together. My breathing echoed across the room as I fought to hold off my orgasm. I know, what moron tries to prolong something like that, but it felt so damn good having his mouth on me that I really could have stayed here, in this moment, in the warmth of this bath, forever.

There was no stopping the spiraling swirl of pleasure which started at my center and ricocheted outwards. I cried out and Braxton held me firmly, keeping his mouth against me and my body above the water. My release went on forever, and yet it was nowhere near long enough. My body shuddered as he moved his mouth against me, the sensations almost too much to handle.

I reached down and dragged him up to me, crashing our lips together, before moaning again.

"Bed, now!" I was all demanding and shit, but it was in his best interest. I was going to return the favor, and there was no way I could hold my breath long enough.

We wasted no time getting out of the water. I snagged a towel, but before any drying could happen Braxton was lifting me up and we were kissing again. Long, slow drugging kisses. The urgency built for me again, and I could see that he was hard ... massively hard.

We didn't make it to the bed. The first time he took me hard and fast on the thick rug in front of the fireplace. I was not remotely quiet as the orgasm flooded through me. Braxton was right there with me, groaning out his own release, my name on his lips.

"Shit, Brax, we didn't use protection," I slurred from pleasure and exhaustion.

He stared down at me, those eyes so mesmerizing. "As far as I'm concerned, you're already carrying my young. I don't want anything between us ... are you worried about it?"

"I love you," I said. "Even if I had a million choices for a mate, I would still always choose you. And no, I don't want anything between us either."

He went motionless above me, our bodies still intertwined, his strong arms holding most of his weight off me. Probably worried about squishing me and his possible baby. "I love you too, Jess. You know I always have. If you had a million mates, I would destroy every single one to get to you."

He shifted to lie beside me, pulling me into him. The heat of the fire crackled against our naked skin and I couldn't stop from running my lips along his chest. He had tasted me and now it was my turn. His eyes were electric as they followed my movements. I ran my tongue along each defined line of his abdomen, down to my favorite V in the world, the one which led to ... damn, he was hard again, even though we'd only just finished. As I let my tongue run across him, tasting the salty sweetness of our lovemaking, I tried to figure out how I was going to fit him all in.

Huge dick was great and all, but I could already feel the ache in my jaw. Still, it was going to be fun to try, and we had plenty of hours left for me to get it right.

The night was almost over by the time we showered again and finally crawled into bed. I was spent, boneless, and as relaxed as a person could be who was not actually dead.

As I lay in the arms of my mate, thoughts slowing down, my animals inside quiet and calm, I did something pretty unusual for me. I prayed to the Faerie gods. I asked the shining ones to protect my loved ones during this battle. I needed this to last forever. I was not ready to lose one second of my life with them. With Braxton.

I hated the dragon king for so much, but if I lost even one person I loved in this coming battle, he would rue the day he decided to create his dragon marked curse and forcibly dragon mate souls. My dragon and I had already decided that we had to kill him just for that alone, for the fact that she should have grown up with her family in Faerie, that she should be the next ruling dragon queen.

Braxton's arm snaked around me tighter, his large palm resting against my stomach. There was something both tender and possessive in his action and it gave me a sense of calm and home. Even though I didn't want to waste one second on sleeping, my exhaustion pulled me under and I was gone into a dreamless slumber.

The sirens violently ripped us from the comfort of sleep. I was disoriented for a second before finding myself really freaking annoyed that my reprieve from the stress and worry of life had ended so abruptly.

At some point during the night we had moved slightly apart in our sleep, although Braxton still had a heavy arm draped protectively over me. That was just how shifters were, we liked to sleep in a big pile of comfort. Without saying anything, we both jumped up and were off the bed in a flash.

"Shit," I said. "I don't have any clean clothes here." I really didn't want to put on my old, dirty Faerie garments.

Braxton was already striding into his walk-in wardrobe. "In here, babe," he said.

I scurried after him, wondering what sort of magic he had cooked up, and as I stepped inside I ground to a halt to see an entire shelf filled with my stuff.

"What the crap?" I shouldn't be so surprised. My mate was nothing if not impressive and organized.

"Did we move in together and you forgot to tell me?"

He grinned. "When you disappeared I might have dismantled most of your room at Jonathon's and moved your stuff in here."

I could see lots of my things now: clothes, shoes, little mementoes of my life scattered throughout the large closet.

"I just needed to feel that you were close to me. I needed to protect these things while I was searching for you." His voice was low as he stood there naked, pouring out his pain and worry.

I couldn't stop myself from crossing to him. "I love this, Brax," I said, standing on my tiptoes so I could almost reach my arms around his neck. "Our stuff should be together, in our dragon den of sin."

He snorted. "Yeah, I think the beast inside was controlling me a lot, and he wanted to protect his treasures."

I knew exactly what he meant.

The siren was still blaring, and a sense of urgency filtered through the room. I knew the others would be waiting for us; we needed to get moving. I rifled through my stuff and pulled on a dark purple long-sleeved shirt and some black jeans. My hair went up into a ponytail; my boots were the heavy, face-smashing kind. Braxton handed me a few knives from his collection and I fitted them into the side sheath of my boot. Our dragons were the best weapons we had, but it never hurt to have a few knives stashed around.

Just in case.

Braxton was silent as we made our way quickly through the room and toward the stairs. Just before we were about to descend, he captured my hand and pulled me against him. I found myself pressed against the closed door of his room, his big body crowding into me.

"I swear to do my best to protect you and our baby, Jess."

It sounded like he had already decided I was pregnant, and in all seriousness the jeans I was wearing might be a little snug in the waist area, although, possibly, that was from the three tons of cake I'd eaten last night.

"Before we join the real world, I just need one more moment in our bubble," he said, and then his lips were on mine. The kiss was soft, just the press of lips and the taste of Braxton. I blinked a few times when he pulled back, trying to regain control of my fuzzy brain. There was so much goodbye and sorrow in that kiss, and I was not freaking okay with any more goodbyes.

"We're going to destroy this asshole," I said. "We're strong enough, I know it."

Braxton was wearing his warrior poker face look, but I noticed the slightest softening. "I have no doubt, but I need you to know that even if this does not work out for all of us, you have to survive. You're everything, and I'm not sure the world will even keep spinning if you aren't here. Make sure you survive, Jess!" He was so fierce, but I could feel my heart fracturing. It sounded to me like he didn't think he would make it through this battle, that he would go down fighting.

"There's no me without you, Braxton Compass. So if you want me to stay alive, you're going to have to do the same."

I held his face in both of my hands, our eyes desperately locked together.

"I don't plan on going anywhere," he finally said. I friggin' hoped he was right.

We spent about eighteen more precious seconds kissing before stepping back into reality. We made our way down the stairs then. Beams of light shone through some of the dark shutters, so I knew it was early morning. The other Compasses, and Grace and Cardia were downstairs, all dressed, all ready to roll.

The air was heavy and no one seemed interested in small talk, which was fine by me. I'd had about two hours' sleep, enough to be functioning, but I'd probably punch the first person to mention some crap like the weather.

I noticed, as we left the Compass home, that there still appeared to be distance between Maximus and Cardia. He was walking with his hand pressed against her lower back, but they didn't lean into each other, which was a very telling sign. I was getting the vibe that he was touching her to appease her and not because he wanted to. But at the same time, why wouldn't he want to touch his mate? I wanted to strip mine naked and devour every single part of him.

A warm, heavy hand landed on the nape of my neck. Braxton splayed his fingers so that they were caressing as much of my bare skin as possible. Case in point. Mates liked to touch each other. It was not only a massive comfort, but also stupidly sexy just having his skin against mine.

The sun was cresting over the edge of the forest, the light filtering across our town as we strode through the streets. The creepy, ghost town feel hadn't gone anywhere, but at least in the light of day I could focus on my favorite buildings and not the lack of living beings around.

The front doors of the town hall were open, and as we stepped up into the room I could see about two hundred supes standing around. Yep, pretty pathetic army – though on power we were packing a lot more than mere numbers. We were the only shot Stratford had.

Louis was up on the dais filling everyone in on what we had learned from the golden dragon, what our battle plan was, and a few other bits and pieces. My pack and I filed into the back and listened in. As soon as the sorcerer noticed us in the room, the blaring alarm died off. Clearly that had just been a wakeup call, and we must have been the last members to make it here.

His powerful voice rang through the large space. "Larkspur is on American soil. He's in Connecticut, and we can only assume on his way here. My spies tell me that his army is slowly trailing across. They're using step throughs, which is getting them here quickly, but also exhausting their sorcerers. I know we have a basic plan in motion, but everyone needs to be fluid. We don't know exactly what the dragon king is going to hit us with, and therefore it's difficult to plan ahead."

That was the absolute worst part of this. We were in the dark. We knew he wanted me and the *Book of Guidance*. I just hoped he was going with brute strength and no hidden traps. Brute strength we could plan for.

Louis was still speaking. "I have arranged for some magic users, truly powerful sorcerers, to join us. Your council leaders have also rallied some of their race members. They'll all be arriving shortly. Still, even with these additions, we'll be vastly outnumbered."

That was an understatement.

"The Craiz and Compass quads are our most powerful weapons. They each have a calling and can stand against the king and his marked. We need to offer them support and protection." His eyes scanned the hall, before resting on me. Many of the supes followed his line of sight. His next words were extra laced with power. "Jessa is priority number one on the protect list. She has a weapon to cut the ties between the marked and the king, which will weaken him enough for us to actually kill him. Plus, he wants her for those reasons I've already explained, so protect her with your life."

I didn't squirm, I just let them look their fill, but I was relieved when attention moved off me again. I hated thinking about anyone protecting me with their life, but it wasn't just about me now. I also had a little one – probably – to protect, and for my young I'd take any help.

Louis stepped away from the front podium and moved through the center aisle. "I'm going to go now and open the doorway for the others who are joining us from around the world. They'll come straight into Stratford. I'll redirect the securities for them, which will leave us unprotected for a few minutes, but I think it's still the safest option. While I'm gone, it would be best if you take all of this information and start formulating some sort of plan of action."

He gave me a kiss on the cheek as he passed, and then was gone from the room. The energy in the hall lessened without him. There was always one thing you could be sure of with Louis, his power was second to none. The supes started to move around, congregating in their race groups. My father and other leaders stepped up to guide those around them.

The Four wandered our way and I forced myself not to snarl. I'd seen them the moment we'd entered the room. I had Four radar now, helped in part by my animals, who considered them to be the enemy and were pretty unhappy about their "still-breathing" status. The four of them moved as a single unit up to the front of the hall, close to the dais.

The room quietened, faces turning toward the identical quads. Some were wary, others pissed – okay the quads and myself were the main ones who looked pissed – but everyone was waiting to see what they would say.

One of them spoke – no point trying to figure out which one, since they were identical and all wearing the same black fatigues. "We'll be joining our power together shortly," he said. "The marked are closing in. We can feel their energy. They'll be here within an hour."

Another one of them said, "When we're joined, we'll have the energy to hold the marked at bay, to almost freeze them to the spot and prevent them from accessing their borrowed dragon energy. However, this will be a far greater number than we've ever faced at one time, and there's no way for us to know if we'll have enough power."

The next one picked up the conversation and I had to laugh. They were like some sort of sideshow, each one continuing the conversation from the last. Maybe they shared one brain or something.

"Louis believes that some of his sorcerer friends can add their power to ours, and as a collective we'll have the strength to contain the marked, thereby giving the rest of you a chance to finish the king."

His eyes found me in the hall. "Jessa must get close enough to break the bonds. She was gifted the necklace from Faerie, and we all know she's strong enough for this task."

I forced myself not to flip him off. He spoke *truth*; that was how magic worked. If you were worthy, it came to you, and therefore it was my responsibility. Even if it hadn't been my responsibility, I was more than happy to take the job.

"We'll stick by, Jessa," Maximus said from where he sat on my left, Cardia at his side. "We've never properly tested our quad power against the king, but we did use it more than once when Jessa went missing, and know how to manipulate the strengths of our bond. I'm confident we can hold the king long enough for Jess to bring the hurt on him."

Jonathon moved away from the shifters then, climbing up to the dais. I looked around for Lienda, surprised to not see her at his side.

Ah. She stepped out of the side door where Mischa was staying. She scanned the room, spotted my pack, and crossed over to sit with us. She leaned across Braxton and gave me a hug before settling back into her seat. Lienda looked beautiful as always, but sort of frazzled, like she had not been sleeping well. Dark circles hung low under those stunning sea-colored eyes. I was sure she was worried about Mischa too. It would be good for everyone when that secret was out.

"The king is calling the marked," my father said, drawing all of our attention to the front. "The call is faint. Mischa is fighting against his compulsion and is still coherent. We expect that he's limiting his control while they're traveling, but that he'll kick it right up once the battle begins."

Weird that I hadn't felt any sort of call or connection. I mean, I still had the on and off ache in my lower back, and the hair on my arms had been standing since I woke. I had figured it was just magic floating through the air or something, but maybe it was the presence of the king as he closed in on us.

"I know that the Craiz and Compass quads have given us a game plan, a place to start. They all have very important roles, along with my daughter, so for the rest of us, we just need to be backup. We need to make sure that our people are not so overwhelmed with energy or magic that they cannot complete their tasks. It's time to take back our town, our world, and the very vital supernatural communities which keep the criminals off the streets."

There were shouts and noisy agreeance. We were starting to fire up, Jonathon's power whipping us all into a frenzy. The crowd began to move out into the city center. I let the room clear out, not prepared to leave until I checked in with my father and Mischa. Braxton and Lienda stayed behind as well.

Jonathon reached me in moments. "Are you okay, Jess? No urges to run off and joined the king's band of merry marked."

I snorted. "Uh, no, I haven't had any strange urges or voices in my head. How's Mischa?"

I couldn't shake my worry about her. Pregnant, fragile, and at the mercy of a dickbag king who could get in her head. I really wanted to protect her from what was coming.

Jonathon rubbed at his temples, signs of stress wrinkling his forehead and adding a few fine lines beside his eyes. "She says she's fine. I'm proud of the way she fights the king's command, but there's so much sadness in her. She's fading away, Jess, and I can't let her go rogue wolf. There's no coming back from that."

Rogues were shifters who let the human side of them fade out to the animal. It happened when they were without pack or hope. And they were dangerous. I knew Mischa wasn't going rogue, she was just a scared, pregnant, wolf shifter who had been raised by humans. She did not know how to handle this world. She needed time to adjust.

I stood. "You all go out and start rallying the troops. Make sure Louis gets the sorcerers in place around the Four and all that shit." I made shooing motions with my hands. "I'm going to check on Mischa, then I'll follow you to the border."

I could see more than one of them wanted to protest. Braxton had that look in his eyes where he was trying to figure out if he was fast enough to throw me over his shoulder before I managed to kick him in the balls.

I shook my head at him. "Don't even think about it. We're equals, remember? I'll be your worst nightmare if you don't respect that part of our relationship.

Blue eyes glittered and his expression was calculating. Still, he didn't say anything more, he just reached out and cupped me around the back of my head before pulling me in for a leisurely goodbye kiss. I knew what the bastard was doing – using his animal magnetism to cloud my senses, reminding me I was much happier by his side.

As he pulled away I narrowed both eyes at him and gave a growl. He laughed before turning to walk away. I seriously wished I had time to punch him in the jaw. *Later*. Definitely something to put on my to-do list for later.

"Thank you for checking in on Mischa," Lienda said as she and Jonathon were readying to leave. "She's so out of our reach right now, and after everything ... I couldn't stand to lose her."

I squeezed my mom's hand. "We won't lose her. I can almost guarantee it."

Jonathon would hear the *truth* in my voice, a truth I was sure of. As soon as this battle was over, Mischa would have the strength again to deal with this. She was a Lebron after all.

Jonathon handed me the key and then they left the building. It was quiet in here with everyone gone, and the place looked absolutely massive. I wasted no time sprinting across the room and unlocking the door.

I wanted to see Mischa in case something went wrong today. We were going into a fight for our lives and if we didn't manage to best the king, I'd either be dead or locked up as some baby-making machine.

Now was my last chance to say goodbye.

Chapter 16

A manic face shot up as I stepped into the room and locked the door behind me. My eyes widened at the sight of her dilated pupils. *Damn, girl.* She was off her rocker right now. I turned and double-checked the door. I did not want to let the dragon marked crack-head loose. Larky's energy was like a bad drug trip.

Mischa scrambled up from her position on the couch, and I wondered if she'd even left that spot since yesterday. Being locked up was no good for her, not as a person or a shifter. We required freedom, fresh air, forests. She probably needed to shift. Her wolf would be making her miserable if it had been too long. There was no problem shifting while pregnant; our bodies adjusted for the young inside, and no harm generally befell the fetus.

She crossed to me, her walk shaky, her clothes definitely still yesterday's. I wrapped my arms around her, wrinkling my nose at the slightly stale smell.

"Misch … tell me you're showering at least."

She laughed against me. "Yeah, every second day. Seems like a lot of effort otherwise. I'm not going anywhere."

Her eyes were less dull as she pulled back. Just being close was cathartic for us. I noticed an untouched tray of food beside her couch, which was starting to resemble a bird's nest with all her blankets and crap on it. I didn't have much time, but getting her to eat was number one on my list of priorities. She'd always been a strange supe, eating sparingly. But now she had another body to nourish, and she was going to eat all of that deliciousness or so help me I was going to kick her in her pregnant butt.

I led her back to her nest, and as soon as she was settled I picked up the toast and handed it to her. "Eat this, Mischa, or I will kick your ass." I hadn't been kidding about that.

Her eyes widened. Like to the point of falling out of her head. "But ... but I'm pregnant," she angry-whispered at me.

I grinned. "Yes, you are, but you're also a shifter and I can kick you fair in the ass and it will not hurt your child. Also, if you're going to use the pregnant card to escape shit, then use it to remember you need to feed two hungry supes now." My voice was as low as hers, but still plenty loud enough to get my point across.

Her wide eyes started to narrow, but she didn't say anything as we held the stare-off. Finally, she reached out and snatched the toast from me.

"I'll try my best to eat, Jess. It's just food is still making me sick. Really sick. I'm pretty much living on dry crackers, water, and jerky."

I patted her on the head. "All I ask is that you try, and jerky ... for reals? That's nasty stuff. Pregnancy cravings are whacked."

She took a delicate bite of the plain toast and grimaced. "You have no idea. It's especially difficult keeping this sort of weirdness from our parents."

I wondered if I had this morning sickness and weird cravings thing to look forward to. Mischa raised the slice to take another bite when her faced crumpled and she dropped the toast to cradle her head in both hands.

"He's here, Jess!" she said, shouting and moaning at the same time. "Go! Go now and finish the bastard."

She started to shake, little tremors at first but then her entire body was rocking, almost like she was having multiple mini-seizures. I was on the balls of my feet, unsure what the hell to do. I knew I should leave. I had shit to do and kings to kill and stuff, but leaving my twin when she was clearly suffering felt like the wrong move.

"Jess!" Mischa shouted at me again, and I could feel our bond kicking in.

I reached out and took her hand and a blast of energy rocked through me. Our barriers were no use today. Neither of us had the control to maintain them. I could feel what was going on inside of her – Larky was wielding a ton of power against the marked. He was so much stronger than the last time I'd been with him in Faerie.

Mischa was connected to thousands of marked, so many consciousnesses crowding her mind, invisible but tangible ties between all of them. I sensed I was connected to this group as well, but not in the same way my sister was. Maybe it was my dragon that kept me separated, protected my mind from the control.

"You have to go, Jess, you have to end this. Otherwise all the entire supernatural races will be like us ... just ... puppets to his madness ... controlled ... weak and without identity.

I shook my head as I tried to fight against the power he held over my sister. She was strong ... holy shit. I'd doubted her when she'd shown so much weakness in the sanctuary, but to feel her fighting him now, locking him out of her mind, keeping him from the knowledge of both of our children, it was damn impressive.

I hugged her hard before breaking our connection. Immediately the tightness in my chest eased and I was finally able to breathe again, back in my own head and with just my two beasts' energy to deal with.

"I'll be back for you, Misch, I promise. Just keep fighting. Don't let him take any more from you."

She nodded, her head dropping and back arching as she continued to battle the call. Her breathing sounded labored and I worried about how bad this might be for her child. If only she'd told someone about being pregnant, they might have been able to help her deal with this. We should have gotten her away, whether she wanted to leave or not. It was crazy for her to be here when we knew the king was coming.

I guess it didn't really matter. If we lost today, there would be no one left to fight him. He would have all the control he needed; every single marked would follow him. Mischa and every supe were putting their faith into us. Into me. I was the last chance for all of them. It was time to do this.

I glanced back for one moment as I closed the door. The shadow dragon was rising from Mischa, her marked powers bursting from her. Shit, I hoped this room was strong enough to hold her. I double-checked the lock and took off.

Once the key was again in my pocket, I found my hand tightly grasping the necklace sitting flush against my skin. I used its cool surface to center myself and my thoughts. My mind was doing very strange things, moving at a million miles an hour, rushing through a multitude of thoughts and worries, and yet it was also calm.

I was ready to end this.

I reached for my wolf and dragon, drawing on their ancient strength and energy. The sense of calm increased and the flood of thoughts drifted away. Even the unnatural pain across my lower back eased, and flashes of light started winding across my vision as I ran through the center of town, past the fountain and houses of Stratford to the forest. I could feel my pack. Their energy was a strong beacon to me.

I rounded out the edge of the town, and followed the mass of trees to the shimmery wall of magic which protected the town. A few yards ahead stood our army, right at the barrier, waiting for it to fall.

Louis had gathered quite a few extras. There were at least three hundred of us now, maybe even more. It was hard to tell with so many of them in scattered groups. I could sense Braxton and the other Compasses to the left of the main gathering. Flashes of the Four's stark hair intermingled with my boys. Those eight were lined up together, and around them stood a crap-ton of energy, enough to have my senses on full alert. Powerful sorcerers. Not quite Louis' level individually, but together they were intense.

As I got closer, my footsteps silent on the grassed path, I counted exactly how many sorcerers were helping out my boys. Twenty. Twenty almost-Louis levels of power.

We might actually stand a chance of holding this shit down long enough for me to kill Larky. My fist clenched on the necklace again; it was my lifeline right now, our one hope of breaking the links to the marked and leaving him vulnerable enough to kill.

Braxton's eyes were on me, his body angled in my direction. I almost stumbled when I realized he was joined to his brothers. A wash of power surrounded them, the visible connection flickering. Braxton was in that massive state of a fusion shift, his scales scattered down his cheeks and arms, which I found immensely badass and kinda sexy.

Everything about my man was sexy.

Focus, Jessa! Now was not the time to go all hormonal chick, even if Braxton was like twice the size everywhere. And I mean everywhere.

His arms were waiting for me, and as I touched him the bond between us flared to life. The Compass' energy stunned me. I was unable to move or speak, locked on to the massive overload of my quads – so much more power than I'd ever expected they held within themselves. I couldn't understand how it was even possible.

Braxton released me and I was finally able to breathe again. I blinked rapidly as I took the four of them in, and the other Four, who still looked like baby stealing fuckwits to me.

Questions burned across my mind: "How is it that you eight are the only quads in the supernatural world? How are you special? How can you even possess pure souls of each race when your parents are hybrids?"

I figured the other Four were the same, but it was still a guess because I didn't really know anything about them.

I was surprised when one of the Craiz men answered. "For a set of supernatural quads to be produced, there must be the perfect blend of the four races in the parents. The odds of two parents containing the four races actually meeting and producing young ... almost no chance. That's why there are so few of us."

"Why do you receive a calling though?" I was still trying to figure out how all the pieces fit together, and most importantly, how Larky fit. Since both of their callings were about him, there must be some sort of reason for this.

The Four exchanged a glance. Somehow they could all look at each other in the same moment. Because that wasn't weird at all.

"We don't really know," one of them said. "But Larkspur really angered the shining ones, and they don't like that. They'll take great pleasure in sending more than a little bad luck your way."

I suppose that could all be true. The golden dragon had admitted that the shining ones were pretty unhappy with him, and would do anything in their power to ensure he never ruled the five races.

"Wait … there are five races. So why do you talk as if there are only four?"

The Four all grinned, shit-head identical grins. "There are only four original races. The fey and demi-fey are essentially the same. Thousands of years ago the demi-fey broke away and formed their own council, demanding a seat in each prison community. It was a good move, it stopped much of the discrimination they had faced over the years."

Okay then. That was not common knowledge. They'd never taught us that in history class. Even the Compasses looked surprised.

The Four noticed our expressions. "The councils removed that part of our history lessons, so as not to isolate the demi-fey even further."

I had nothing but respect for the demi-fey. Torag was one of my father's oldest friends, and the troll leader was as solid as they come. In all ways. He'd be right there on the front line today, I knew that without any doubt. I was glad they were given a seat on the council.

"Are you ready for this, Jessa babe?" Maximus' voice was deeper than usual, his hair almost black. All of the quads' features had blended into one another again, although they were nowhere near as identical as the Four.

Cardia popped her head out from behind her mate. "Yeah, Jessa, ready to save the day again and have all the men in the world fawn over you?"

There was the snark that had been in her the very first time we'd seen her, which, to be honest, I preferred over the false friendship crap she'd been trying to feed me. I just smiled at her, all polite, but with more teeth than was warranted for a friendly grin. I wasn't going to react, because I understood. Maximus was holding her at arm's length for me, and no mate wanted that to happen. If the future didn't end for us all today, I'd have to corner my vamp. Find out what was truly bothering him.

I turned my back on Cardia, no time at all for her shit. "Where's Grace?" I asked Tyson, not seeing the witch around.

"She's across with the other healers. There're about twenty of them in Louis' little posse. They'll be helping out during the battle." He sounded all casual, exuding so much I don't-give-a-crap-what-Grace-does, but he was pretty informed for someone who didn't care.

"Okay, well, I'm going to stick close to you four," I said to my quads, "and when you figure out how to lock Larky down, I'll crush the locket into his chest. Then we can kill him without having to destroy all the marked." Sounded so simple when I said it like that, but we all knew that nothing to do with the dragon king was simple.

I heard footsteps, and spun to find Louis and Jonathon approaching our section of Stratford's defense line.

"The king's army is gathering to the west," Louis said, wasting no time. "I think they're waiting to be at full capacity before attacking, but according to Mischa the king is already here, so the leaders have decided to hit him now, before the rest of the marked arrive."

I nodded. Sounded like a plan to me. Less marked for the Four to contain, and less minions for the king. Win-win. Louis stepped closer, lurking inside my personal space, but lucky for him he was one of the few supes I liked enough to let this close.

"I'm going to stick with you, Jess. That way, if the Compasses are busy, I'll be able to step in and help you with your task."

I bristled. I was almost a hundred percent sure I could do this shit on my own. It wasn't like smashing through someone's chest cavity was really that difficult. But I wasn't willing to risk my loved ones, so I'd graciously accept his assistance.

"Thanks, Louis, but if you get in my way I'll kick you in the face."

Totally gracious.

His long arm came out and ruffled my ponytail. "Looking forward to it."

I swatted his arm away and stepped back into Braxton, not touching him, because his energy was just a little too much for comfort, but close enough that my mate was satisfied. See, I was not only gracious but an excellent mate.

My dragon was restless inside of me, as if she could sense all of the marked power outside the barrier. Not to mention that damn Larky. We just couldn't get rid of him.

"Prepare yourselves." Louis's power-laden voice carried to all of our people. "I'm preparing to drop the securities. The quads will then lead the way. We let them do their thing, and the rest of us fit our powers in where necessary. No matter what happens, we must stop the king before he controls us all. No single leader should have dictatorship over our races. That's why we have the councils, that's why we all have a higher power to answer to. Now it's time for Larkspur to answer to his."

A sense of unity, of comradeship, filtered down the line. For many of us, our supe natures were violent and power-hungry, but we were also civilized and structured to an extent. We had to be for the supernatural communities to work. Putting five powerful races together, it would be a disaster if run any other way. Larky had forgotten that in his quest to be the most powerful, and I for one was willing to die trying to stop him.

Louis reached out, his hands almost touching the shimmering barrier that surrounded Stratford. I felt the rise of magic, ancient like Faerie magic – elemental, from the earth and sky, the wind, and the living entities which dotted around us. The shimmer started to fade away, and the outside, which had been just visible through the veil, came into clear focus. The noise hit me first. It was loud, and the scents were strong and varied. I was going to go out on a limb and say that dragon dick had not given his marked any downtime for bathing and clean clothes.

I fought the urge to cover my nose; shifter senses were way too strong for this stench. "No need to direct us toward the sweaty ass-crack crew. Larky is clearly not going for stealth with his marked."

There were a few chuckles around. "It's pretty intense," Tyson said, "but maybe your senses are heightened for another reason, Jessa babe?" And thankfully his voice was a whisper.

I hadn't told my father yet about my possible pregnancy. I would rather wait until after Louis could test me. No point announcing my magical baby until we were sure. Then, if I was pregnant, my plan was to drop Mischa's news first. After that no one would worry about mine. See, having a sister could come in useful at times.

We surged forward as a group, the power of the eight quads ricocheting around us, making it really uncomfortable for me to be in the center. I ended up moving to the edge of them for a reprieve. Louis then dropped in to cover my vulnerability, but at least his power was contained within his body and not arcing around like a friggin' lightshow.

Our line of defense was spread out to not leave gaps, but with just enough space so that each supe was able to utilize their power and abilities. We were trained for this type of situation – not that I'd ever had to use my training in actual mass battle before. The magic users were rocking their distinctive golden eyes, connected to their gods and earth power. The fey were wrapped in the four elements, the demi-fey in their most lethal skin. Torag was looking very tree-like at the moment; he would be much harder to kill like that. Each of us was as prepared as we could be to finish this today. There was no way everyone here would survive, because the odds were way stacked against us, but now was not the time to worry about that or let doubts cloud our minds.

Now was the time to fight.

As we closed the gap between the lines, the noise increased, but only briefly before silence descended across the line of the dragon marked. Our pace picked up as we headed straight for where they were flying their dragon spirit flags. Specters were high above, mingling between each other, and it was scary and intimidating.

Larky moved out to stand front and center, his height and golden sheen distinct from the rest of the marked.

"Remember, they have extra speed and strength when they are connected to their mark," I said. "They can mentally communicate with Larky and each other."

The males around me nodded. Cardia just looked bored. Even as we ran, she appeared to be examining her nails. The vamp needed to get her head in the game or she was going to be in trouble. And if she got Maximus hurt or killed because she was a stupid, selfish bitch, I would rip her head off and not even lose a moment of sleep over her death.

We moved swiftly, still some distance between us and the stinky-assed marked minions. I could feel the king's eyes on me. The intensity of his gaze was hot, like someone had directed the sun to focus on me. I was ultra pissed when my mark began to tingle along my side, responding to his energy.

Thankfully my heart and bond remained firmly with the male at my side. Even my dragon, who'd basically been stolen solely to be the mate to Larky, had chosen Braxton. Would it have been harder for me to resist the dragon king if I hadn't already had my own true dragon mate? Thankfully I'd never know. So even though a huge part of me still wanted to kick the fates in the face, another part wanted to kiss them for making sure I had choices, great choices, so I'd never be tempted to the dark side.

My attention zeroed in past the dickhead to the slight form at his side. *Rose*. Why the heck had he brought her along? She looked unhappy, arms crossed over her chest, and I wondered if she'd be a help to our side. I still wasn't sure what her endgame was. She had sent me into the labyrinth, which led to this necklace, but if I hadn't been able to shift to dragon I'd probably have been killed by the creatures in there. So was she helping me or trying to get me out of the way?

The dragon king lifted both of his arms, holding them shoulder-height, palms facing up. His voice boomed across the field to us: "All I want today is Jessa. I'll leave your community alone. You can keep your *Book of Guidance* and seats on the council. You don't have the numbers to best us, so why forfeit your lives so easily? Give me Jessa and I'll forget this rebellion against me, but if you do not … I will wipe every one of you from existence."

Truth. There was a lot of truth in those words, but also deception. Our strides remained strong as we moved toward his massive army. We would not be stopping or making any deals. We didn't negotiate with tyrants.

He must have seen that in our determined faces. I saw his shoulders lift in a shrug. Just like in Rose's memory projection he would kill every supernatural here today, for no reason other than we refused to bow down and allow him to control us and all the power of our races. He would destroy our communities. Criminals would be back in the population. And the human population would face a massacre.

Larky waved his arms in a signal of sorts and my mark started to burn and tingle in a way it had never done before. I had the brief thought that he was issuing some sort of command. My dragon's presence shifted closer to my mind as if she was adding her strength to keep me protected.

I had no idea how Larky had the power or control to be in a collective presence of thousands. Surely that many "voices" would drive him crazy, like drowning in a sea of energy.

The marked started to move, a single mass, the front line a few steps ahead of the rest. I couldn't see any small children, although a few looked like teenagers. I felt the call of energy around me and knew our side was preparing themselves. Larky was not holding back, he was sending them across full force, determined to finish this today and to retrieve me. Which, lucky for him, was what I needed to happen also. The moment he was close enough, I was going to end it.

Chapter 17

It was like time stood still for that second, our two groups raging toward each other, power and energy flying around, chaos in its purest form, and I wondered how many of us would still be standing in the end.

When we were a few dozen yards from the marked minions, the Four dropped back. I could hear the murmuring of sorcerers and magic users as they joined their power to the Craiz men. This would be our best chance to halt a large portion of the marked and give me and the Compasses the moment we needed to take the king down. I just hoped he didn't know about the necklace. If he was prepared for my attack, it would be so much harder.

The Compasses and I didn't stop. Braxton, Maximus, Tyson and Jacob were glowing with power, the swirl of energy above their heads strong and prominent. I could see the focus in their faces; they wanted the king and nothing would stop them. Cardia remained off to the side of Maximus, and just like me, she wasn't getting too close.

I felt the whoosh of the Four's power flutter across my hair then, and I almost gave a shout when the marked froze in front of us. Tendrils of the Four's energy caressed my skin, but my dragon roared to life and sent her energy out to push through theirs. *Thank the gods.* Would have been a bit of a disaster if I had frozen too.

Not waiting for the others to catch up, I went straight into the fray, dashing from one marked to another, cracking them in the temple. We didn't want to kill them. This was a fight most of them had not signed up for, but we needed to make sure they were down and would stay that way for a while. The Four's power had frozen them, but they were still awake and aware. We were just shutting their lights out for a few extra hours.

The Compasses were right with me, all of us moving at super speed to get through the masses. The rest of our people were doing the same. Louis was wicked useful, knocking down about eight at a time with his blasts of power. On top of that he was adding his energy to the Four, and helping in other areas. Dude was an overachiever; we were damn lucky to have him.

The further we moved through the minions, leaving prone bodies in our wake, the more aware the marked were becoming. The Four's power only had so much hold, and we were reaching the edge of that control. I'd lost sight of Larky once the fighting erupted, but I could feel his presence close by. My mark continued to burn and tingle, reminding me that we needed to move our asses and find the king.

"Jessa!"

I looked up from putting down a marked woman and found Rose barreling through bodies toward me.

"I'm so glad I found you. The king is just over there." She pointed me toward the edge of the group, and I caught glimpses of his golden hair above the fighting masses. The marked who were not controlled yet were reaching us now and starting to fight back. I was distracted from Rose when two marked charged me. I sidestepped the first – a fey – before smashing him in the temple. He was down fast. The second was a shifter, but with no fight training. It took me a few moments longer, but I managed to land a solid uppercut that had him seeing stars. It was hard to knock out supernaturals, but when you were strong and knew exactly where to hit them, it was doable.

Rose grabbed my arm. "If you have any way to stop him, you have to do it now."

She was shaking and I wondered what was happening to her.

"What's wrong?" I had to shout to be heard.

"His brothers are coming, and the four together are too strong to fight."

My quads were close, each occupied with fighting and immobilizing marked, but she caught their attention. "What brothers are you talking about, Rose?"

Her big eyes were rimmed in red, tears sprinkling her lashes. "Larkspur is a quad. He and his brothers are the original quads. You weren't the first he dragon mated, his brothers were. But it went wrong. I think because only he's a shifter, the others are pure blooded: fey, magic user, and vampire. Their energy wasn't built to be shifters, and by forcibly dragon mating a soul to each of them, it destroyed their minds – but not their strength. They're close to invincible."

I sucked in a deep breath, trying to figure out what she was talking about. "The shining ones said those other three souls were never mated. They returned to the sky."

Rose clutched me closer. "They did almost die, the souls and his brothers. Larkspur found a sorcerer strong enough to put them into a deep, healing sleep. They remained in this stasis for almost a thousand years, and now they're healthy and strong. They can shift and they're here to destroy your pack. They've come for your mate."

The Compasses tightened ranks around me. They'd heard the entire conversation, even whilst smashing any marked who came at us.

"He knows or suspects that you're pregnant, Jessa." The urgency in Rose's voice increased. "He promised the shadow spawn the first dragon shifter from you, the chosen one, and that's enough for them."

Panicked screams were lodging in my chest, trying to burst free. Braxton's arms wrapped around me, pulling me back into his body. I didn't even care about the surge of power from him, I took comfort from his strength. His massive chest shook around me, and I knew he was close to letting his beast take over.

"Go to Larkspur," Rose said as she glanced back in his direction. "You have to fight him now before his brothers come."

The quads moved even closer, and Braxton set me back on my feet. "Why did he bring you today?" I asked her.

Sorrow had her face dropping, shadows crossing the cocoa color of her stunning skin. "To control the marked he must channel the energy through me. I'm the original. My blood was used to cast the spell. He uses me to issue the commands. That way the crowd of voices and energy doesn't drive him crazy."

Motherfucker. That's how he was doing it. Rose was the conduit for them all.

"I don't think I'll survive any more of the channeling," she said, her voice low enough to be muffled. "In this sort of situation, with close proximity – well, one more time and my mind will fracture. I'm desperately holding on to it. You have to stop him."

I was relieved at the reassurance that she was on our side. All of the sympathy I'd felt for her in the floating castle kicked in again.

"I'm going to kill him," I said to her; the five of us were already moving toward Larky. "Just hold on to your sanity for a little longer."

She sobbed again and my urgency upped another notch. I was running out of time. I had to get to the dragon king before he destroyed her and everyone else here.

We started to run. I dodged to the side to kick out at a marked demi-fey who was choking one of our wizards. My boot hit her in the throat; she choked and gagged for a few moments before a well-placed kick from Tyson shut her lights out. We continued moving, doing what we could to help those in our path, but unable to really stop. I was kind of enjoying smashing marked as we passed them by. Poor minions. Couldn't catch a break.

An opening in the crowd paved a path right to the golden king. He was lazily standing there like he was just waiting for a bus or something. A grin lit up his face when he saw me, and I could tell by the look in those dark eyes that if he captured me today he was not going to let me go again.

Immediately, about ten marked came at us, trying to separate me from the boys. No way was I stupid enough to take him on without help. I threw back my elbow, catching one of the minions in the face, before spinning around to stomp him, hard. The next few minutes were a flurry of activity, the quads and I making short work of putting the rest down.

A charging troll hit me then, knocking me back and barging through to get to Maximus. I managed to stay on my feet, but Braxton's growl rocked over the crowd. There was no way to miss the worried glance he cast at my stomach. I rubbed at my side, giving my mate a smile of reassurance. The troll had only smacked my hip, which was smarting like a bitch. Those troll fuckers hit like steam trains.

Braxton hooked me under one arm, Tyson under the other, and they lifted me free from the mass of bodies blocking my way. As we regrouped, I realized we'd lost Cardia somewhere in the mess, which explained Maximus' distracted glances around.

Not the best thing to be doing when he was right in the middle of fighting that troll who'd hit me. Luckily, the vamp was skilled in many different fighting techniques, and the troll was young and untrained. If Larky had taken the time to actually train his marked, we'd have been screwed for sure.

The second Maximus was free I grabbed his hand. "Come on," I shouted, knowing he was going to double back to find Cardia. "If we can stop this, we save them all. It's our only chance."

The moment I spoke there was a roaring rumble, like one of the magic users had called on a storm. A quick glance up into the glow of the rising sun and I realized it was far worse than a storm. Three dark beasts were cruising toward us, quite distant now, but would be here in moments at the speed dragons moved.

"Shit!" Braxton said. "I'm going to have to shift. Otherwise those three will destroy everyone here."

He was right. Their speed, flames, claws and massive fang filled jaws would cut through the supernaturals. On both sides.

Braxton was strong, I knew that. He held his own against the king, but three versus one ... they would tear him to pieces. I grabbed his arm, the quads' joined energy thrumming across me strong enough that I almost dropped it just as quickly.

"You can't go alone, they're too powerful. There is no way."

I jumped as Louis popped up from somewhere. Sneaky sorcerer. "I'll stay with Jess and help her until you can return. Braxton, you need to shift. It's the only chance. Jacob, Tyson, and Maximus, you need to stick close to him, protect his back. Your calling will work on the king's brothers as well. They're quads, joined together the same as you four are."

Damn. It was all starting to make perfect sense now.

Louis continued: "I didn't know until those dragons appeared, but now I can tell that this is why you and the Craiz brothers have a calling, to fight the original quads who messed with what was not theirs to mess with. The king controls his brothers, their minds were damaged from the forced dragon mating, but they're strong. Do not underestimate them."

Rose's warning had been accurate. The king started all of this when he messed with the sacred bond of dragon mating. Now we had to clean it up. Funnily enough, now that I saw more of the puzzle pieces, I was starting to notice some real parallels between Braxton and Larky. Both were quads and powerful dragon shifters. Arrogant. They loved power and were destined to control and lead, it's just that Larky took it multiple steps too far. I wondered if the dragon king would have followed through on the forcible dragon mating of his brothers had he known the end consequences? That his quest for total domination would destroy his family. Maybe that was actually when he lost the last part of his soul.

My thoughts were put on hold as I was gathered up in the arms of my pack. They had dropped their joining briefly, so I wasn't zapped, although I could still feel the panic and frustration from each of them. Braxton was the last, and as he wrapped his arms around me, his strong body cradling and protecting me for one last moment, I had to fight down the tears.

"Don't die!" I said fiercely as I pulled back from him. "Don't you die, Braxton Compass, because your child and I need and love you more than anything."

He pulled me close enough to drop his lips onto mine. "I promise you, Jess. I will always come for you. Not even death could stop me. Remember, we're a team. Where you go, I will follow."

He kissed me one last time. I didn't want to let him go. Then everyone had to step back to give him space. Louis sent out a wave of energy, scattering those around us. In a blink, my mate was no longer on two legs, but on four massive black and blue, scaled legs. Those large, unblinking yellow eyes locked in on me, and my dragon wanted so badly to shift as well. We had to defend our mate.

Not yet, I reminded her. *We have to stop the king or everyone will die, and Larky will take the baby.*

I loved Braxton with every piece of my heart and soul, but I was pretty sure I loved my child just a little bit more – my young who was vulnerable and needed my protection.

The Compasses climbed onto the back of their colossal brother. I refused to believe that this was the last time I would see them all. And as my boys rose into the air, Braxton's powerful wings lifting them at a rapid rate toward those three beasts, I swear my heart went with them.

"Come on, Jess. You have to trust that they're strong enough to do this."

Louis' hand on my arm forced me to focus. Larky was no longer where he'd been lazing, and my senses were suddenly on high alert. Shit! Where was the creeper now?

Roars split the air above us and I couldn't stop myself from spinning to find my boys in the sky. The king's brothers had circled around the Compasses and were preparing to attack as one from all sides.

"I need to shift," I said to Louis. "I can't leave them up there with just Braxton."

I was in full panic mode now. The king's brothers were huge, each about the same size as Braxton. He would be torn to pieces.

The sorcerer wrapped himself around me, cupping the back of my neck and pulling me in so that our eyes were inches apart. I had no choice but to stare into his mesmerizing purple depths.

"Give them a second. I know you're worried about them, but I think their power will work on the king's kin."

My upper lip lifted as I snarled into that perfect face. "You think? You better pray you're right, sorcerer, or I'm going to rip your freaking head off."

He smiled. Smug bastard. Why was he never afraid? It was disconcerting to be faced with so much confidence. Even the Compasses had their moments of doubt and fear, but besides a little guilt-laden moroseness regarding the death of his chosen mate, Louis was cool as ice.

The roars increased above us, and more than one set of eyes were locked in on a once-in-a-lifetime sight. Four dragon shifters. Three Compass males. One epic battle.

The boys must have let loose with their energy then. I gasped as the dragon-minions halted mid-air as if in suspended animation. Braxton then dived low, the others clinging to his back as he came up underneath the first and the air was saturated in blood and innards as those razor sharp claws eviscerated its soft underbelly.

I could scent the dragon magic. It was strong, especially as the blood flew free.

Braxton changed trajectory, doubling back to dragon two. Jacob and Tyson leapt off his back and landed on the second beast, and in that moment the Compasses must have lost their connection. As the fey and wizard landed, both of the beasts who were still in possession of their guts started to move. The third plummeted from the sky, and all those in the vicinity below had to get out of the way immediately or risk being crushed.

I was distracted from my pack by a bunch of marked storming toward me, their dragon specters spinning dizzily above their heads. I dropped lower, calling on my dragon and wolf, forgetting the sorcerer was at my side. With a lazy flick of his hand, and some well-placed power words, those marked flew off into the distance.

I turned back to my boys, relieved to see that all of them were still fighting. Braxton was going head to head with one of the black dragons. Gouges littered both of their hides, but the other dragon was definitely covered in more injuries. Tyson and Jacob looked to be inflicting plenty of damage on their beast, each of them using blades they had pulled from their own personal arsenal. The quads were always weaponed-up, even if they were just going for breakfast. The dragon was struggling to dislodge them from its back, even with all the dipping and diving going on.

"I told you they'd be fine," Louis said with that humor in his tone again.

I whipped around. "Shut it!" I might just punch him for fun. I knew my eyes were blazing, cheeks flushed as I glared my displeasure.

Louis' reply was cut off by a sweep of air behind us. As we turned, I had a terrible feeling about what I would find there.

Larky, in his dragon form.

"Does your magic work against dragons?" I asked Louis, both of us stepping closer together.

"Not very well," he said. "I have a few tricks which might hold him, but probably not long enough for you to get through the body and into the heart."

About fifty yards separated Larky's beast from us, and there were a lot of marked in between, but I could feel his focus on me. He was coming to get his prize, and I couldn't let myself be taken. He would strip me of my one weapon, our one shot to end this.

The screeching above increased, and a quick glance over my shoulder told me that the Compasses were not doing so great now. The third dragon had somehow repaired that original damage and was back up, tag-teaming with the dragon fighting Braxton and Maximus. Was Larky's marked curse unnaturally keeping his brothers alive too?

"We have to do it now," I said.

With a roar, my dragon pushed herself to the front of my being, desperately trying to force me to change. I knew now why she was so much stronger than a regular dragon spirit, so much more in control and independent from me. She was never supposed to be a mated soul. She was the queen of dragons and her soul was pure power.

But I loved her as much as my wolf, meant to be or not.

"I'm going to shift," I said to the sorcerer, trusting my dragon's instinct. "It doesn't look as if the quads are going to be back anytime soon, and at least in dragon form I'm fast and strong. With your help I might be able to take the king without them." The odds were slim, but I would always give it a fighting shot.

Louis nodded, and I immediately removed the necklace and handed it to him. "Keep this until I need it, I don't want it broken in the fight."

I didn't give him time to answer, and I didn't bother taking my clothes off. I gave free rein to my beast, immediately connecting to the shifter magic inside. The change was seamless and no longer caused me any sort of pain. As my senses heightened, and vision sharpened, I felt calm and in control. My claws sank into the ground, gaining traction, and my tail whipped around and knocked back many of the marked who had been getting a little close.

Hell to the yes. I was awesome – okay, my dragon was awesome, but I was coming a close second just by knowing her.

I bound across the space between Larky and I, covering the distance in seconds. My dragon wanted to connect with Braxton, but I wouldn't let her distract him while he was in such a precarious position. It was up to us to finish Larky first.

The king roared and strode forward. His beast was almost twice the size of mine as we barreled toward each other.

I'm going to kill you, I mentally projected.

You're mine, Jessa. That dragon young you carry inside of you is mine. And I've come to take what's mine.

That jovial nice-dude persona he'd worn around me was gone. I could hear the cold oppressor in his tone and I knew the real Larky was finally rising to the surface.

We clashed, and even my dragon winced at the weight behind him as he slammed into me. I shook myself, long neck swaying in an attempt to get my wits back. I couldn't go at him front-on like that again; he'd just about knocked my head off. Rising to my full height, the two of us starting to circle around, I could feel Louis' magic at my back, along with some familiar scents.

Cardia and Grace had found us.

I continued circling, keeping Larky as my main focus, although I was catching glimpses of more familiar faces. The dragon recognized them as friends and therefore was careful not to hurt them with her sweeping tail or bursts of flames.

Fiery anger clearly swirled in the eyes of the dragon king. I wondered what had him so extra roiled up. His voice slammed into my mind.

You should have been controllable like the rest, but as always those damn shining ones somehow knew this would happen. They knew that after I cursed the most powerful dragon soul and sent it out to be dragon mated to a shifter, together you would be stronger than my command.

Thank the gods for that. Imagine if I'd just capitulated. We'd all be screwed.

You should be at my side, standing against those quads, not carrying a bastard dragon child. We were destined to rule them all. I waited a thousand years for you to be born and unlock the mark. A thousand years for the perfect dragon mating which would produce shifter babies. A thousand years! His voice rose, his cool and calm demeanor disappearing under his rage.

He was losing control, and I was glad about that. Anger would have him make a mistake. Loss of emotions was the worst thing to happen in any fight.

I'll rip that young from your belly and dump it in the barren prison of the shadow spawn. They'll torture and control your dragon shifter child and then unleash him on the shining ones. Faerie will fall to the rule of the shadow spawn and Earth will be ruled by me.

Yeah, because the shadow spawn will be satisfied with just ruling Faerie.

He didn't answer me, but I sensed that my words had struck a chord with him.

What a fucking idiot. He was going to release the shadow spawn, and let them annihilate the one race who could have fought against them, and then he expected they would contain their destruction just within Faerie. Sure. Not a single thing wrong with that plan.

He lunged toward me again, clumsier this time, almost as if he couldn't help himself – like that time in his castle. I knew it was the tie between us. It called to the king.

As he stumbled another step, I thrust my wings sideways and pushed myself up and over the top of him, landing heavily on his back. Immediately my four claws dug in and I tore against his armored hide. He roared and bucked. I didn't have enough traction to keep my footing and ended up flung free, claws full of scales coming with me.

I had to get beneath him. It was where he was most vulnerable, and the easiest access to his heart. I was wasting my time anywhere else.

Louis and the girls caught my attention. The sorcerer had his hands joined with Grace, their lips moving as they cast their spell. I felt the magic; it was strong, starting at Louis and extending outwards. More sorcerers joined in, all linking their magic, trying to offer me a shot at taking down king dick.

A black and gold flecked netting flung from the circle of magic users, skimming across my head before settling over the dragon king. He roared, and slashed out, but the spelled mesh held for that moment, the magic infusing it with an unbreakable bond. I ran at him, lowering my head at the last second to crash into his side, hoping to knock him over and expose that underbelly.

Our two beasts went down in a mass of dragon, and despite some pain from the tumble I started blindly ripping into him. The netting was holding him down on his side, his powerful wings restrained. This was my best shot.

I dug at the dirt surrounding us, and was able to get in under the barrier with my two front claws. My talons sank easily into the softer belly flesh, but before I could get in far enough to smash through the ribs to his heart, the netting flickered and disappeared.

The magic users had been set upon by about a thousand marked. *Shit*. Larky had put out a call for help, and it looked like his second group of minions were finally here. There was no one left to hold them at bay. The Four were either dead or still stuck keeping some marked contained; our people were so vastly outnumbered.

That didn't stop Louis and his friends from letting loose. He and the magic users were brutal, smashing through the marked with graceful death. Cardia was also in her element, snarling with brilliantly white fangs as she pounced on a marked and ripped his head clear off his shoulders. Dammit, so much for trying to keep them alive; the marked were dying left right and center. But so were our people. There was nothing I could do, I was still locked in a deadly tussle with the dragon king, and one wrong move could end it all.

Chapter 18

Even though Larky was free from the netting, I hadn't given up trying to gain traction against him. I clawed and bit, my mouth filled with flesh as I tried my best to inflict enough injuries to slow the king down.

His wounds healed almost instantly. I couldn't even keep them open long enough for decent blood loss. It was so frustrating, and a huge reminder that he was pretty much impervious to injury while still connected to the marked. I had to break that bond to stand a chance.

Larky roared again, flames shooting skyward. Dragon dick was pissed and there was no doubt that things were about to go bad for me. He kicked out with those powerful back legs and I was flung far, my wings flapping to stop me from completely eating shit. As my adrenalin hit an all-time high, my dragon and I merged closer, more in sync than ever. Both of us had the same goals, and there was no way we were going to give up.

I rolled to the side as Larky landed heavily in front of me, squishing about eight of his own marked supes in the process. The battle raged around us. It looked like my boys were back down to fighting two dragons, their group flying a lot closer to the ground now. As they lost strength, they lost elevation.

My attention was diverted as Larky slashed out at me. I avoided the front set of claws, but wasn't quick enough for the follow-through. His back talons sliced through my body, severing part of my right front leg. He was so much faster and more dexterous than me. I just didn't have enough experience in my dragon form. The injury was deep. He'd severed my muscles, leaving me no way to hold my own weight.

Jessa!

Braxton's voice filled my mind. I wanted to growl. He'd been keeping an eye on me, probably distracting himself in his own battle. Still, that rumbly tone was the best sound in the world, somehow drowning out my pain and the worry. The same way my dragon filled me with confidence, Braxton did also.

I'm okay. Focus on your fight. Finish those bastards and then get back here and help me.

I'll be right there, my mate.

I could hear the promise in his voice. He'd be there for me as soon as he could. I spun as Larky slashed at me again. I was already off kilter and could do nothing but flap my wings and take to the sky. My injury was already healing, but not quickly enough.

Larky followed me, and despite wanting Braxton more than anything, I made sure to head away from the other dragon battle. I skimmed across the land, and as a large shadow crossed over me, I dropped down again, into a space at the back of the fighting. I wanted to be clear of the marked before we fought again. I wouldn't kill more than I had to. They had already been dealt the shit-life hand.

I landed heavily, front leg still useless. The king was right up my ass. I couldn't shake him, and I got the sense that he was going to finish this now – injure me badly, force me to shift back to human. Then he could carry me off to his baby-making lair.

My leg was getting stronger and the bleeding had slowed, so when he dived on me I found the strength to roll away. Larky definitely had not expected me to do that. Slipping beneath him, I clawed straight up into his gut.

Hells yeah!

I clawed with all my strength, my jaws clamped onto his throat, tearing and fighting. He was trying to break free, but I held him down for as long as I could, ripping away at the layers of his underbelly.

Louis!

I mentally screamed for the sorcerer, hoping like hell he was close by with the necklace. There was no answer at first, and I was losing traction – and hope – when his voice echoed across me.

"Jessa, you need to hold him for another minute."

Louis was close but there was no easy way for him to get between our fighting beasts. Larky freed himself from one of my claws, and as I struggled to hold him I heard a long, bellowing roar laden with dragon energy.

Larky ripped himself from the rest of my claws and turned the tables on me, locking his jaws over my throat, lifting me up. I hung there for a split second before my fighting instincts kicked in and I thrashed out at him. I was slower now. I was starting to weaken from my injuries.

The king's voice sneered in my head. *You know, I don't think you're worth the trouble. I can rule the supe world with the marked alone, and if I don't have any offspring, the shadow ones will still be locked away, unable to exact revenge on me.*

He murmured like he was speaking to himself, but it was clear he wanted me to know I was no longer valuable to him, that he was preparing to kill me and my child.

I fought harder, but that only forced his claws and teeth deeper into my body. I slashed out and tore into the ribs on his right side, inflicting an injury which might actually slow him down. In fact … his heart was visible. *Shit.* I didn't have the necklace and I couldn't see Louis.

My head went fuzzy as Larky crushed my throat, and at the same time tore across both of my wing joints and shoulder blades. I tried to bellow but no noise emerged. The pain was everywhere and all encompassing. He'd completely disabled every avenue I had to escape.

That other roar sounded again, and I tried to remain focused, needing to know which dragon was closing in. Usually I'd think Braxton, but for some reason it sounded different. A weight landed on us; the hold Larky had on me eased and I was flung free.

I caught a glimpse of Louis as I sailed past. Air expelled from me in one huff as I hit the ground, my eyes closed, my dragon and I both struggling through our pain. I almost couldn't handle it. Energy washed over me then, cool hands touching my side.

Normally that would make this supe very stupid, touching an injured dragon, but I was in no position to fight now.

"Jess! Girl, you have to change back." I knew that voice, that scent. *Grace.* Her gentle energy wrapping around me.

I opened my eyes, struggling to lift my head. Grace was disheveled, her hair everywhere. Dirt covered her face and there was a gash along her chin and down to her collarbone. Cardia stood protectively over her; it looked like they had been working together for most of the fight.

The healer witch appealed to me again: "I can't heal you in your dragon form, the magic just rebounds back to me." Her large eyes were glassy; she was swaying on her feet.

I'd say Grace was pretty much at the end of her ability to heal anyway. Still, I knew she was right. I had to change back to human and hope she could patch me up enough to give me another shot at the king. I reached for the magic, the shifter energy which made up the core of my being. My dragon had already let go of her control; she wanted me to shift and save both of our lives.

Internally, I scraped myself toward the energy, trying to hurry because I was losing a lot of blood. Finally, by the tip of my fingers, I managed to yank a strand toward me, sobbing as the change washed over me.

The shift back was brutal. My energy was low, and the agony of trying to change around massive damage had black dots dancing across my vision. When I was about halfway done, a shadow loomed over the back of the two girls. I tried to shout a warning, but my vocal cords were stuck between dragon and Jessa.

Cardia sensed the marked at the last moment and whipped around so fast she was a vampire blur. But it was a second too late for Maximus' mate. As the sword swung around, slicing clean through Cardia's neck and partially severing her head, my vocal cords returned. Screams ripped over the battlefield as I watched on in horror.

It was like the world was moving in slow motion. Grace, who was the gentlest of supes, suddenly went feral and blasted out at the sword-wielding marked with some sort of spell. By the time she was done, the vampire who had ended Cardia was a scorch mark on the earth. Grace then dropped down beside the vampiress, sobs ringing from her. Finally finished my shift, I dragged myself to them, willing to offer whatever energy I could to help heal the fallen supe.

"No, no, no ... too much damage." Grace was murmuring through her sobs and I knew that it was too late for Cardia.

There was no saving Maximus's mate. My heart squeezed tightly in my chest, nausea rocketing through my gut. My vampire was going to be devastated by this. He would never be the same daredevil, carefree, over-protective, larger-than-life Compass again. This would ruin him, reduce him to a shell of the supe he was now.

More energy flowed as Grace tried again; she hadn't given up. I could tell how much she cared for Cardia. The two had probably spent a lot of time together while the rest of us were stuck in Faerie. Grace finished sealing the wound on Cardia's neck, basically reattaching her head, then she sliced across her own wrist, feeding blood into the vampire's mouth. I watched in silence, not surprised when there was no movement, no beat of Cardia's heart and no signs of regeneration. She was gone.

Still Grace wouldn't give up, and as she bled her paleness increased to worrying levels. Finally, I shoved her aside.

"Heal your wrist," I managed to mutter, before taking Grace's knife – I was naked and weaponless – and slicing my own wrist. I placed it against Cardia's mouth.

I was only doing this for Maximus, so he knew that we did everything we could.

Despite my pain and injuries exhausting me, tendrils of panic thrummed through me. I couldn't see anything through the mass of sorcerers which surrounded us and had no idea where the dragon king had disappeared to. Energy brushed against me, strong and ancient, and relief surged as Louis and some of his sorcerers pushed through the crowd.

He dropped down at my side, laying both hands on Cardia. His eyes fluttered closed, and when they reopened the dull emptiness there confirmed what I'd already known. There was nothing more we could do.

"She's gone. Her soul has moved past this world and can no longer be retrieved." He touched my wrist. Clothing covered me, followed by the burn of a healing. I almost collapsed as the warmth spread everywhere, accelerating the healing which I'd already started with my shift.

Beside us, Grace was hunched forward, her hands on her legs, head hanging low. Tears silently dropped off her cheeks; the pain she was exuding was tangible. I was also mourning, and not because Cardia had been my friend, but because she had been mated to Maximus, and that made her important, made her my pack. I couldn't stand to think of his pain right now. He would already know and was probably incapacitated; hopefully the boys had him, and wouldn't let him plunge to his death in grief or something. It had been known to happen.

As my body finished its repairs, with Louis' help, I was able to focus on my task again. The king needed to die and he needed to die now. Where the hell had he gone? I thought for sure he'd have been here, trying to finish me off when I was at my most injured, but there had been that roar and then nothing.

As the last of Louis' power evaporated, a sense of rejuvenation filled me and I stumbled to my feet, before straightening to my full height. A sparkle of gold caught my eye.

What the actual fu–

Five dragons were fighting: two of the king's black-as-night brothers; Braxton's blue-black beast; Larky, who glowed black, red, and orange; and the last larger than all the rest, and pure gold.

"She came," I said, my nails digging into my palms. "That's the queen of the dragons. She just saved my damn life."

She had torn the king off me before he could finish crushing me, saving my life, Josephina's, and the young who resided inside of me. We might actually stand a chance now; she was stronger than any other dragon.

"Should I shift?" I said, not really asking anyone in particular. "I could help."

Louis wrapped a hand around mine, and when he pulled away the necklace rested in my palm. "You're still weak. I haven't had time to heal you properly. I think if you shift one more time today you'll probably fall into a healing sleep. You can be just as helpful down here, making sure you finish it off when the queen brings him down."

He was probably right. I could still feel the recent injuries, the weakness inside my blood and muscles. Louis normally would have fixed that right up, but the sorcerer was spent. He'd maxed out his energy today.

"I need to get closer," I said taking off at a stumbling run, my legs needing a few moments to get the blood flowing.

I pushed through the marked, most of whom had stopped fighting and were all staring up into the sky. I thought at first they were just captivated by five dragons in battle, but then I noticed the dragon specters. They were swirling high, higher than I'd ever seen before, and linking directly to the king. He was calling on every ounce of power to beat the queen.

"Knock out the marked!" Louis was yelling. "Knock out the marked now!" His power-laden words drifting through the crowd. All members from our side – those still standing – lurched into action. This was the perfect time, as the marked were all distracted assisting the king, and the more we took out, the less power Larky had at his disposal.

"Jess! Are you okay?"

Jonathon was sprinting toward me across the bloody field, and I found myself swept up in his embrace. "I saw your dragon fall. I thought the worst. I'm ... I'm so goddamn happy to see you."

I collapsed against him, allowing a second of comfort before I started urging my father to run with me. I had to get closer to the battling beasts.

"Is Mom okay?" I asked as we scrambled through the crowd, both of us knocking out as many marked as we could on the way.

"Yep, I sent her back with Mischa. Your sister managed to get free. I had to knock her out."

I winced. My sister really had to tell our parents that she was pregnant. Although, I'd bet Lienda knew now after carrying her back to the hall. It would be hard to miss that little belly. One consolation was that Jonathon knocking her out was better than someone else mistaking her for one of Larky's and killing her.

Jonathon followed my line of sight. "Where did the golden dragon come from?"

He had heard the story from Faerie. All of the leaders knew what the shining ones had said about Larky, but seeing it in the flesh was quite another thing. She was even bigger than the dragon king, and still too stunning to stare directly at, sparkling pure gold in the sunlight.

I quickly explained again the true majesty of Chrysandra. She was queen of dragons and had joined the battle for one reason only. Larky had killed her child.

Awe crossed Jonathon's features; my father wasn't easily impressed, but Chrysandra was a rare exception of power and beauty, even in our world. They were directly above us now. Braxton had separated out and was fighting against the two black dragons again. From my angle it looked as if the rest of the Compasses were on his back, but it was hard to tell. Hopefully the third of Larky's brothers was down permanently. Braxton did not need another beast to fight.

Clenching my sweaty hand around the charm, my fingers flexed as I waited for an opening.

Larky and the queen swirled closer. The golden dragon struck out hard and fast, leaving bloody gashes along the king's hide. For some reason, whenever she did, the wound lasted longer than when I had, her magic working against him.

The marked dragon energy was still swirling into the sky, slowly filtering to the king. I could see a large cloud of specters about to hit him, a ton of power, and I was suddenly afraid for the queen. My dragon bellowed within me, her emotions a mess as we were forced to wait on the sidelines, helpless. My poor Josephina; it was colossally unfair that such a majestic creature had become a prisoner. I loved her enough that I wished things were different for her. Unlike the other souls who had chosen to be mated, she should be free.

When that dark, misty mass of marked energy finally reached the king, the air exploded around him. I could see vibrations of power absorbing directly into that fucker. He grew in size, quickly reaching the girth and length of the golden queen. There was no hesitation in his attack now. He went in straight and fast, wings heavy and strong. I jumped as his talons caught hold of her tail and ripped a large chunk out. At the same time his jaws clamped down on her flank. She twisted, her back talons gouging his underbelly.

The pair of them clutched together; neither could break free, both losing blood, but nothing too serious. Then the king released her flank and went straight for her throat. The queen snaked to the side, avoiding the first hit, but was unable to dodge the second. He had her in a vulnerable position, but somehow she slashed up with her lower half, nearly tearing Larky in two.

Jonathon had me up in his arms and was running. The dragons were coming down, and we were right beneath their massive bodies. As the pair hit behind us, the ground shook like a mini-earthquake and both of us were flung sprawled out in the dirt. I rolled over and clutched at my stomach. *Shit.* That was a hard fall straight onto my front. I couldn't think about it yet, about how I might be pregnant and my child might be hurt. I had to focus on the dragons.

My fear and adrenalin were high and I sprang to my feet. I was going to end this shit before anyone else died. The pair were still locked together. The golden dragon was slowing, her movements less sure, and because her head was facing in my direction, I could see how glassy her eyes were. The red jewels had lost their shine.

Her chiming voice, filled with ancient energy, rang through my mind.

I will hold him. Use the blood.

I still held the necklace in my hand. I ran, not looking left or right, unable to see anything but the entangled dragons, determined to get close to Larky without being speared to death from flailing talons.

The queen had pretty much totally eviscerated his beast, and yet he was already starting to heal.

With his head locked on her throat, he didn't see me dashing up behind them. I dodged a flying tail and the spray of blood which followed, before ducking beneath a large red wing, spread wide and flapping frantically to try and gain traction. I was quick and small, slipping into gaps, and then with a deep breath I dived over the locked bodies to land in a small gap between the two. The king was still looking in the wrong direction. Here's hoping that his blind focus on killing the golden dragon would be the reason he lost his life.

Do it, my child. Take care of my ... my daughter.

My heart was trying to beat out of my chest. The queen was falling and I couldn't stand the agony of watching her die. Beat by beat, minute by minute, she held on and fought with everything she had, giving me the time I needed. My dragon snapped me out of my agonized fear and mourning, forcing me to focus, shifting my hand into a talon claw. Without thought, I moved and when I was close enough I plunged my hand straight into Larky's chest, breaking through scales, skin, bone and muscle.

His dragon heart was massive, no way for me to miss it. The second I felt the beating rhythm, I clenched my claw tight. It took a moment for the glass to give, stronger than I expected, but it broke at the very instant Larky released the golden queen and turned to repel me. I plunged the bleeding jewel deep into his heart, leaving it there as I yanked my hand free.

I knew I had seconds to get free from my position between the two beasts, the dragon king was hurt, but not dead and he would be coming for me. I was also trying to contain my panic for the golden dragon, she lay still, too hurt to move, though I could still feel her essence. All was not lost yet. Just as I was backpedaling, trying to get free, I was grabbed roughly from behind.

Chapter 19

The binding across my middle felt unbreakable. But I'd come too far now to just give up. I threw out both arms, hands shifting to wolf claws so I could fight, but just as I struck I caught a glimpse of a very familiar pair of blue-black scaled legs. *Oh thank the freakin' gods.* Braxton. It was too late to halt my attack, but luckily my claws just grazed his hide.

My mate had yanked me out of the dragon pile just in time. Larky was on his feet, unsteady but still preparing to go after me. Had the necklace worked? Why was he still moving and healing? Screams started around us, and one by one the marked started to fall, literally falling to their knees and then onto their backs, as if they couldn't stand for a moment longer. The frantic cries surrounded us on all sides; it was deafening, and I tried in vain to lift my arms to cover my ears.

Braxton set me on my feet a few meters away, and immediately fell into a protective pose. He used his bulk to block my body from Larky, who was coming straight for us. I had half my attention on that asshat and the other half on the golden dragon. Her eyes were still open but she was not moving, and blood continued pouring freely from her.

Finish him, my child. I will wait for you. There is something I must tell you.

Don't die, I choked out. *I'm on my way.*

There was no reply, but at least her eyes remained open. I returned my full attention to the massive scaled beast advancing on us. I was overflowing with anger, and was just about to shift into dragon when I felt the pull of energy around us. Larky shifted back to his human form.

Okay, he wants to do this on two legs.

More energy rocked the air around us, and then Braxton was back in his hot-as-fuck skin. Larky clothed himself, clearly still possessing enough borrowed magic to do that simple spell. A nearby sorcerer, who ducked out of the crowd, clothed Braxton. The dragon king strode toward us, looking a little shaky on his feet.

"I'm going to destroy you both. I killed the queen of the dragons and shining ones. There's no way you two stand a chance."

He was already bragging, which is how I knew he was much more worried than he let on. No one talked a big game unless they were trying to figure out what the hell to do. Nope, they attacked and got it over with.

"Jess, baby," said Braxton, "you know I love you more than anything in this world, but if you don't give me the pleasure of killing this fucker, I'm going to be a real pain in the ass to live with for the next few years."

I snorted, my heart flip-flopping at that confidence. My mate might be looking a little battle weary right now, but I knew he could take the king. Not to mention with the parallels between Braxton and Larky – which were probably due to the shining one's interference – it felt like Braxton was the one chosen to end this. Still, for the sake of future relationship decisions I wasn't rolling over for him that easily. Hands on hips, I tapped my foot.

"Give me one good reason why you should get the pleasure of killing him. I deserve this kill. It's mine."

Braxton captured my face in both of his hands. His lips were hard and fast as they crashed down onto mine. "The kill might be yours, Jess, but you're mine. I've had to watch him kidnap and hurt you over and over. It's my turn now to protect you."

I sighed, and with a wave of my hand, let him have this one. Damn pregnancy hormones were making me soft. I settled back to watch the show. There would be no unfair advantages today. Larky was no longer impervious to true injury and Braxton was going to make him hurt bad.

As the pair started to circle each other, I found myself bouncing, as if preparing for my chance to be tapped into the fight. Wasn't going to happen. I knew Braxton. There would nothing left but spatter for the supe council to clean up.

"You're a dead man, Larky," I said, throwing as much attitude as I could. I'd love to put him on the defense straight up.

He turned those stormy eyes on me. "I tolerated that horrible nickname initially, in deference to our mateship, but no more will you disrespect me."

I snorted, before cracking right up. He could not be serious. Disrespect was the last thing he needed to worry about.

"You need to take your eyes off her now," Braxton said, not a lick of emotion in his voice.

Uh oh, Larky was in trouble.

The dragon king gave me one last narrow-eyed glare, before facing my mate. "You're powerful, I'll give you that, but you don't stand a chance against me. You're young. A child. And after I kill you, I'm going to kill your brothers. Every single one. Then your mate, and lastly the child she holds nestled in her womb."

I heard the sharp intake of breath behind me, and saw that both Grace and Jonathon were close enough to have heard his words. My father's eyes, a cobalt blue, stared at me with both shock and awe.

"Is it true? You're pregnant...?"

It took two steps for me to reach his side and capture his hand. "We don't know that I am. There's been no time for any confirmation spells, but the possibility is high."

I had always talked a big game about not wanting children, and, truthfully, until I was faced with the prospect of having one, I had never wanted any. Now though...

"If I'm pregnant, Dad, then you should know that Braxton and I are already madly in love with our rugrat."

He blinked a few times, as if trying to wrap his mind around that. "I think I'm a little young to be a pa, but Lienda is going to be overjoyed."

There was no more time for hugs. I wanted front row seats to the end of Larky. Braxton looked like a statue, his features hard, eyes blazing blue. The taunting from the dragon king had struck a chord with my mate. The thought that he could lose his brothers, or me and his child ... it was enough to have his temper flaring. Thankfully he had enough fight experience to compartmentalize those emotions, to focus on what he had to do.

Braxton side-stepped the king's first well-placed jab before swinging around to clip the douchebucket up the side of the face. Larky stumbled and then righted himself, coming at

Braxton again. My mate dodged for a second time and kicked out with a roundhouse, which knocked into Larky's throat, slamming the golden-haired male to the ground.

I thought for a second that Braxton was going to draw it out, make him suffer, but he must have decided that this piece of shit was not worth one extra second of his time or attention. In his mind Larky was already dead. He'd been a dead man walking from the second he stole me away. Braxton yanked up the so-called dragon king, wrapping his arm across his neck and flexing tight enough to cut off all his air.

"How does it feel to know you can die now? That no longer will the lives of others keep yours unnaturally long." Braxton's voice was low, controlled. "Make peace with your gods, because this time when your head is removed, there's no coming back."

The king started to buck and kick out. His arms were flailing, knocking into Braxton – who looked quite immovable. I gasped as my mate released his hold, but I didn't have to worry. He was fast enough to grasp Larky on either side of his head, and twist. The first crack was barely audible, and then in the same beat a much larger snap heralded the removal of the king's head. Ironic that he would die again, in the same manner as a thousand years ago, only this time, as Braxton has said, there was no coming back for Larky. His curse and reign of terror were over.

We'd gathered quite a crowd, and a cheer rang out. Braxton tossed the head behind him before speeding toward me. I met him halfway, throwing myself into his arms. Our kiss was hot as hell, his tongue stroking against my own. Still, my joy was short-lived. There was no time now for the make-out session which I was dying to have. I needed to get to the queen of the dragons.

Braxton must have sensed that need, because he spun and started to run. The sky was darkening, an unnatural shadow descending across the land. The death of the king and the breaking of his curse had fractured some of the magic from Faerie, and the end result was a magical storm.

We reached the golden beast in seconds, and Braxton let me go free to fling myself down beside her. My dragon, who'd been quietly waiting, started to mourn again. Tears streamed down my face at the aching keen of her cry.

Mother, we cried, and those large red eyes flickered open again. I saw the history of our land in those jewels, so much knowledge, so much power.

Child, well done. You have achieved so much. Your strength makes all of us from the royal line proud. You're a true queen, and so is your friend Jessa.

I was still crying and trying to push myself back so that my dragon could be as close as possible to her mother.

I'm dying, my child. There is no reversing the injuries. They were fatal from before I crashed into the ground ... I did not tell you ... better you focused on ending Larkspur. I held on long enough to speak with you, but now my souls are ready to be released to our gods in the great blue sky.

No! No, she couldn't die. The world needed her leadership, the dragons needed her. There was no other to take her place. My dragon strained against me, and I wished so hard that I could let her go. It hurt my heart more than I thought possible to consider losing her and our bond, but I would let her go in an instant if it were possible.

The queen's voice was faltering, her eyes barely open.

Josephina and Jessa, you have a choice to make. My dragonling, there's a chance that your soul can take the place of mine. If Jessa releases the bond, there will be enough energy to repair the dragon body. It would be a great sacrifice, Jessa. You would lose much strength, and the ability to shift to dragon. More importantly you will lose the ability to have dragon babies.

Am I pregnant now? Will it hurt my child?

Her reply was so faint I had to strain to hear. *You are indeed, twin souls. And no, they will be ... healthy. Perfect. So much responsibility...*

My dragon swirled inside of me, and I could sense that she wasn't sure what the right decision was. She didn't want to leave me, but in the end the decision was mine to make, my hard choice.

I don't know what made me look over my shoulder then, some sort of sixth sense that knew eyes were watching me. Sure enough, standing along the line of trees in the distance was a row of jinn, a black and red line of death. There were at least fifty of those fortune-telling asstards there, and I remembered the message from the jinn in the labyrinth. They would not interfere if I made the right decision. Was that what they waited for?

Turning back to the golden queen, I clenched my hands so hard that my fingers ached. There was really only one choice I could make in this situation. Josephina deserved to be free.

The golden dragon faded away then, but in one last burst of energy she placed in my head the knowledge of touching and removing dragon souls.

I pretty much hadn't stopped crying since I'd knelt at the queen's side, and as she left us in a flash of bright light and ancient power, I screamed out in pain. The agony of her death was enough that for a moment I lost all sense of time and space. My dragon was in the same place, her hurt fueling mine further. In the end it was the wolf soul which gave us focus, reminding us that we needed to act now or lose the golden dragon body forever.

Breathing deeply, I let the knowledge of how to free Josephina wrap across my mind. It was almost easy to open up the part of my soul which belonged to my dragon, and before she could protest I tore her beautiful, glowing energy free. Somehow I didn't die in that moment when the pain of a thousand fires flooded me. Weakness tore along my limbs and struck through my heart.

My dragon cried out, her soul fighting the parting; we didn't want to lose each other, but there was no other choice. I found myself curved around the golden body, clinging to her, sobs ripping from me. I felt lost and broken without my dragon, empty inside, like I was half a supernatural now.

My wolf soul wrapped around me, using pack warmth to offer whatever comfort she could. Arms enveloped me also, and with a snap like a rubber band, the bond between Braxton and I sprang to life, hard and complete for the first time since the sanctuary. I gasped as his energy flooded my mind and heart, visible ties which bounced free before disappearing completely.

Baby... His voice was filled with something that went beyond joy, like pure awe. *This is right. We're truly bonded.*

We were, but I was no longer dragon mated, and that small part of my soul felt like it was dying. I was not so far gone in my own misery that I didn't notice the group of jinn cast me one last look before fading back into the trees, taking with them that uneasy feeling of eyes crawling all over me. Seemed I had made the right decision after all. I'd righted the wrong from so many years ago. I just wish it didn't hurt so badly. My soul literally ached.

The golden limb closest to us started to twitch. I huffed in and out, my breathing rapid and shallow before stopping completely as the golden dragon lumbered gracefully to her feet and lifted her snout to the sky. She roared, smoke flowing freely, and followed with a long plume of red hot flames tinged in blue.

I knew I should be happy – the dragons had their queen back, and the soul of my beast was free – but it still hurt so much. In that moment, Braxton's dragon and energy intermingled with mine.

We're here, Jess. You're not alone. You're still dragon mated, to me and my beast. We're one.

I closed my eyes and truly felt those words, felt all of the emotion zooming between us. It took me some time, almost as if I were going through the steps of grieving in mere seconds, but for some reason his reassurance made the hurt a little less intense. He was right, I was going to be okay. I had him and his beast, and it was comforting to be able to touch the familiar dragon energy.

A snout brushed against me and I opened my eyes. The golden dragon had her head lowered and she looked to be smiling as she snaked herself closer.

Hello, my Jessa.

She sounded like her mother, only her energy was a little different. Softer.

I miss you already, I cried out to her. There were extra fractures in my heart, and the sorrow was seeping out.

I will always be with you. I'm just a short trip to Faerie. We can visit anytime.

I nodded. I knew this logically, but it wasn't going to be the same.

I will be dragon mother to your offspring, loved by me as much as I love you.

I reached up and wrapped both of my arms around her, and I could feel the humming happiness from deep in her chest.

I have to return to Faerie now. I must bond with the wild ones and we must reinforce the prison of the shadow spawn. Then I need to spread the word of my mother's death – a time for mourning. And

Larky's – a cause for celebration. We'll see each other again very soon.

If I wasn't so miserable, I'd have laughed at her use of *Larky*. I had definitely rubbed off on her. Forcing the next lot of tears to remain at bay, I gave her one last hug before stepping back. I knew I had to let her go now for good. She was very important, and had much to do to cement her new role.

Will you be okay? Faerie can be dangerous.

I have the memories of my mother to guide me. I will make mistakes but I will learn fast. You taught me that. To never lie down. To never give up. You're the strongest of any supernatural, and what I learned from you will make me a good leader.

She touched her snout to my brow. The heat of her energy caressed my skin and then she was gone, strong wings flapping her up into the sky. A step through flashed in the storm, then she disappeared. I wrapped both arms across myself and tried to hold it together.

The supes around me were scurrying about, healing each other, moving the dead, cleaning up this massacre so that no humans stumbled upon the absolute carnage we'd wrought here. But I couldn't move.

I knew that all of my pack was close by, and since I hadn't been sure I'd ever see them all again, I should be celebrating. I told myself to cross over to where Grace was healing Tyson – my wizard Compass had a massive gash along his face and half his eye was hanging from his head. Or step closer to Louis, who was waving his hands over Maximus, putting him into some sort of sleep stasis. The vampire looked like shit, emaciated worse than I'd ever seen; the death of his mate had brought him down when the dragon quads couldn't. Even Jacob could have used some help. His body was riddled with massive burns, third degree in most places – he'd been caught in dragon flame.

I still couldn't move.

Arms cradled me again, lifting me. I cursed myself for my weakness, knowing I had to snap out of it. No one else was falling apart, no one else was allowed to wallow in misery when there was still a crap-ton of work to do to fix this mess.

"Jessa!"

The twin connection flared to life, and before I thought twice on it, I was running into Mischa's arms.

"Jess, you're okay." She hugged me so tightly I feared for a second that I was going to pop her preggo belly. "The king is gone from my mind. The mark is gone from my back. We're finally free. There is no more need to fear the dragon king."

I wondered then. Pulling back, I lifted my shirt … the swirl of my massive mark was visible in the half-light of the stormy sky, black and red, though no longer moving. Now it was a solid tribal, tattoo-like print.

Braxton reached out and lightly dragged his fingertips along it. "This was never about Larkspur. You weren't really dragon marked, you were dragon mated. This is the mark of the queen's line, and you will forever wear it." His voice went into that lower growly timbre which wreaked havoc with all my girly parts. "Still the sexiest thing I've ever seen."

He looked straight into my eyes and more of our bond clicked into place. The strength of my ties to my twin and my true mate were so much more intense now. The loss of Josephina had allowed my soul enough freedom to bond properly with them.

In that moment I mentally accepted my loss ... and felt all of my gains. As I let go of so much of my sorrow, a sense of completeness washed through me. It was as if my mind simply had to understand that it was okay to lose my dragon. She was still there, she still lived, and now I was complete in other ways.

I hugged Mischa again. "I feel the true bond of twins now. I'm so glad you're back in my life."

"Me too," she said, a little muffled. "I love you, Jessa."

Just as I was pulling back, I felt her stiffen. We were touching, so I could have tapped into our bond and listened to her thoughts, but it was better to let her tell me when she was ready.

"What happened to Max?" she finally murmured.

Right! My vampire. I linked one hand with Braxton and the other with Mischa before dragging them toward the boys.

"His mate was killed," I said, my words catching. The pain of my loss was dulling now, allowing me to feel the pain of other losses. "He needs us."

Braxton's relief was palpable. I was mentally and emotionally back with him and we could now focus on Maximus. This was his brother, his quad; they shared a bond even stronger than Mischa and me.

"Were there any other deaths?" I asked as we made our way to the small gathering around the Compasses.

"The Four didn't make it," Braxton said. "One of them was mobbed, and their bond was so strong that to take one out took them all out."

"I meant any other deaths I give a shit about."

Harsh maybe, but those fuckers deserved to die. I was just glad they managed to at least help a little first.

"We lost more than half of our people, and I believe that Torag, Julianna, and Galiani were all cut down. Besides Jonathon, Stratford is basically leaderless."

My heart ached at the death of the demi-fey leader, Torag. He had been a family friend and a good troll. All of the others, especially our leaders, were also massive losses to the supernatural world.

"Louis lost ten sorcerers. No doubt we'd have had many more casualties if it wasn't for the healers. There are also at least five hundred dead marked, and a thousand injured. All of them should make a full recovery when they awake."

As more lightning crashed in the magical storm, I was reminded of the fighting that went on above us. "What about Larky's brothers?"

"When you broke the curse, a step through opened behind us. They were pulled through. I assume they're in Faerie right now, probably having those stolen dragons ripped from their souls. They were tough bastards, but empty, just puppets."

The supernatural world was in utter chaos, supes scattered all around, prison towns all but abandoned. New leaderships would have to be called early for all of the towns Larky hit, and I knew what that meant. The Compasses would have to step up. Responsibility would fall on them two years before it was meant to.

We reached the boys, and I freed my hands so I could wrap myself around Jacob. "I'm so glad you're okay, Jake. I love you so much."

He returned my hug, wincing as I rubbed against his burns. "I love you too, Jess. Thank you for kicking his ass long enough for the golden dragon to arrive."

I snorted, enjoying the moment of being wrapped up in the elemental magic of my fey Compass. "He did a lot of the ass kicking actually. But somehow we made it."

His lips grazed my cheek, a gentle kiss, before I was passed off to Tyson. The wizard was looking a lot better. His magic hummed as I wrapped myself around him.

"Feeling a lot like a sorcerer, my friend."

I was teasing him, but there was that distinct sorcerer hum to his energy.

"You always know what to say, Jessa babe, to keep a male happy."

I patted him on his cheek, the one which had no damage, and pulled myself up. Next on my list was Maximus. He was not conscious, but I couldn't stop myself from reaching down and sprawling across his broad chest. I slowed my heartbeats to match his, and lay there offering comfort for as long as I could.

"We love you, Max. Please come back to us. Cardia would want you to live, to return to your pack. You know we can't exist without you. You complete us."

Mischa knelt down beside me, and even though she wasn't as friendly as I was, she still placed a gentle hand on his shoulder. "You have more reasons to return than you know, and when you're ready, we'll be waiting for you."

I widened my eyes at her. His baby might be the one thing to snap him out of this massive darkness, but Mischa shook her head. She wasn't ready to tell him like this; I could sense that the timing felt wrong for her. She was hoping he'd come back on his own and be the father that she envisioned in her head. I didn't have the heart to tell her that Maximus would never be the same again. She would have to adjust her mindset to fit the new reality of our pack mate.

Jonathon and Lienda were standing off to the side, arms wrapped around each other. I could see in their faces that they both knew of Mischa and I – they were going to go from no grandchildren to two, practically overnight.

Wait a freaking minute ... the golden dragon had said twin souls. Did she mean?

"Shut the friggin' door." I spun and pointed a finger at Braxton. "Dude, why you always got to be an overachiever?"

I could tell from our bond that he knew exactly what I was saying.

His grin was all the response I needed to jump to my feet and tackle him to the ground. I spent a few minutes pummeling him, and he pretended not to let me win. My wolf was satisfied with our performance, and I was pleased to find out that even without my dragon I was still dominant, still an alpha.

I was still me.

Chapter 20

The next few hours were not fun, like ... at all. We gathered up the fallen and laid them out in the town center for one large sendoff to the gods. Each of the races had their own death rituals, but in times of war, a mass burning was always the way it went.

I was walking along the line, Braxton on one side, Mischa on the other, the rest of my family and pack trailing along at different paces, all of us intermingled with other survivors. We were silently blessing the bodies, thanking them for their service to our people. I was keeping my emotions in check ... until I was about half way along one of the long rows...

A small, familiar face caught my attention. "No!" I cried, falling to my knees beside her. "No ... Rose! I can't ... fuck!"

I was devastated, wanting to sob, but was too numb to cry any more. She was laid out all perfect, pretty and petite, the first dragon marked, who had suffered more than any of us, the channel for the king's power, whose blood ran through all the marked. She deserved so much more than this, to finally have a chance at freedom…

"What happened?" I asked, unable to see any injuries. Her skin was still that perfect mix of color, dark and smooth, but without any of the warmth she had held in life.

Grace answered me. The witch had remained blank faced since Cardia was killed, but continued to use her healing for as long as she had the strength.

"I heard that when the marked were sending their energy up into Larkspur, she went crazy, screaming, blood pouring from her eyes and nose and mouth. Some of the healers tried to help her but she just collapsed."

Larky had been so desperate to win … he had channeled too much energy through her, destroying her … before I could stop him. What the fuck? Life shouldn't be this unfair.

Even though I knew she was dead, and there was no one left there to hear me, I picked up her hand and leaned closer. "I'm so sorry I failed you, Rose. You deserved to have a shot at a free life, and now I can only hope you find your place amongst the gods, and that the afterlife is peaceful." I silently added prayers and blessings for her safe journey home.

I had no doubt that I looked like shit as I stumbled to my feet. This had been the longest asshole of a day, and even though we'd won the battle, we had lost so much.

Braxton wrapped himself tightly around me, as if somehow, with his physical strength alone, he could keep me safe from the pain. No one could do that, but our mate bond certainly made it easier to deal with. I managed to keep my shit together for most of our blessings. There were many of us wandering through the masses of dead, so many who had lost friends and family. Not to mention all of the supes around the world who were yet to know that their loved ones were not coming home.

I lost it again when I reached Jonathon; he was with Torag, kneeling silently at his friend's side. At first I thought he was simply praying, but as we moved closer I could see the tears trailing down his cheeks, and that was what completely broke me.

Jonathon was a strong alpha, a leader. He felt his emotions, owned them like most shifters, but he was always so contained. Today, though, his grief was so great that it was pouring out of him and crashing into all of us. I couldn't stop myself from crossing to him and crouching down to hug him from behind, resting my head on his back and offering whatever comfort I could.

More of our pack members followed. Braxton. Mischa. Lienda. Dozens of others. Some who had been marked and some who weren't. We all crowded in and mourned with our alpha. The keening howls would have been heard all the way to the closest human city if it wasn't for the protections back up around Stratford. Eventually, we had to release the pain. We had to rejoice in the time we had shared with our loved ones. We had to move forward.

The burning ceremony was both incredibly moving and releasing. Supes believed in an afterlife – well, most of the races did. It was comforting to know that those who had sacrificed so much, who had died today, would find their place with the gods. We would meet them again one day. Death was inevitable for us all, and we couldn't stop living just because some were taken from us too soon.

Jonathon and Louis were contacting communities around the globe, letting them know the threat had been eliminated, and that all of those who had been marked were free of the king's control. Their dragon symbol was gone, along with the increased benefits from the spirit of the dragon.

I was the only one still bearing a mark, and I would wear it with pride. It was the evidence of my dragon mating, the only connection remaining to me of the golden one, Josephina. My dragon.

It had been a long day and I was pretty much dead on my feet, but we all found time to eat together in the great hall. Yeah, who was I kidding? I'd always find time and energy for food. You know … except if I were actually dead.

Maximus wasn't here, and his empty seat was a massive kick in the guts, reminding all of us that there was a break in our pack.

"You have to tell him, Misch." I lowered my voice so only she could hear. "He needs something positive to hold on to."

She was silent, pushing her food around on her plate. "Don't you think maybe it would be an added stress he doesn't need right now? Something else to deal with when he is already consumed just dealing with his loss?"

I sighed, my battered heart clenching. "You're probably right, but I think we give him a few weeks, at most, to try and work through some of the pain and anger. Then there will be no choice but to let him know."

"Agreed," she said quietly. "I don't want to spring it on him after the baby is born."

Yeah, I totally wouldn't recommend that. Maximus was likely to completely lose his shit if he found out that way. Vampires were very protective of their young. Most of the supe races were, except for some of the demi-fey. Pretty sure mermaids ate their young. Ugly bitches.

I devoured everything on my plate, which was harder than usual because Braxton kept shoving more food onto it. Eventually I reached out and captured his hand, the one holding another plate of chocolate cake.

My eyes locked on the dripping ganache and cream center. "Okay, after this piece of cake, I'm definitely too full to move. You're already going to have to carry me from here."

His blue eyes sparkled and he leaned in closer. That scent of his, wild and rich, reminding me of the forest, wrapped around me. "I plan on carrying you out of here and straight to my room. Then I plan on staying in there for a week. After which I will have to leave to accept my council leadership, and then I will take you straight back to my room again."

I snorted, but deep down my entire body was tingling with excitement and anticipation. Some might think it was too soon after the battle to be getting naked and happy, but what better time to rejoice in love and life? There were no guarantees for tomorrow and I would take and embrace every second I had with Braxton.

**

My boys stood straight and beautiful on the dais, towering well above the community members of

Stratford who filled the town hall – and the elite gathering of elders and leaders from other countries standing off to the side. The Compasses weren't smiling, their expressions an equal amount of somber and awed. I had spent a lot of time with them over the past few days. We slept in a big pack puppy pile – which Maximus needed more than anybody. He didn't speak much anymore, but he rarely left our sides.

When we weren't resting, we just did simple things: watched movies, talked about everything and nothing – Maximus just listened – and ate a lot of food. Damn, so much food. My curves were beginning to show again, and I was pretty sure that a baby belly was in my very near future. I still hadn't done the ritual with Louis. I trusted the word of the golden dragon, so there was no real need.

I knew the boys were a little nervous about their premature elevation into leadership roles, mostly because the time they should have spent learning about leading this community had instead been spent with Kristoff trying to lock them in Vanguard. But they would be brilliant. I knew it. They were young, yes, but they were born for this role and they would do it as fairly as they could.

I was in the front row with my family and had a perfect view of the dais. My father was on one side, Mischa on the other. Her belly was growing by the day, but the secret was mostly still contained. For now, it was just my parents, Braxton, and me who knew. Oh, and one healer who had checked her over and declared everything was developing perfect and healthy. Now that her nausea had died down, and she didn't have the stress of the dragon king in her head, she was able to eat more, and was making weight gains to match my own. I knew she planned on telling Maximus today, after his elevation to council leader. I still wasn't sure how he was going to take it; the loss of his mate was still very raw.

Time ticked away as we waited for the final select to arrive. The demi-fey were secretive about how their leader was chosen, waiting right up until the last moment to announce them. All heads turned as they finally entered the room, their chosen leader making his way up to the front to stand beside the Compasses. It was a troll, one which I did not know.

Jonathon leaned over. "Jerak, he's a good male. He was Torag's hopeful successor."

I settled back into my chair. If my father was satisfied, then so was I. Plus, I liked when trolls were on the council. They were steadfast and resilient of mind; they could not be easily swayed to the decisions or beliefs of others, strong like ancient trees. Always a good quality in leadership.

As soon as Jerak joined the Compasses, the room quieted. Every seat was taken, all of the township had returned, and the ghostly feeling of Stratford was gone.

It was time to begin.

I had never been to one of these ceremonies before. My father's had been just before I was born, so I was really interested to see what would happen. Five elders stepped up behind the boys, each holding a large ceremonial blade in their right hand – gold, with a curved blade and glittery red stones embedded in the handle – and an ancient-looking book in their other hand, diminutive in size, with the sort of binding popular centuries ago, like a tiny version of the *Book of Guidance*. And speaking of, the large tome was in the center of the dais, waiting for its part in the ceremony.

The five elders, who had travelled in from communities across Europe, where the majority of supernatural resided, started to read from their books. The language was fey in origin. I recognized some of the words, but since it wasn't one of the classes I took advanced studies in, I was out of practice. I was pretty sure they were thanking the shining ones and also the gods of other races. They spoke of the five supernatural souls which make up our races, and the leadership of these. The last part sounded a lot like a spell, calling forth energy from the people to empower the leaders to govern.

The words were flowing, mesmerizing. I could see the boys swaying as if they were caught up in the ceremony, unable to stop themselves. Finally the elders asked them to lay their right palm out in front of them, and with a quick slice the ceremonial blade cut into each one. Then they each took turns placing that bloody wound down onto the *Book of Guidance*.

I was on the edge of my seat, barely breathing, as much in awe as the rest of the silent room. The energy was arcing around, flowing into them, and since I was bonded to Braxton, I felt the power flooding into him. The quads had already been blessed with a massive overload of power – hence their leadership at such a young age – and it was so much more now.

As the five males bled onto the book, the energy of every supernatural in the room, and from across the continent, surged from us and flowed into the new leaders. It was subtle, just a small amount – you'd never notice it missing. And now I could sense them, like a shining beacon that drew all of us, that gave us a small piece of ownership over our new council members.

You already own me.

I wasn't sure I would ever get used to Braxton being able to talk in my head, but I wouldn't change it for anything.

As the five newly-appointed council leaders stepped back, the elders picked up their books again. They read a few more lines, bestowing their own blessings, and then it was done. I was up on my feet and flying across to the quads in seconds, wrapping my arms around each one. Jo and Jack were right there beside me; those two were so proud of their boys. It's funny that the perfect mix of races, and love between those two supes, was the reason we had a set of quads strong enough to take out Larky and his brothers. Jo and Jack were really the heroes of the day, and they had not even been there for the fight.

Nash bumped me as he dashed past to jump on his brothers. No one had been able to find his parents. It was thought they were killed by the Four when Nash was first captured, so Jo and Jack were taking the steps to adopt him. He was going to officially be a Compass.

Fucking Four. I was beyond thankful that those bastards were dead.

Jacob twirled me around when I reached him. Tyson did the same. Maximus simply closed his arms around me, holding me tightly for a few long moments. I relished the closeness. He had been so lost since Cardia.

"I'm going to go away for a few days, Jess," he said as he pulled back. I forced my face to go blank, even though I was already opening my mouth to protest. "I promise it's nothing you have to worry about. I just need some time alone to get my head together ... to deal with the fucked up darkness inside."

"What about your council duties?" I knew the boys would be straight into learning their roles. Louis and Jonathon – my father was an elder now too – were going to be their teachers. They had to fill a lot of roles since there were no previous council leaders left – well, except for Kristoff, but that dude was a dead man the moment he surfaced.

Maximus' eyes were black and glassy. "They'll just have to wait. I'll never be any kind of leader if I don't find peace with ... everything."

I swallowed down my pain and pulled him back in for another hug. "Call me whenever you can. I swear I will carry my cell phone around day and night. For you I will."

He actually chuckled and I held tight to this moment.

"I love you, Jess, and I will be back soon. Can't let my nephews be born without me here to keep Braxton from losing his mind."

I elbowed him. "They might be girls."

He dropped a gentle kiss on my head and then he was gone. I had been his last goodbye. I just hoped he didn't do anything stupid while he was gone. My throat was all choked up as I turned to the rest of the gathered.

Mischa's lower lip was wobbling as she stared after Maximus. Looked like her plans to tell him about her pregnancy was not happening today. She hugged herself, the loose shirt draping across the small bump. I really had to look to noticed it, but there was a definite size increase. So much sorrow laced her downturn face, and I was starting to see that for her the feelings had never gone anywhere. Mischa still cared deeply about the vampire who was never destined to be her mate. I just hoped they could work out their soap opera drama, for the sake of their child.

"Jess…"

I turned to find Grace. She had been different since Cardia's death, lost somehow. I could still see the torment on her face.

"I'm going away for a while," she said, no hesitation.

What the crap? Was this the day of people saying goodbye to me?

"What the hell!" Tyson popped up at our side, as angry as I'd seen him in some time, gold already threading his honeysuckle eyes. "You can't leave. We've already lost so much … you have to stay."

Grace swallowed hard, and for once didn't run from the wizard. "My family is having some problems, Ty. They need me right now, and frankly I'd like to escape from the painful memories here. I need to do some cleansing of my soul, my chakras."

She reached out a hand and placed it on his chest, the first time I'd seen her touch him outside of healing. I held my breath, expecting for a moment that a mate bond would kick in between them. Unfortunately, nothing happened except for Tyson's eyes – they went full gold, like he was completely immersed in a spell.

"Will you come back to me?" he asked her.

Grace sucked down a sob, then nodded, and with a last moment of something between them, she wrenched her hand free and ran from the building. Tyson started after her but I caught his arm.

"Let her go, Ty. She said she'd be back. Let her make the choice. If you want her to choose you and Stratford, you cannot force it to be."

I could see him fighting for control. Eventually his head fell forward. "I'll give her some time, but if she doesn't return to me soon, I'm going to find her. She's mine, even if she doesn't realize it yet."

I let him loose, reaching up to pat his arm. "That's my boy."

Tyson flicked me under the chin then, before turning to make his way slowly from the hall. I trusted that he would let Grace go for now, but the healer was soon going to feel the full attention of a

Compass quad, and she was not going to know what hit her.

Louis popped up then, scaring the shit out of me. My hand slammed against my chest. "For shit's sake, Louis. Don't you dare tell me you're leaving town too."

He laughed, flashing white teeth, before shaking his head. "No, Jess, you're stuck with me for now."

I gave him a hug. "I'm happy to hear that. I've been waiting for you to get back to town. Tell me, what happened with your brother?"

Louis had left to deal with the mystics' fallout a few days after the fight. Some of them had been a little unhappy about their forced exclusion, and we'd been worried for Quale.

"I got there in time for the war of the mystics, but in the end they found peace with their situation and all decided to stay in the sanctuary. Turns out they quite like running a safe place for supernaturals. It's going to be open to all now, all that need to escape. They can change the protections to let in supes who are seeking safety."

I smiled. That was kind of perfect.

Louis lowered his head so we were eye to eye. "Besides that, I need to tell you two things. Firstly, your trial had been pardoned as a thanks from the supernatural councils across the world. They acknowledge that the incarceration of dragon marked was not sanctioned, and that you were simply doing your duties to free them."

Frig, I had sort of forgotten that I had a trial pending, the one from when I attempted to sneak into Vanguard to free the marked. Nice to have one less thing to worry about. I wasn't sure those prison grays would look stylish with my soon to be massive-ass baby bump.

"That's great," I said. "So what's the second thing?"

"I know you're satisfied with the word of the golden dragon, but I was wondering if you'd still like to do the pregnancy ritual now? You'll be far enough along to know the sex of the babies."

A surged of excited adrenalin hit me and I nodded enthusiastically. I turned around to find my mate. He was still at the front of the room speaking with the elders. Everyone wanted a piece of the dragon who had killed Larky. He was a hero. I guess we all were – right up until we did the next stupid thing and found ourselves neck deep in trouble. For now we'd take the accolades and gifts, especially since a lot of said gifts were food.

Braxton noticed my gaze, and the moment I held out a hand to him he gave a brief goodbye to the elders and crossed to me. He was dressed more formally than usual, all black, button-up shirt – open collar exposing tawny skin – and dress pants. He looked tall, dark, and dangerous, my three favorite things.

The moment we were close enough, he pulled me in for a kiss; touching like this now was second nature. His hands dropped down to rest against my stomach, which he did at least eight times a day. Louis cleared his throat a few times and eventually Braxton and I parted long enough to follow him from the town hall.

It was nice to look around and see all our friends, pack, and family celebrating. Soon all of Stratford's inhabitants would be on their way to the elegant dinner tonight in celebration of the new leaders. It would be party central here for the next few days. More than one supe would end up naked in the town center. For once, that was not going to be me.

My heart was both light and heavy as we pushed through the crowds, making our way out into the quiet of the forest. "So how does it feel to be the leader of the shifters?" I asked the darkly handsome councilor.

I was legitimately curious to know what changes were going on inside of my Compasses. I always knew they were going to experience this without me, and I was cool with that. I'd never wanted to be a leader. I was content in my power.

Funnily enough, since Braxton turned out to be my true mate, I could actually experience this with them – tap into my mate bond and access his mind. But since we preferred our privacy most of the time, only sending thoughts when words were not readily accessible, I let him tell me instead.

Braxton rubbed his hand down my spine, sending lovely chills across my body. "It's strange, the power has always been intense with my dragon, but now I feel like it's actually calmed down. The fact that so many souls are tied to my own, in a very small way, allows my energy to be doing something, almost as if I am constantly sending out reassurances to our people."

"So you can actually feel thousands of shifters' energy?" It was mind boggling.

Louis chuckled. He was a step in front of us, but clearly still killing it at eavesdropping. "You'll learn to separate the mass from your own energy. Don't give too much back to them, no matter how powerful you're feeling. You'll learn how to use it to enforce our laws, and to bring order to the chaos. Until then, enjoy the boost of power. It only lasts for a blink."

Yep, twenty-five years was a blink.

Once we were safely ensconced in the tranquility of my forest, we began the ceremony. Louis removed a small pouch from his pocket, and I knew we would find the richest soil from Faerie, along with a few other herbs and stones inside. These were the five points of the fertility pentagram, and from each we would learn something of the babies I carried.

Braxton stepped back, allowing Louis to paint the symbols around me with magic chalk. Then the five elements were scattered in even coatings on all sides and the sorcerer started to chant. The pull of energy was immediate, and I knew the results would be faster and much more accurate with a magic user of Louis' power at the wheel.

Braxton's eyes were soft, a light sky blue, as they stared into mine, both possessiveness and tenderness in that gaze. I loved the way shifters adored their pregnant mates, loving the changes in our bodies, worshiping the fertility of females.

Braxton was happier than I'd ever known him to be. He'd been completed in that moment when our bond was made whole, when he knew the sacrifice I had to make was about tearing my dragon away from my soul, and not about choosing another mate.

I wanted to express how blessed I was feeling. Words weren't exactly my thing, but I was going to give it a shot. I tapped into our bond, opening the communication path. *I couldn't have survived the past week without you, Brax. I could never have found the strength to release my dragon, my Josephina. I love and adore you and I'm more than blessed to be having your children.*

I didn't speak in his mind much, but when I did I made sure it was sappy and sentimental. That way there was no ammunition for the other Compasses to use against me.

Braxton's reply was cut off by Louis' laughter.

"Well, not that I expected any different, but you two are having some seriously strong-willed children. I'm not getting much from them; they're hiding their energy from me. But I'm very happy to tell you that it's definitely twins, a boy and girl. Your son is protecting his sister, protecting both of them, keeping me from reading their energy. I can't tell if either are a dragon shifter, but they're both developing rapidly and are healthy."

I bounced a little, and broke the circle so I could climb Braxton and reach his face for more kisses. "I don't need to know anything other than the fact that they're healthy."

Braxton chuckled. "Yep, if our children end up being dragon shifters, able to control all races, then we'll deal with that when it happens. For now we celebrate our blessings."

He lifted me closer and twirled me around. By the time my feet hit the soft layer of leaves and decaying forest matter, his lips were already on mine. Our kiss went on forever, and when I finally came up for air, I noticed a rain of petals cascading down over us – odd, because there were no flowers above us; the winter months had left the forest in its barest of states.

I caught a flash of gold in the corner of my eye, but by the time I looked there was nothing to be seen.

"She's happy too," Braxton said, clearly having caught on to what was happening. "Josephina was bestowing a blessing on us."

My heart ached to think that she'd been so close and I had missed seeing her, but I was also overjoyed to know that she was watching over me. She was still so much in my life and heart.

Louis must have left us alone, because the forest was now empty of all but Braxton and me. The quiet closed around us, and as my mate reached forward to place both hands over mine, resting against my stomach, I knew this was the first day of the rest of our lives. As cliché as it was, until this moment I had never been free to love Braxton as he deserved. I had been tied to the king, unnaturally dragon mated, bonded to a race who needed me to save them.

But now … I could give myself wholly to my mate and children, and I knew that even with the multitude of trials we would face over the next thousand years, as long as I had my family and pack by my side, I'd take those trials and kick them fair in the balls.

I couldn't freakin' wait.

Stay tuned for more Supernatural Prison Stories featuring:
Maximus
Tyson
Jacob
Louis

Sneak peek of Maximus Compass' story

Each night the emptiness claims me and each morning I force myself to awake. Aimlessly, I wander the streets of the human world, feeding to survive. At times I briefly contemplate ending it all, but I refuse to leave my brothers or Jessa.

Speaking of my number one girl, a buzzing illumination indicated I had another text. She was relentless, never letting me wallow in my misery.

Jessa babe: *Maximus Compass, where the fuck are you? Seriously, dude. I'm as fat as a house and my eyes are literally falling from my head, I'm that tired. Mainly because two babies are kicking the shit out of me every night. I need you to come home. Braxton won't stop feeding me. I'm starting to waddle. WADDLE.*

An actual smile forced its way across my face. She was the one light in my darkness, the reason I was actually heading back in the direction of

Stratford. Though I wasn't sure I could step into the community again. That was the place my mate had ... *died*. I was actually able to say the word now, but it still burned like the hottest fires of hell. I needed to start accepting what had happened. Truth was, the guilt was killing me. Guilt and pain. I hadn't protected Cardia. I was too busy trying to save everyone else. My duty should have been to her first, and yet it never was.

I didn't deserve a true mate, and so the fates had taken her from me.

Those fucking evil bitches. I wanted to kill them. But that was not something I could do. One day, though, I would find the fates who had manipulated my life and I would kick the shit out of them.

My phone buzzed again.

Jessa babe: *I'm serious Max. You need to come home. There's stuff happening, Kristoff has been seen again, and the shifter bears are planning some sort of coup against Braxton. We need you. The council needs you.*

She was pulling out the big guns now, reminding me of my responsibility, of my brothers. I missed those assholes. We had barely been separated since birth, and it was our birthday next week. Twenty-three. So fucking young. And yet I felt like I was a thousand years old. Old and completely done.

I hit her back with a brief text.

On my way.
That was all she needed to know.
   ***

Please, if you loved this book, could you do me a huge favor and post a review on Amazon and/or Goodreads. Reviews are so valuable to independent authors and I'd appreciate your feedback. – Jaymin ☺

Facebook: http://www.facebook.com/pages/Jaymin-Eve
www.jaymineve.com

Mailing List: http://eepurl.com/bQw8Kf

Acknowledgements

Wow! Another series finished and I'm again torn between excitement and sadness. I have to thank all of the usual wonderful people, those who make this life as an author doable. I would be nothing without you all.

Travis, Lola and Silvie: you three not only make this author job doable, you make life worth living.

My parents: your love and support is priceless. The girls and I are blessed to have you.

Cody and Laura: you're the best friends and family to us. I appreciate everything you do for me and the girls.

Lee from Oceans Edge Editing: thank you for the countless hours and advice you have given to this storyline. I have learned so much from you, and there's no way the Supernatural Prison series would be what it is without your input. You go above and beyond. Thank you so much.

Tamara (cover artist): Sometimes I think you have a direct link to my mind, I give you some vague idea and you produce a masterpiece. Thank you for all of your hard work. I was completely blessed to discover your talent. I love every single beautiful cover.

My beta readers: Marice, Andi, Sarah and Laura. Love you all so much. Thank you for all of your support, there are no real words to describe how much it means to me. You take my stories, love and embrace them, give me feedback to better the story, and encouragement to keep me going. Hugs and cocktails are on me the next time we're out! <3

My author BFFs: Leia Stone and S.t Bende – without the both of you keeping me sane I would be rocking in a corner somewhere. I love your positive attitude. Not to mention your insane talent, thank you for all of the hours of entertainment, conversations and love. Big Author Hugs!

My Nerd Herd and Release Team: You all rock! Seriously, I don't have enough amazing things to say about how awesome you are. The way you enthuse over my books, and the book world in general. I have made a lot of great friends, and learned of some really fantastic books. Hugs to you all! <3

The readers: I can't even express the pure love and adoration I have for you all. The way you have embraced my worlds, loved my characters, and brightened my day. I never take any of you for granted, and count my blessings each and every day. The fact that I have such an amazing career is thanks to you all, and I hope that we all remain friends for a very long time.

Hugs!
Jaymin Eve xx

Other Book Titles by this author:

<u>A Walker Saga - Young Adult Fantasy Series (Complete)</u>

 First World: A Walker Saga Book 1
 Spurn: A Walker Saga Book 2
 Crais: A Walker Saga Book 3
 Regali: A Walker Saga Book 4
 Nephilius: A Walker Saga Book 5
 Dronish: A Walker Saga Book 6
 Earth: A Walker Saga Book 7

<u>Supernatural Prison - New Adult Urban Fantasy</u>

 Dragon Marked: Supernatural Prison 1
 Dragon Mystics: Supernatural Prison 2
 Dragon Mated: Supernatural Prison 3

<u>Sinclair Stories - New Adult Contemporary Romance</u>

 Songbird: A Sinclair Story Book 1

<u>Hive Trilogy - Young Adult Urban Fantasy</u>

 Ash: Hive Trilogy Book 1
 Anarchy: Hive Trilogy Book 2

About the Author

Jaymin Eve is an International Bestselling author of Young Adult and New Adult romance novels (both urban fantasy and contemporary). She has a passion for reading, writing and arithmetic ... okay maybe not the last one but definitely the first two. She loves surrounding herself with the best things in life: her two girls, a good book and chocolate.

She'd love to hear from you, so find her at Facebook:
http://www.facebook.com/pages/Jaymin-Eve
Mailing List: http://eepurl.com/bQw8Kf
Webpage: www.jaymineve.com
Email jaymineve@gmail.com

Printed in Poland
by Amazon Fulfillment
Poland Sp. z o.o., Wrocław